DAGMAR

Last of the Olympians

By

Angus Thomson

ISBN-13: 978-1519520098
ISBN-10: 1519520093

To Frances.

CONTENTS

The Blood Imperial

The stunned boy became aware, aware that he was bleeding. He was destined to grow up to be the greatest, most powerful person on Earth, have anything, everything, command anyone in the world, as long as he did not bleed, and now he was bleeding.

He must not, must not, must not bleed. And yet he was bleeding. He heard whimpering and then that shattering noise again, the huge clatter of gunfire in a closed room. He turned his head and looked sideways, glaring like a horse startled by lightning. Even here, close to the floor, the smoke swirled and stank but through it he saw Stasia, sprawled against the striped wall. She stared at him, blood smeared across her face. Stasia opened her mouth. Then a hulking body and a plunging arm, a bayonet thrusting into her chest like a sword, and blood spurted from her mouth.

He raised his head but before he could scream a boot hit the side of his face. For a moment, only a moment, he felt a revolver muzzle behind his ear.

Chapter 1

Dagmar rose, carefully removed her hair binding and slipped a dressing gown on over her nightgown. Some tea perhaps, she could send for tea… no, there was no one to answer the bell – there was no bell. This was an English house in the Crimea – did the English have bells? She couldn't remember.

She would find some tea to help her rest and, please God, to sleep. This was a troubled night. What was it the bible said? The king's horses killed one another… or was that Macbeth? The mantle of the temple was rent? Yes, that was the bible. Everyone, it seemed, had troubled nights, and this one was hers. One of many, so very many troubled nights. If only she knew that Nicki and the children were safe. In this chaos she could stand anything if she could be sure of that. She must stop this interminable worrying about them in the night; it did no good and God would provide. Please God, make them safe. More than anything, don't let Alexei bleed.

In the doorway she paused, disconcerted. Where was her Cossack? She remembered Nicki saying, "You can always rely on the Cossacks." Yes, there he was. It was Yuri, sprawled asleep in a chair on the landing; he would not stir. Down the shadowy stairs, along the corridor… there was a line of light beneath the kitchen door. Dagmar did not turn back; it was not her way.

A Tartar guard, dark, unshaven, looked up as the door opened. His eyes widened and he leapt to attention. This was a unique moment for each of them. He had been sitting half asleep when he was confronted by an Olympian, an aristocrat so far removed from his humble life that he had never supposed she would ever even notice him. She found the meeting equally extraordinary. But she felt unable to turn round and leave – and the man had a glass of tea in front of him.

"I did not know any of the men stayed in the house overnight," she said.

"Just one to raise the alarm if necessary," said the guard, with an accent so thick she could barely understand. "Your Majesty. Just one to raise the alarm if necessary, Your Majesty."

"I could not sleep," she said, sitting down. "I thought some tea would help me."

His own tea steamed before him. "May I pour some for Your Majesty? I have biscuits. Would Your Majesty like a biscuit?"

"The tea would be kind but no biscuit." She thought for a long moment, then added, "Thank you."

There was a pause while he prepared and passed a glass of tea. "I can bake biscuits," she said. "Or at least, I could when I was a child. There was a time when I would bake biscuits whenever we could afford the butter."

***

"It is a fine thing to be a princess," the storyteller had told her, "but it is an even finer thing to be able to bake a biscuit as excellent as this."

The child gazed up into his long Nordic face. The high forehead, heavy lidded eyes, the half-smile that hinted there was always one last untold secret. "Is it a finer thing to bake an excellent biscuit than to tell an excellent story?"

"Certainly," said the storyteller, "for no story can ever be as delicious as a well-made biscuit."

"But a biscuit is soon gone and forgotten, while a good story is forever and ever," said the child.

"Nothing is forever and ever. Not the story and certainly not the storyteller. Everything is soon gone and forgotten, just like a biscuit."

"Is being a princess like a biscuit?"

"That is a very important question but I don't know the answer, for I am not a princess, nor shall I ever be," said the storyteller. "But you will become a princess on Sunday and, when you have been a princess for a very long time, you must find me wherever I am, and tell me whether it is like a biscuit. Then your question will be answered and we shall both know. I shall be able to rest, once we know."

***

Dagmar took a cigarette and lit it. As she drew and inhaled, she noticed the guard watching so she extracted a second cigarette from her case and handed it and her petrol lighter to him.

"Thank you very much indeed, Your Majesty." He

lit the cigarette clumsily, then inspected the lighter. It was not one of the ornate confections of the court jewellers but a simple one, made of gold, several of which she had herself ordered from Mr. Alfred Dunhill of London. She was fastidious about her smoking paraphernalia. Suddenly she realised that he had probably never operated one before.

"That's worth more than I could earn in a year," he said, and handed it back to her.

They smoked in silence, then the guard sipped his tea. "I didn't know biscuits could be made with butter," he said. "We only ever had pig fat. I thought that was what everyone used."

Chapter 2

His Serene Highness Prince Christian of Schleswig-Holstein-Sonderburg-Glucksburg was, by natural inclination, an honest man who loved his family, his country, and a good joke, in that order. He despised hypocrisy, which was ironic because hypocrisy would make him King of Denmark.

The tiresome and divisive politics of the disputed duchies of Schleswig-Holstein had been the pea under Western Europe's political mattress for years. British Prime Minister Henry Palmerston said that only three people ever understood the Schleswig-Holstein question: Queen Victoria's deceased husband, an academic who had gone mad, and himself, but he could not now recall the details.

In 1848 the Schleswig-Holstein saga had taken yet another disputed convolution, leading to war between Holstein and Denmark. Christian by natural inclination sympathised with Holstein, but the King of Denmark had generously created a comfortable home for him and his expanding family in Copenhagen. His support was lightweight, he calculated, but siding against his host would be churlish. So he gave his backing to Denmark and within months was rewarded by having his family accepted by law into the line of Danish succession, usurping those who had committed themselves less prudently. He might have been forgiven for deciding that honesty had never done him much good and taken to a life of duplicity, but he did not. He did have a quiet glass or two with Hans the storyteller while Louise tended the new baby. "Some you win," he said, "and some you lose. Mostly you lose but it's nice when it goes the other way."

Nobody cared less than his daughter Marie Sophia Frederikke Dagmar of Schleswig-Holstein-Sonderburg-Glucksborg who was seven months old at the time and already recognised her name as Minnie. She was to have so many names – Princess Dagmar, Empress, Dowager Empress, Comrade Romanov – but Minnie was good enough for now, for the large-eyed grinning infant who lived at 18 Amaliegade, Copenhagen.

Christian had previously fathered three children by the slender but quietly forceful Louise, and two more would follow. Now, if he was destined to occupy the throne, they could all be expected to do rather well. Here was a pedigree Danish stable of aristocratic, healthy, politically non-controversial breeding stock. There would be no dowry but, if the mother were anything to go by, the girls would be fecund, bedworthy, and socially decorative, which was as much as any aristocrat was likely to ask. Powerful men in monarchies throughout Europe made note of Denmark.

But at the halfway point of the nineteenth century, Christian and Louise were impoverished fringe royalty living frugally but quite contentedly with their expanding family in a grace and favour house called, because it had been injudiciously painted, the Yellow Mansion. It is still yellow and it is still called the Yellow Mansion. Danes like to tell it the way it is.

Frederick was the eldest; he would become King of Denmark too in his turn. Alexandra would marry the dissolute son of Queen Victoria and become Queen beside him when the Widow of Windsor eventually died. The third child was William; he would marry a Russian Grand Duchess and become King of Greece. Then there was Minnie. Yet to come at that time were Thyra and Waldemar, who would be the materially least successful, respectively marrying the ugly Ernst August, Duke of Cumberland, and Marie of Orleans. Ernst's father had lost the Hanoverian crown to Prussia but, as Hans the storyteller scribbled in his notebook one night in the Yellow Mansion: "Some you win, and some you lose. Mostly you lose but it's nice when it goes the other way." Marie was closely related to the pretender to the French throne and detested Prussia for its brutality to France. Frederick would collapse and die from natural causes in 1912; William died the following year with an assassin's bullet in his heart. The others would live through catastrophic upheavals beyond their wildest nightmares.

High in the Yellow Mansion, Minnie, growing rapidly, shared a Spartan attic bedroom and all her childhood thoughts with Alexandra. There was little enough wealth in a world where hand-to-mouth was a fact of life for most people. In Denmark, there were a few relatively well-to-do bankers and merchants, but most aristocrats were as impoverished as commoners, with neither means nor inclination for heaping luxury on anyone. Christian's income was inadequate so, while a respectable face was presented to Copenhagen, the girls learned to mend clothes, to cook and serve at table, to conserve and make do. That was expected. They were taught essential skills: the piano of course, dancing, horse riding, drawing and painting, and languages. But the only book that carried weight in their home was the bible, and it carried a great deal of weight. Christian and his lady were sensible but they were not cerebrally inclined and noticed with amiable indifference that Minnie liked to read books. Simple pleasures satisfied the family and none more than gathering round Hans the storyteller when he visited, to hear the soft voice recount his extraordinary tales, watch his lidded eyes flash with surprise or fear, his mouth twist with emotion to emphasise the stories of pathos and heroism, loss, and recovery. When he came, smoked fish was served for an honoured guest, usually on visually opulent open sandwiches. Everyday food was basic; stews of root vegetables, thickened fruit, torn bread in sweetened, lightly fermented beer. Danes like the way things are, even for royalty. Hans was liked and always welcomed in the Yellow Mansion; the girls cooked for him, competing for his compliments.

Although highly esteemed by all the family, in one way he occupied the outer boundary of privilege. He called the child Minnie; to anyone beyond the storyteller, her name was Princess Dagmar, to be addressed as Your Highness and, from a day close to her eleventh birthday, Your Royal Highness. Such things mattered, and cost nothing.

The years of happy family life passed, until Alexandra had grown tall, willowy and exquisite, while Dagmar was slight and gamine, too vivacious and too emphatic to be thought lovely. The older girl was almost ready for market.

In England in 1859, Queen Victoria and her husband Prince Albert were despairing of their son and heir. They decided that a German princess would quieten the libertine antics of the Prince of Wales and, as for his brutal inclinations, well, she would have to fend for herself. With luck, he would not amuse himself by driving her over the brink to her death, as he had a flock of sheep he came across while walking the hills. When asked, the Prince said he didn't much care whom he was mated to but she must be a looker and know how to look after a chap. This was edited to become a desire that candidates should be charming and beautiful.

Prussia was by now bickering with Denmark over Schleswig-Holstein, which was still the grit in Europe's Vaseline. Queen Victoria's mother, husband, and son-in-law were all German so there was no doubt of her inclinations: "What a pity the Danes can't be reasonable," she said. "They would never do for Bertie. Whoever he marries will need to be very reasonable indeed." Then she saw the photographs and read the reports. Here was bloodstock to restore vigour to the attenuated Saxe-Coburgs. The British royal couple's eldest daughter Victoria was married to the Crown Prince of Prussia, so she was sent on reconnaissance. She reported back that, while Dagmar had a delightful personality to compensate for a careless lack of glamour, Alexandra was bewitching. Nice, calm, and not so clever as to create problems. Young Victoria recognised that her primitively inclined brother, known amongst the London swells as the Brute of the Brothels, could never cope with the sharp intelligence of Dagmar. He was much better suited to the placid Alexandra.

The manipulators resorted to a stratagem so crass that it made Christian cringe with embarrassment. He and his family would go to church. There was no need for security and no requirement for pomp or ceremony. Off they went to Speyer Cathedral. And in that great building, to their obvious amazement, they bumped into Victoria with her Crown Prince... and Bertie, Prince of Wales.

Meanwhile, other fillies were being unwittingly paraded before prospective purchasers. Princess Victoria thought Dagmar would make a suitable bride for her own brother Alfred, but Queen Victoria, having had a casual meeting in Belgium with both girls, ordained that one Dane in the family was enough.

The British Prince of Wales did as he was told and proposed. Alexandra did as she was told and accepted.

All families go through busy years and, what with Alexandra marrying the heir to the British throne, her brother William being proclaimed King of the Greeks, and the direct heir to the Danish throne dying (leaving Christian as next in line), there hardly seemed time to attend to anything. To cap it all, before the year was out the Danish King was next to go boots backward into the vaults and Christian became Christian IX, King of Denmark. "Never a dull moment when you're King in Copenhagen," he remarked to Hans, who jotted it down as soon as he was on his own.

But to Louise, Christian said: "I'm afraid the peaceful years are ended."

Emissaries of the Czar came sniffing around. Few things increase the collateral value of a princess more than her relatives acquiring stable thrones and, although Greece was somewhat dubious, England and Denmark were top quality except, they claimed, for the imperial throne of Russia.

Everything would have been splendid except for Schleswig-Holstein. Taking up his monarchic duties, Christian found that his predecessor had decided to absorb Schleswig into Denmark but had neglected to sign the relevant requisition form. Christian, with a flourish of the pen, dutifully rectified the omission, at about the same time that Prussia decided to step in and grab both Schleswig and Holstein. An untimely signature can have various consequences; on this occasion, it meant war. There was evidently more to being a king than having your ass kissed by all and sundry, the novice Monarch reflected, but he was careful to avoid saying so to anyone who carried a notebook.

In early 1864, Prussian and Austrian armies invaded Denmark. Cavalry churned the farmland into mud while infantry shot and bayoneted Danes to die in it. Britain, like all the other great powers, knew that Denmark's cause was just. It was also aware that the Prussian-Austrian alliance fielded an awesome war machine, so Britain happened to be looking the other way at the time. So was everyone else. Probity in international affairs was, as ever, subservient to expediency.

Denmark stood, pale and alone, facing annihilation or humiliation by Germans. Christian, blamed by many Danes because he had German blood, preferred humiliation to the destruction of his and their national identity, so he gave in. Denmark survived. Smaller, more subdued, but still a sovereign state, and one with a deep and bitter grudge.

The conflict did Dagmar's value no harm at all. Manipulative political advisers saw that there could be no allegations of political hidden agenda in a marriage between the children of defeated Denmark and magnanimous Russia. The Russian court was disinclined to fool around with informal meetings on the way to church, especially when the pair they wanted to bring together belonged to very different churches of Christ. The Lutheran faith was anathema to Russian Orthodoxy so compromise would be required – Danish compromise. Czar Alexander and his Empress Marie Alexandrovna sent their eldest son, Czarevitch Nicholas, on a world tour with a stop at Fredensborg. Louise could not miss so blunt a message. Any vendor who wants to make a sale lays out his wares; that was what the Czar was doing – clearly he was ready to do business.

Chapter 3

There was something strange about the Czar's eldest son Nicholas. Unlike his father Alexander and his brother, also Alexander, who were sturdy, the twenty-year-old was slender and cultivated. Czar Alexander must have looked at the boy sometimes and wondered whose head had been on the Imperial pillow. Still, at least the lad had more between his ears than his brothers.

Nicholas had been given a photograph of this sprite of a girl Dagmar three years before, and had built a collection of them. Now she was sixteen, and when they met each recognised a kindred spirit. Within weeks Nicholas dutifully asked his own parents for permission to propose. Then he asked Christian for her hand. To give him his due, her father said that was a matter for Dagmar but whatever she decided, her decision would have his blessing. God alone knows what a Russian Orthodox Czarevitch might make of a Lutheran blessing, but Nicholas was past caring. He was in love.

He proposed, she accepted, and everyone displayed astonished delight.

There is nothing as intoxicating as young love, fresh and undamaged by experience. Dagmar feasted on it, growing ever more alive, but there were those who noticed that this was not so with the Czarevitch. He was happy; indeed, he was undoubtedly in love. But he was not growing ever more alive and sometimes he was in pain.

Nicholas left to continue his tour; gifts and letters showered on the ecstatic young princess. But the pains that had hindered Nicholas while horse-riding with Dagmar in Denmark returned. Courtiers who encouraged him to sow his premarital wild oats were rebuffed. In Florence he stayed in bed for more than a month, undergoing treatment for an old riding injury.

At the beginning of 1865 Nicholas was taken by naval vessel from Italy to Nice. His mother was there, amongst the strong Russian community that had adopted the French Riviera. The Empress Alexandra Feodorovna, widow of the Czar's father Nicholas, had launched the Russian aristocracy's interest in Nice eleven years before when she began going there in the hope that her fragile constitution might thrive in the Mediterranean climate. Simultaneously a Russian naval base was established around the headland of Mont Boron in Villefranche.

Dagmar was learning Russian, taking instructions in the Orthodox religion – much to the disquiet of the Lutheran clergy – and planning her journey to Russia. The Russian community in Nice closed ranks but rumours were spreading, rumours of deadly disease. Dagmar, protected from gossip, did not know he was ill but became increasingly anxious. She wrote, reproaching her betrothed for three weeks without a letter.

On Easter Monday a telegram to Copenhagen announced that Nicholas had suffered increasing disturbance until cerebral haemorrhage left him part paralysed. He had meningitis. For weeks his treatment had been inappropriate, leaving his real condition neglected.

Another message from the Czar summoned all who could to gather in Nice; the Czarevitch had been given the last rites.

Scheduled trains across Europe were halted to make way for speeding locomotives as Dagmar and her party converged on a rendezvous at Dijon with the Czar and two of his sons.

Stopping only for fuel and water, her train sped south. Dagmar, far from home and taut with anxiety, tried to be civil, exchanging greetings as she was introduced to members of the Russian party. But always she seemed to find herself withdrawn into a corner, staring east towards the Alps, huddled over her grief for what might be, and for what might never be. She turned at the Czar's voice: "This is Nicholas's cousin, my dear. Your Nicholas is Nicholas Alexandrovitch; this young man is Nicholas Nicholaevitch, son of my brother. We call him Nikolai and he has a role to play in Russia's destiny." He winked.

She saw a boy aged perhaps nine or ten. Straight backed, restrained and yet vibrant with eagerness. "How do you do, Nikolai Nicholaevitch. I am glad to meet you, even on an unhappy occasion."

"Yes it is sad," he said with the pompous candour of youth, "but while we sorrow, we must look to the future. The future belongs to Russia under the Czar."

"But we are all mortal, Nicholas, even the Czar."

"There will always be a Czar. People die but the Czar is forever."

"What do you think it is like, Nicholas, to be Czar?"

"I've never thought about it. It isn't my destiny, it's the destiny of Nicki or maybe Sasha. My destiny is to serve the Czar as a soldier. To live and die, devoted to the service of the Czar – it must be the aspiration of everyone in Russia. People are only people. The Czar is Russia, has always been Russia. And always will be. I can think of no way to live nobly except in his service, can you?"

Alexander stepped forward. "I shall sleep the sounder for your commitment Nikolai, but now I think the princess would like to rest. Come with me and take tea."

As they walked away she heard the boy ask: "Did I speak foolishly, sir?" The great man murmured something she could not hear, and laid a hand on his shoulder.

On Friday, in the Villa Bermond, Dagmar again took the loved hand in hers. They spoke but not much. What could they say with the Emperor at one shoulder, the weeping Empress at the other, and an ikon of a gaunt Saint Nicholas, miracle worker and the dying man's patron saint, propped beside them? They were not to have their happiness, he said. It was not to be. But she was now part of the destiny of Russia and, with or without him, she must fulfil that destiny. He asked for her promise that she would still be Czarevna, would still tread the carpet that led towards the throne. "We are Olympians," he said. "But you must climb Olympus without me." She replied that she would have given him anything – her own life if she could.

A promise was such a little thing. She promised, as the Czar nodded his encouragement.

Dagmar held his hand as he died, surrounded by relatives and clergy, the ikon, guards and court officers. In that room full of Orthodox chants and the smell of musk, her young love died with tears in his eyes, and her youth went with him. She went dazed through the funeral at the Russian Orthodox church in the rue Longchamp; she gazed vacantly as the horrid casket was carried aboard the frigate *Alexander Nevski*, bound for ceremonial interment in Petersburg with his forebears.

All the parents – her own and Nicholas's – became profoundly concerned about her. She seemed so shattered that she was beyond grief. If she could grieve, they said, perhaps she would recover, but somehow she did not seem to understand what had happened, what was happening. Or perhaps she understood too well.

Although the elders discussed and even planned the pragmatic way forward – marriage between Dagmar and the new Czarevitch, Alexander – nobody bothered her with it, but within months the Russian lessons and religious instruction were resumed. Dagmar knew that Russia would not allow so valuable a brood mare to escape to another stable but she was past caring. If she was to marry, she would marry Nicholas. If not Nicholas, she had promised him her destiny. If it was his wish, they could mate her to whatever fur-shrouded barbarian they chose.

She had written to the Czar a year or so before, a sweet, naïve, personal letter asking him to save her father from the massive humiliation that the Germans' terms were imposing. Alexander had not replied. Now another Dagmar wrote, one who had suffered unbearable loss and had somehow survived. If Czarevitch Alexander wanted to marry her, really wanted to, then she would be his bride. All she required in return for her commitment was his.

Commitment was one of the few gifts he could claim to have to offer but she had already heard that he had offered it to another. Unencumbered with cerebral qualities, graceless in speech and conduct, he had shambled through life with a general goodwill towards most people and an unwavering commitment towards Russia under the Romanovs. Now he had to give up his undemanding life and reluctantly prepare to be Czar, all for Russia under the Romanovs. He would do it. He needed to marry for Russia under the Romanovs. That too, he would do. And if Dagmar was good enough for Nicholas, she was good enough for him. But he had given his simple heart to Princess Marie, one of his mother's maids of honour.

Through the summer he fought with himself… Marie, he must have Marie… Dagmar… he had no choice but Dagmar.

In the end, he had no choice. He had to be as one with Russia and his father ordained that Russia needed Dagmar. He was sent to Copenhagen to do whatever was necessary while lovely Marie, who was without fault in all this, was ordered to France for a forced marriage to a minor prince. Within three years she was dead from blood poisoning following childbirth.

Dagmar need have no concern about Alexander's commitment to her. Within months of Marie's departure he was declaring undying love for the Danish princess. It was not that he was fickle; he was simply shallow, but he gave commitment with sincerity, and he adhered to it. When he demonstrated his social skills by asking her where he stood in her affections, compared with his dead brother, she said she could love no other living person. They remained physically faithful to each other for the rest of their lives.

The marital recruitment of a fine young woman to the hothouse of a powerful and luxurious court always arouses intense public interest. There were those who said they feigned love while others accused them of superficial affection, but Europe revelled in the fairytale of young love bathed in privilege. Hans the storyteller wrote paeans, factories churned out souvenirs, Dagmar dresses hung in shops, hairdressers developed the Dagmar look, her name was imposed everywhere – from English pubs to Russian ships.

This exultation will turn the head of any recruit and that is its purpose, for it is an initiation ceremony. From a life of under-funded, modest privilege, Dagmar was taking a short journey to a world where the good sense and kindness that distinguished her childhood environment would be entirely displaced by etiquette, autocratic control, and luxurious privilege as of right. From now on her word would be law to all her social inferiors, which would be almost everyone. For some, like Alexander, the gift of authority exists as a birthright. The same gift takes ordinary incomers and makes them extraordinary. It transforms unremarkable people into the potential occupants of catafalques, while those about them embrace subservience, and so remain nonentities. It is called celebrity and, although it is entirely illusory, faith makes it effective. Many people are duped by it and the most convinced are those whom in reality it fails to improve.

Accompanied by her dog, her bible, and a crowd of family, attendants, and officials, Dagmar said farewell to the exuberant Danish masses on her way to the harbour at Amalienborg. She had very little clothing with her because she took only unmended garments; it was impossible that she should let Russian servants see the repairs and darns that now hung, discarded, in her wardrobe at home. She had been told that a Romanov never asked the cost of anything. How would she ever make a purchase if she didn't know the prices?

Once aboard the Royal yacht there were tearful embraces and endearments for her mother, father, and two younger siblings, while her favourite brother Freddie leaned on the rail and smoked. His parents could not afford the costs of going to Petersburg and in any case, it was not wise to be out of the country just now. Even Alexandra could not come, being pregnant by that gross oaf of an English Prince of Wales. Worse, the Prince himself would be there at the wedding, a lecher in a foreign land.

Freddie was going as personal escort for his sister, a mere token attendant who watched the celebrations with a bittersweet knowledge. One day all this would be for him: the nation would rise up and hail him as superhuman. But the father he loved would not embrace Freddie then as he now embraced Dagmar. On that day, his father would no longer be there.

As soon as those who would stay in Denmark had left and the yacht sailed, Dagmar retired to her cabin. Freddie stayed close by, gazing over the rail, hangdog and unhappy. Why couldn't they have been simple bourgeoisie, unburdened by privilege, and without the curse of responsibility? They were well out to sea when his nineteen-year-old sister emerged onto the spotless deck, those large eyes bloodshot, her cheeks flushed, her manner bright and brittle. She took his hand. "I am to be Empress of the largest Empire in the world," she said, taking his arm. "I should like you to be the first to review my destiny."

Chapter 4

The country, court, and culture that lay ahead would demand much of the little princess. Efforts had been made to educate her about Russia but she had no real idea what lay ahead of her. This great, sprawling, ungovernable Empire had in many ways failed to emerge from the dark ages. Russia wrapped the earth's northern hemisphere like a shawl: when the sun set on Russia's Baltic coast, it was simultaneously rising to gild Vladivostok. Rich farmland surrounded costly villas in flower-strewn Crimea on the Black Sea in the South West. In the North East the icy eternity of Siberia had for centuries provided life in death for the beaten, broken, branded multitudes, processed and ejected by draconian control.

Three in four Russians were peasants and one of those three was, until only five years before Dagmar arrived, a serf, a slave, a saleable commodity; landowners who chose to torture or kill a serf, who ordered a serf to be raped or mutilated, did so with impunity. A serf was an ox, a beast of burden. To put out the eyes of a serf was not a crime, it was a valuable lesson in social behaviour for which those serfs who witnessed it should be grateful. In theory individuals had the historical right to defend themselves and their own from others, and to exact vengeance as appropriate, but not serfs; autocracy had years before introduced a hierarchy of privilege that turned rough justice into a system that Kafka would have recognised. The administration of justice was taken from the individual and the community when bureaucracy claimed it for its own, gathering information secretly, considering it in private, handing down judgement and punishment without accountability. The inevitable abuses, from vanity, corruption, ignorance or any combination of the three became so absurd that regulations were introduced to control them. Ingenuity created more obscure abuses; bureaucracy developed more convoluted regulations.

Peasants who displeased their landowners, derelicts, prostitutes, Jews who persistently failed to pay taxes, political dissenters: all disappeared into the Siberian wastes. Branding criminals on the face provided reliable identification. Many, especially the political prisoners, had been extensively and inventively interrogated. Deportation to Siberia was often used when other punishments had failed: mutilation was favoured in some districts. Some prisoners were flogged with the knout, a powerful, long-handled whip that had a fearful reputation. Twenty lashes by experienced arms could kill and would at least cause permanent maiming injury; being sentenced to one hundred lashes was to be condemned to die. Capital punishment was abolished in the mid-eighteenth century but many landowners, feeling the need for robust punishments and deterrents, resorted to the knout instead. It could be as effective as a noose and was far better entertainment. Another imaginative punishment that compensated for a lack of hanging had its roots in peasant history, although its name, Spitzruten, was originally German. The victim's wrists were tied together before he or she was forced to run the gauntlet between two rows of people armed with canes, whips, or what they had to hand. This enjoyed high fashion status under Nicholas I, especially in the army, and remained in the traditions of some regiments long after he answered for his own sins in 1855.

His son Alexander II was on the throne when Dagmar arrived. Alexander would be given scant credit by history for his enlightened attitudes. He succeeded Nicholas, declaring that he intended everybody to enjoy justice, mercy, and impartiality. Regulations officially replaced the knout with less damaging flails; provincial committees were instructed to discuss the implications of emancipation while central bodies examined the need for judicial reform. Massive reform on a massive scale takes time, but inside nine years the foundations had been laid for a judicial network with simple justice, justices of the peace for petty cases, tribunals with juries for criminal trials. Equally important, the Emancipation Manifesto had been published.

The enthusiasm that greeted these legal reforms soon evaporated, especially amongst the influential and privileged. Abuse and corruption persisted but now were more easily seen in a more open system, so the system brought to reduce them was blamed for their existence. Anecdotes abounded at all levels of society; justice for all meant a levelling for all and nobody welcomed that except the lowest – everyone else had something to lose. One notorious example occurred when a military grandee, who not many years before had regarded maiming an insolent serf as his duty, was fined for insulting his cook.

The well-to-do closed ranks at such an outrage but they need not have worried; their saviour was not far off. A revolutionary bomb would replace Alexander with Dagmar's husband, a reactionary Czar who would set about reversing the progress. When, in the years to come, his kidneys failed, his son, the last Czar, would carry on with the retreat into the dark ages.

At a time when nations like the United States were already complex modern social economies, a curious civil servant took the trouble to order a count of the number of exiles who were leaving Tomsk to drag their leg irons 1,000 miles on foot into Siberia, or as far along the road to that graveyard as they could. In one month more than 10,000 set out. Some dependents accompanied the exiles, some from the bond of human love, others from the knowledge that certain starvation faced them if they stayed where they were.

These were the scrapings of the criminal barrel. More able-bodied malcontents faced different penalties, like nearly 200 students at Kiev University, who protested over the cover-up of the rape of a young girl and so were drafted into the army as punishment for rioting.

Those criminals who could scrape together the fare rode in trains into Siberia. The Trans-Siberian Railway even had fourth-class train compartments, especially for them. Third class was for the poor; fourth was for the desperate. Anything was better than becoming one of the trudging multitude, every one an individual human tragedy, out there where a sound pair of boots was worth more than a life, where a coat could make the difference between waking and freezing in the night. All the corruptions and cruelties that human ingenuity and greed could devise developed among guards, their commanders, the distributors of food, the resident peasants, the blacksmiths who shackled and repaired the shackles. Murder, rape, and abuse were commonplace, kidnapped innocents were substituted for criminals with influence. And the ghastly implement that had by then been proscribed from use as a weapon of punishment had been retained as a tool of correction. Guards used the knout.

A prisoner who fell would be hauled up by others chained to him or her; they knew that a glancing blow from the knout could put them down too. If they failed, a guard would knout the fallen figure, either stirring up the dregs of energy or destroying whatever was left. Shackles were struck from dying prisoners and thrown into wagons. The shackles were more valuable than the people to whom they had been riveted: the shackles would travel this way again.

Guards on the exile trail lived little better than the prisoners, enduring the hatred of the prisoners, the contempt and brutality of their commanders. For some the best recreation was to be had beside the trail with a dying prisoner. Slashing a hamstring was one of the least creative parting rituals: there was nowhere to escape to but guards had to be sure they would die. Wolves, forever watching pale-eyed through the undergrowth a few dozen yards away, would close in at nightfall.

Chained in fours and fives, the groups would

move on. Better to shuffle on than risk the knout. There was little enough reason to go on but a powerful incentive not to fall.

Heat was cruel, cold was worse, but when the rains fell the mud became a nightmare where wagons bogged down to their axles, whole groups fell and could not regain their footing and the cold penetrated to the bone. The enforced pilgrimage ceased in deep winter but in a land of two seasons, cold could strike suddenly. When an icy night was expected after a day of rain, the prisoners were taken further from the road to sleep overnight. This was better, in case they did not waken.

Not all Siberia was penal servitude. It is a vast land, with rich soil, infinite forests, and immense panoramas. Incentives were developed to encourage Russians to migrate there: they were given land, implements, grain, financial support. They were shown that summer in Siberia was delightful. These excited pioneers arrived at Cheliabinsk, spent weeks living in the holding stations before paperwork could catch up, then were absorbed by the landscape. They came, but not the multitude that was needed; people knew that summer was short and when winter closed in, the land was locked solid until summer came again.

Forest, undamaged for thousands of years, stretched from horizon to horizon. Trees germinated, grew, aged and died without encountering the interference of human kind. The largest freshwater lake on the continent, Lake Baikal, lay there, an inland sea and a vast obstacle to the East and Vladivostok. Boats, assembled on the lake, provided ferries while throughout the winter, ice formed so thick that its pressure burst upwards into forests of impenetrable shards. Still people prospered there, mostly from the endless toil of those who laboured in mines. Irkutsk, a trading town on the sole river flowing from Lake Baikal, was enjoying its golden age, handling gold and diamonds. This brought additional employment for slave labour but no relief or luxury. The riches they helped create only increased their despair.

Some people recoiled from the draconian system that passed for justice and 'Not Guilty' jury verdicts became more common, even in cases where guilt was obvious. A general inspecting a prison believed a young political prisoner was disrespectful of him so he had him severely flogged. A young woman took exception to this; she shot and injured the officer. None of this was questioned during her trial but the jury found her not guilty. The Establishment, particularly the Czar, regarded such reaction as an attack on his authority and responded accordingly, weighting the system against acquittal.

But in 1866, as Dagmar travelled towards this extraordinary land where clocks could run backwards, reformation was still in the air. The whole tragic-comic carnival backdrop that was Russia would condition everything Dagmar would do and be for the rest of her life but now, at this magical moment, the immediate environment stunned and amazed her. The yacht sailed past the sea defences of Petersburg, a city not 170 years old. Czar Alexander, with the Czarevitch, was approaching the Danish yacht in his own imperial vessel, through a guard of honour of a dozen man-of-war. Bands played, cannon fired, flowers floated on the water, and under a clear blue sky the Princess surveyed the gateway to her Empire. Freddie stood back and watched; Dagmar, quick-witted, uninhibited and full of laughter, had lived her life and was transforming into someone else. The woman before him was becoming Empress Maria Feodorovna, mother of all the Russias. He turned away. These barrel-chested barbarians would have no respect if they saw his sorrow.

Everything was fresh and new, everywhere there were celebrations. Guns thundered a salute as she drove with her new family along Petersburg's Nevski Prospekt to the Winter Palace.

Never, in her wildest fantasies in the Yellow Mansion had she imagined anything of the magnificence and dimension of the Winter Palace. Built for Elizabeth, the daughter of Peter the Great, who died without having seen it completed, the Baroque grandeur had been the dynasty's principal residence for 200 years. "This," said Alexander, as he led her through some of the palace's 1,056 halls and chambers, "is Olympus – home of the Olympians."

She was puzzled; she had heard that reference before. "What are the Olympians?"

He took her hand and laughed. "We are the Olympians. That is what autocracy means."

He led her to a window so they could gaze across the immensity of the Palace Square towards the panoramic classical building on the south side, and the triumphal arch through which they had ridden from the Nevski Prospekt. Between them and the arch stood an immense red granite column surmounted by a triumphant angel. "That is the

Alexander Column," he said. "Alexander I was the Emperor who faced Napoleon."

"And it was Alexander who destroyed him?"

"Well, yes, with a little help from General Winter and one or two others."

"Was General Winter an Olympian?"

Alexander laughed. "Alexander was an Olympian. General Winter? He is the marauder who massacres those who invade us, and our men too if they are careless. He clears the drunks and the derelicts off our streets. No, General Winter is not an Olympian. He is a primeval force and a damned nuisance but we often thank God for him. Come and see Catherine's paintings. They say it's one of the greatest collections in the world but I wouldn't know."

"It must be extremely valuable."

Alexander looked at her, almost angry for a moment. Then he softened and said: "Money has no meaning on Olympus so nobody ever mentions the cost of anything. Not cost, or price or value. We don't ask and everyone knows better than to tell us."

"I'm sorry."

"Don't be sorry, just learn. Most of us Olympians are born to it. You are the new recruit and I suppose there is a lot to learn."

The woman who as a girl had always changed her better clothes for worn ones as soon as she came home, found exquisite garments laid out for her three and four times a day, attendants to help her into them. Jewellery of a magnificence and value she had never imagined was casually given to her. There seemed to be no food that was not exotic and delicious and it was served on porcelain plates and dishes, each of which would have been recognised as a work of art in Copenhagen. And everywhere there were objets d'art, sculptures, paintings of the most perfect… a face she had never thought to see again gazed back into her eyes. Nicholas, whom she had watched breathe his last, was there, in a gilded frame and, so expertly was the portrait painted, he seemed to breathe again.

The eyes that had lost their lustre so short a time ago continued to gaze into her heart, even when she closed her eyes. Freddie found her helpless there and held her to him as she shook. "It should have been him," she whispered. "It should have been him." At last she could grieve.

The marriage contract was signed and ratified, Dagmar would be rich as long as she was married to the Czar or lived on as his widow. Living abroad would drastically reduce her income; remarrying would end it. Her value was in the job she had been given and she would do well to remember that.

The Empress sent for her. She did not rise as Dagmar entered but sat on a couch covered in heavily patterned floral chintz, with more of it on the wall behind her and still more on the windows. That was the fashion.

"Come and sit down my dear," said the older woman in French, the language of the Russian Court. "We are quite alone. I shall help you, but you must be candid with me."

"Thank you," said Dagmar. "I had not thought to

be anything but candid with you, ma'am."

Maria Alexandrovna was six years older than her husband but the difference could have been much more. Dagmar conjured up her father-in-law in her mind: fleshy and florid, while the woman before her was sharp featured, thin-faced and birdlike. Eight pregnancies, how could she have managed it?

Dagmar needed to concentrate. The Empress was looking searchingly into her face. "I need to know," she said. "Do you truly love Nicholas?"

There was no point in lying, even if it had been in her nature. She knew her face told everything. "Yes ma'am. I truly love Nicholas."

There was a long pause. "Then why are you marrying Alexander?"

"Because Nicholas asked me to and I promised I would."

"Why?"

"He asked because he believed Russia needs a bride. I promised because he asked."

"Can you give Alexander all that you would have given Nicholas?"

"I shall give Alexander everything in my power, if only for Nicholas's sake."

The Empress rose and walked to look out of the window. "I have never loved his father nor has his father loved me. But I too love Nicholas. He was my true son. I pray every night for God to take me to him."

This was more candour than Dagmar was able to

deal with so she sat silent, staring at the blue chintz flowers. The Empress came and stood close, looking at the neat hair, the clear eyes and the set of those pretty shoulders. "You will be a better Empress than I have been," said Maria. "I believe you will hold your husband. Mine wanders and I do not care."

She was as good as her word and guided Dagmar through myriad details of behaviour. As a Lutheran, Dagmar had never crossed herself in her life but now, at Maria's request, she did what she had seen Catholics do. "No my dear. Not like that." The Empress placed the first two fingers of her right hand and her thumb together; then she touched her forehead, her sternum, her right shoulder and her left. "They used to touch up, down, right, left as we do but they changed. We never have."

"Why did they change?"

"I have no idea. We did not because we don't. It is not our way to change."

"Is it a bad idea to sometimes adapt, just a little bit?"

Maria smiled. She was lovely only when she smiled but she did not smile often. "Probably, but we never have and we never shall. I expect one day progress will sweep us aside but I shall be with Nicholas by then and perhaps you will too."

Etiquette, ritual, and tradition controlled almost everything at Court and certainly a wedding of this status. Maria Feodorovna had to study, rehearse, and rehearse again. Guns wakened her to a crisply snow-covered morning on 9th November, guns saluted as she set out for the church and guns marked the end of the incense clouded marriage ceremony. The swinging kadilo, with its burning charcoal and pungent incense, represented the benevolence of Christ and Christ, it seemed, was very benign in that respect. Dagmar reflected that providing seats or pews might have indicated a certain compassion but apparently the incense was there to do that. Even the infirm stood if they had the strength.

There are no voices on Earth like those of Russian choristers and today they rose like the exultations of the heavenly host. "We have no musical instrument to lead the choir because they have no need of it," Alexander told her. "There are no pianos in heaven and that is the standard we aspire to." The corner of Dagmar's mouth twitched – the riposte was on her lips – but as the voices soared in extraordinary harmony into the cathedral vastness, she said nothing. He was right; their singing touched the hem of God's garment; there was nothing any artifice could add.

The Petersburg capella choir, founded in the fifteenth century, was key to the celebrations. Mikhail Galinka had died a decade before but he had been Court capellmeister for thirty years and his influence was still upon the choir, with its two dozen basses, eighteen tenors and fifty boy contraltos and sopranos. Wealth, privilege, autocracy created the magnificence. The capella choir made it glorious. Alexander leant close to her and said: "This is all for us. We are the Olympians."

But Galinka was only human. Dagmar had to sit through his opera, *A Life for the Czar*. By the end, human was not the word she would have chosen. Written for Alexander's grandfather, Nicholas I, *A*

Life for the Czar celebrates the sacrifice by a naturally noble peasant of his life to save his hierarchically noble Czar. This had done more than any other piece of music to both mould Russian music and develop the Russian people's relationship with the Czar. Nicholas had said: "He who gives his life for the Czar does not die." Galinka had given the concept credibility.

He invented Russian opera, making *A Life for the Czar* an essential part of all Czarist events, but he did much more. He took the folk songs of peasants and made the music of the people the anthem of the nation. Before Galinka people belonged to communities; afterwards they belonged to the Empire – and thus to the Emperor.

To the sound of gunfire and the smell of incense, Her Imperial Highness the Grand Duchess Maria Feodorovna turned her back on the girl she had been and faced her future as woman, lady, Czarevna, and then Empress. To family members of sufficient status and to the Copenhagen storyteller she would, in Denmark, Russia, and England, always be Minnie. To Danes she would always be Princess Dagmar. With her betrothal she was granted the Russian titles Grand Duchess and Imperial Highness; marriage brought the illustrious title Caesarevna. Here we call her Dagmar. It was the noblest of all her names.

She seemed perfect for the role she was to play. Small, neat, and nicely made, with an enquiring oval face and large eyes, she played well to crowds. She had a lovely smile, a charming and spontaneous bow, an instinct for seizing the unscripted moment, shaking a hand, accepting a flower, bending to speak to a child. She and Alexander tried hard to forget other loves and concentrate on each other and, day by day, affection grew. She was little more than a child and loved social contact, parties, balls, music and dancing. He recoiled from such things. Fortunately he was not part of the boisterous, roistering groups of young bloods who night after night celebrated their privilege, but he avoided social formality. A quiet night, drinking heavily with a few male cronies, a little bullying and making loud music – he was a man of simple tastes. Gradually they developed a balance that worked for both of them; it helped that neither was promiscuous, so that he could smile at her coquetry with other men, while she was equally confident of him.

And there was too something strange about her personality. She had lost the man she loved and, though distraught, accepted that she should marry his brother. She went through a form of service that required her to spit her contempt for her family's religious beliefs; she did not like it, but she did not demur. She tried hard to teach her clumsy, sometimes boorish husband some grace and even history and literature, but accepted without question the reactionary teachings of his tutor, Konstantin Pobedonostseff. She seemed too readily to accept that she was unable to alter some things, and then to conclude that whatever cannot be cured must be endured. Her recognition and acceptance of her own limitations could be both a quality and a fault. In her eldest son, the same self-knowledge without the determination to act on it would one day be catastrophic.

An authority on Russian law and history, Pobedonostseff was profoundly committed to the Russian Orthodox Church and the Czarist autocracy. As a tutor to the brothers, Nicholas and then Alexander, he used his considerable intellectual gifts to oppose freedom of any kind. He was implacably opposed to democratic and religious freedom, rights for the masses like voting or jury service, and any relaxation of controls on the press. He defended laws that oppressed racial and religious minorities. Especially, he believed that the Czar's liberation of the serfs had been a dangerous folly. Free serfs could bring sedition, which Jewish money could develop into revolution. "All change is dangerous," said Pobedonostseff. "Giving power to the people is like giving gunpowder to apes." His face was not the kind that smiles much and nor was his soul.

Chapter 5

Petersburg was a city with its modern foundations in autocracy. Peter the Great, one of the few truly great and incomprehensibly brutal Romanovs, had gone to war with Sweden in 1700, to restore Russia's access to the Baltic Sea. He never doubted that he would win and, as his troops fought, he began to use forced labour to build a city on the delta of the Neva River. In water and mud, flooding, frost, ice and snow, driven multitudes toiled to create Petersburg. Few of them lived to see the day in 1712 that it was declared the capital city of Russia, replacing twelfth-century Moscow as capital for administrative purposes. Peter used forced deportation to populate it; even a substantial landowner, a peacetime warlord in his own environment, did not disobey Peter if told to take his wealth to where it suited Russia. The war would go on for another nine years but Petersburg was strong now. It would grow and prosper.

Simultaneously Peter was reforming, creating organised defence forces, dragging Russia forward economically. He had shown no compassion for the troops and peasants who died in the war and the construction of his capital city, and he certainly showed none for anyone who challenged his authority. Mass executions demonstrated his single-minded determination; he was a keen attendant at them and was willing to demonstrate his own skill as an executioner. His own son questioned Peter's omniscience and was very fortunate to evade a noose. The war ended in 1721, when Czar Peter was declared Emperor. Less than four years later he died, aged fifty-three. One of the greatest features of Petersburg is the Peter and Paul cathedral and fortress, and there his 6ft 8in body was laid to rest.

His lady Catherine had established a country retreat nearly a score of miles from Petersburg, at Czarskoe Selo. Her own name had been given to another of Peter's conurbations, Ekaterinberg, a focus for industry and commerce he had created in the Ural Mountains. Czarskoe Selo was close enough to Petersburg, the seat of administration, for functional purposes but far enough from it to be comfortable. Here the Czar and his family could live an epicurean life of unequalled luxury. Amber and semi-precious stones were sliced into veneer, tailored into beautiful panels and used to line entire rooms. Art was commissioned on a Renaissance scale. Silks, gilding, marble in architectural quantities, sculpture, paintings of the finest quality, no expense was ever spared, no cost ever questioned. Successive Czars expanded, developed, and improved Czarskoe Selo, installing the most advanced energy, water, hygiene, and communications systems, and overwhelming the town with vistas of palaces and parks.

This was less self-consciously selfish than it might seem. The rulers of Russia did not regard themselves as parasitic but rather as the only people who could possibly accept the burdens of rule and who very reasonably accepted the standards of being rulers. If they indulged their whims, kept their mistresses, what of it? They needed their relaxation; if their young men drank and brawled and occasionally scarred or killed a social inferior, well, young men are always boisterous and accidents will happen. "Each man is as important as the job he does," Peter told his son when interrogating him in prison, "and my job is the most important on Earth." A landowner who had a peasant beaten to death was not murdering an equal; in the unlikely event that he found a peasant's bride sexually interesting, claiming the first night was not a sin. He was simply administering a God-given right over insignificant beasts of burden. The Czar of course, owned everything, including the land and the landowner. And, for that matter, the bride.

Alexander II brought Czarskoe Selo to its pinnacle of magnificence and there in later years he was to lead a self-indulgent life, free from marital restraint. He had married Princess Marie – Grand Duchess Marie Alexandrovna – when she was sixteen years old. One of the best ways of preventing a bride having an embarrassingly scandalous past was to marry her before she could develop one. She bore him eight children but lost one in infancy, while Nicholas died when barely out of adolescence. Her fragile health was undermined by childbirth and grief. As her husband's affairs became more blatant she increasingly devoted her time to the comforts of God, the Crimea, and the South of France.

The Czar was more conscientious about his work than his marriage; he listened with respect to a close friend, Prince Baryatinsky, who had played a hand in his many reforms, including freeing the serfs, and now urged him to encourage private ownership, which might block the path of communism. Russia had become intensely stratified, so that it was virtually impossible for people to cross social boundaries. The aristocracy ruled, both by influencing the court and as patrician landowners. An aristocrat would rather starve than do anything profitable, apart from owning land and living off the toil of others. There were growing numbers of enablers, manufacturers, organisers, but many of these were Jews; Jews held an unenviably unique position in society.

Jews were easily identified, tended to amass reserves and, far from believing in the true Christ, had demanded his crucifixion. Cut a Jew's throat and pour out the gold, they said. Persecuting Jews could be profitable and there were seldom any repercussions; many Russians enjoyed persecuting Jews and, God forgive them, some still do.

When Russian peasants were not burdened with endless labour or chilled beyond endurance, they toiled without hope or opportunity for improvement. Instead of hope in this world they had what Karl Marx called the opiate of the people. Sceptics around the world have tried to justify their own reservations about religion by quoting from his introduction to a critique of a work by Hegel, but when Marx made that remark he was focused upon Russians. They were a special case.

The commitment of a Russian peasant to the Russian Orthodox Church was total. The Church was more than the family, the community, more than Russia, more than life itself. It was more, even, than the Czar. In recognition of this total devotion, the Russian word for peasant was simply 'krestianin' – Christian. The Church had the key to eternity, so they would endure whatever misery this life imposed. Suffering would be rewarded a thousandfold. If the Czar had the blessings of Mother Church, then he shared its powers.

Inevitably, the stratification of society had an effect on faith. More than half the days on the calendar were fast days of one sort or another. Certain foods – notably oil, flesh, and alcohol – were frequently forbidden, pleasures proscribed. For most serfs, to whom meat was a luxury anyhow, temporary abstinence was comparatively easy; staying off the alcohol meant some serious work could be done, and the liver rested, ready for the next bout of abuse. For the rich and privileged, however, surely a little self-indulgence was harmless enough, wasn't it? After all, God wasn't going to damn a soul for the sake of a couple of lamb chops, was he? And a deity whose son turned water into wine would not begrudge a glass or two...

The vast mass of the population knew that their masters did not live as they did but they held their peace. They knew that the eaters of skorum (forbidden foods), the cruel and the wicked, were on borrowed time. A peasant did not need to judge a landowner, indeed, it was forbidden; God was keeping watch. God's vengeance was inevitable, inescapable, and would be eternal. The actions of Satan were swift, opportunistic; God moved slowly, inexorably. There was absolutely no room for doubt; God could see doubt and he detested it. The punishment that he would exact upon the privileged was a secret he shared with those who had no privilege. This was the secret that kept them warm.

Lenin would write: "The concept of God always dulls social issues, deadening reality, imposing the worst kind of slavery – inescapable slavery." Had he looked elsewhere on Earth he might have had doubts about his thesis. But he observed only Russia and anyway, Lenin never had any doubts. He recognised that the greatest hindrance to revolution is inertia, and the peasantry, satisfied by the narcotic of religion, was the inert mass he must overcome to create justice for the proletariat.

Dynastic rulers embrace churches which preach an omnipotent God; people are so much more forgiving when they are convinced that their deity will certainly punish the transgressions of their rulers while rewarding those who forgive in this life. The historian Polybius, writing before the birth of Jesus, said that superstition was the foundation of Roman greatness, introduced into every aspect of life to restrain people by fear of punishment and hope of reward. Whatever the merits of the Russian Orthodox Church, Russian autocracy seized and built upon the union, God and the Czar.

For a very long time it worked, at least for successive Czars, but the world changes. Industry was progressing, transport and communications systems advanced, attitudes, understanding, and the needs of the individual altered. Things would have to change in order to stay the same. Only by opening for peasants the door into trade and commerce could a decent, self-satisfied, self-interested class be created to provide an inert middle-class buffer against revolution. Acting on Baryatinsky's rhetoric, Alexander took cautious steps forward. "I'd rather liberate them than have to try to stop them liberating themselves," he said. A bank to finance the aspirations of peasant farmers was a good idea; progress, however, was slow. The bank would not exist until 1883. Had Alexander been able to continue indefinitely as a reforming Emperor he might have saved his throne and his dynasty. The year 1918 would have seen magnificent one hundredth birthday celebrations in Petersburg instead of an obscene war and squalid slaughter across the land, not least in Ekaterinberg. But he would not live ten decades; he would not even live seven.

Extraordinarily he took no interest in teaching his son Alexander the business of government, simply leaving him to the mercy of a warped tutor with a powerful and dominant intellect. The student had no difficulty embracing Pobedonostseff's view that no interest could be permitted to interfere with the concept of Russia under an autocratic Czar supported by an Orthodox church. And Dagmar, who did know better, never questioned it. Only in hating Prussian aggression did she try to influence her husband, and in that she was forceful. They both developed an almost paranoid loathing of 'the Predators of Potsdam.'

Prussia had begun small but in the seventeenth century, after lying dormant for two centuries, it had started to expand. During the next 200 years it grew to enclose two thirds of all German territory. Its unsatisfied territorial ambitions had been written in blood, not least across Schleswig-Holstein. Other countries with coastal frontiers on the Baltic Sea also feared Prussia; only in Austria did it find a kindred spirit.

Towards the end of 1867, with the marriage just past its first anniversary, Dagmar declared that she was expecting a child in the spring. In July, while visiting her family in Denmark, she had miscarried and her husband had despaired of ever having an heir, but now that was forgotten. When her time came she had to endure giving birth while her husband held one hand, his father grasped the other, and the Empress sat, observing her while toying with a sal volatile flask. On the day that the Orthodox calendar dedicates to Job, the biblical character who suffered unjustly to test his loyalty to God, she gave birth to a puny son, Nicholas. There was rejoicing, an amnesty for some non-political criminals, and another good day on the incense market.

Dagmar had been raised to be courteous, considerate, and reasonable. Her husband had not and was none of these things. At events of any kind, in Russia and abroad, he would on a whim simply not attend. When he did come along he would say whatever came into his head, which fortunately did not seem to be much. If the fancy took him, he would abruptly depart. Dagmar frequently found herself apologising, filling in, and later stamping her little foot at her substantial, sulkily unrepentant husband. She was also by nature candid, while he was brutally frank, so their disagreements often rattled the chandeliers and delighted the servants.

Luckily they both recovered their tempers as

rapidly as they lost them so within thirteen months Nicholas had a brother. Alexander was a robust baby, which comforted the court immensely. Nicholas was fragile and most could remember the contrast between Nicholas, Dagmar's first love, and Alexander, her husband. It was well to have a reliable second string to the bow, said the wiseacres.

Baby Alexander did not last a year. Meningitis, which had cut down Nicholas in the previous generation, now took the new generation's second born. Both parents sat with him into the early hours as he died, then stayed to watch over the tiny corpse until the Eastern sky was smeared with light. The child's father only partly undressed before he collapsed in exhausted sleep but Dagmar walked away to stand for hours, silently shaking and wet cheeked, gazing into a portrait of a sensitive young man.

One of the tragedies of an infant's death is that the child seems to have had no opportunity to participate in the complexities of life, but this was not the case with baby Alexander. His little life left his parents closer to each other, more reliant, more loving. It was as though his mother buried the past with her child and began a new life, looking forward, not back.

Although Alexander still shrugged off the niceties, he did care. From army exercises he wrote to Dagmar, who was relaxing in Denmark with her family, to complain that she did not write as often as he would like; it brought back memories of her reproachful letters to Nicholas, when nobody had told her that he was too busy fighting for life to write.

Meanwhile war clouds gathered dark in the skies of Europe. The storm burst and inside a few weeks

Prussia had defeated the French.

Napoleon III, nephew of the original, had fought for and achieved power in France, won some of his overseas campaigns, and set France on the path to redevelopment and success. Then, concerned at the aggressive swagger of the Prussians, he allowed their Otto von Bismarck to goad him into war. He was captured at the disastrous battle of Sedan and, deposed in France, went into a deep depression and exile.

The Czar and his court were still feeling aggrieved with Napoleon III over the Crimean War but Dagmar stayed with her Danish prejudices against all things German and inculcated them in her husband too, so that he and his father had opposing loyalties. Arguments followed. The Czar had advised her father to keep Denmark neutral and, when Christian asked for Russian support in trying to win back Schleswig-Holstein during post-war realignment, he received no satisfactory response. Dagmar spent time with the Empress, whom she liked, but she had reservations about her father-in-law and, as marriage partners do, she shared them with her spouse.

A third boy arrived but George was another fragile child. His weak chest and Nicholas's ailments worried Dagmar and she took them to Denmark whenever she could. Everyone wants to go home when illness strikes and Dagmar still saw Russia as an extraordinary adventure she was duty bound to perform. Alexander's military activities kept him away from home anyway so they spent frequent periods apart.

They did get together for an informal visit to England, to repair relationships with the British Court, ruptured by the Crimean War. Unfortunately the Shah of Persia – larger than life and much more colourful – upstaged them with a tour which culminated in London at the same time that they were there. Dagmar and her sister Alexandra had co-ordinated their wardrobes so that they could dress identically at key events throughout the Russian visit. It was a brilliant publicity device and captivated the ladies of the Court, but the crowds and the press were more interested in the strange and exotic Shah. To Dagmar, playing girls with her sister, the Shah's visit provided an amusing diversion but Alexander was furious at being upstaged. He had abandoned his pleasures to be admired by the effete English and here he was, merely a sideshow for this outlandish barbarian. With difficulty Dagmar dragged him through the formal itinerary but, as soon as they could escape, they sailed for Denmark.

A fourth child, and the best: Xenia was her mother reborn. Small, alert, with large eyes, she would grow as gamine and charming as her mother. There would be two more: Mikhail and Olga but between those two births, the children's father would become Czar. Of the five, only Xenia and Olga would outlive Dagmar and die of old age. But now parenthood and the social round ate up the years. Dagmar, maturing splendidly into the role of heir to the First Lady of the Empire, frequently visited London and Copenhagen. She loved the luxury of Czarskoe Selso but preferred the climate of the Ukraine. Alexander enjoyed family life and, when he tired of it, he revelled in his leisurely role in the command of troops. There he was surrounded by family and friends, for senior Romanovs were often senior officers. A few took the military arts seriously and were mocked for their commitment. Alexander thought his nephew Nikolai Nicholaevitch took it a bit far, going through the full rigours of the staff college. He was rapidly becoming a highly professional and competent leader of men; that could be useful one day, just as long as the lad didn't get ideas above his station, thought Alexander. The Czarevitch's drinking was substantial but he had learnt to hold his liquor with no less dignity than he exhibited the rest of the time. Anyway, he was always surrounded by his own kind.

Those anxieties Alexander did experience sprang mainly from his relationships with the previous generation and the next. His father recognised that dynastic survival depended on a less total domination by the few of the many, while young Alexander did not. On the other hand, Czar Alexander II failed to admit to himself that he would not live forever: he refused to confront the fact that Alexander was an entirely unenlightened Czarevitch. An unenlightened Czar Alexander III would be a misfortune from which Russia might recover but the Romanovs could not. But the Czar let the younger man have neither experience of nor influence on matters of state. He regarded his offspring as a dolt, which was understandable, but he ensured that he was an ignorant dolt, which was unforgivable.

And there was another point of conflict between father and son. A friend of the Czar had wasted his own fortune, then died having asked Alexander to be guardian to his children. The Czaritsa had been aged by childbirth, grief, and disappointment; Alexander gradually turned to one of his wards for comfort. In 1865 the girl, Princess Catherine Dolgoruky, was eighteen and he declared undying love for her. She accepted his devotion the following year, although she was nearly thirty years younger than Alexander. In due course she was appointed a lady-in-waiting, to bring her into the court. She lived in villas convenient to the Czar, bearing him two princes and two princesses.

Dagmar, who had exchanged many confidences with the Empress, was only slightly younger than Catherine. She was appalled, as was the Czarevitch, and they cut Catherine whenever their paths crossed. The Czar responded with animosity, and so relationships deteriorated.

Still the Czar did not see a need to prepare his son to be leader.

The dynasty was founded in 1613 when the fabled original, Mikhail Romanov, left Kostroma on the Volga to claim in Moscow the Russian throne to which he had been elected. The Byzantine title of Czar had strong paternalist undertones and the Romanovs came to believe that the Czar owned all the land, an estate owner on a gargantuan scale. Towards the end of the nineteenth century, the last Czar would describe himself in a census as a landowner. He meant nothing less than that he owned Russia. And because all political, social, military, civil, judicial, and ecclesiastical authorities found it convenient to recognise every ruling Czar during 300 years as an all-owning, all-powerful father answering only to God, others believed it, and because many believed, it was so. And until the last few decades, because it was Russia, he who owned the land, owned the serfs. Division of ownership had moderated the systems of other countries. The cataclysm of the French Revolution had rectified many matters there, while the Magna Carta, signed at Runnymede near Windsor, gave the edge of reason that would trim the flight feathers of English Kings; but the wings of the Russian Imperial Eagle had never been cropped.

During the reign of Peter the Great there had been a serious effort to develop a system that moderated power and authority. The Petrine doctrine sought a legal system controlled by the Czar who it suggested, by having control, came under his own laws. The autocratic State would be the ultimate authority. On the other hand, the Muscovite model insisted that the Czar ruled as the personal representative of God on Earth; his perception of what he should do and how hc should do it was God's perccption, and denying God's perception was inconceivable. Czar after Czar rejected the Petrine model, and Russian Orthodox people, multitude after multitude of them, lived and died with neither hope nor light except their love of the father of all the Russias and faith in the hereafter.

All this was generally accepted and it remained as long as it was accepted. But the world was changing and some people learned new ways of seeing things, doctrines like all property being theft. They considered the proposition that one man could own all Russia and the labourers and their labour, their love, life, and destiny, one man who passed that ownership on, father to son, for centuries. Having considered it, they would gather in hidden places to talk among themselves. And the muttering could be heard in high places.

The serfs were emancipated by Alexander in 1861 but disenchantment, like corruption, had become endemic, and that did not change. If a landowner nominated a social inferior as a subversive, that person was guilty. That did not change. Police investigations were infrequent and incompetent. That did not change. The result was that many ordinary people were condemned unless they could bribe their way out of it, and if they could not afford the train fare, shackled to tread the road eastward. Others were killed, some by judicial process, many more by injudicious violence.

There were wars, of course. In 1876 the Serbs and the Turks started killing each other and Russia saw a chance for some righteous anger, which could coincide with expansion of its national frontiers. Dagmar devoted herself to hospital work while husband Alexander went off to command the Russian rearguard. Greece – under Dagmar's brother William – intervened to ensure that Russia won. England, under Dagmar's sister's mother-in-law, intervened to ensure that Russia did not swamp Constantinople. Prussia's Otto von Bismarck was called in to adjudicate (Astute? Certainly. Objective? Hardly) and organised the peace so that the Balkans remained precariously unstable.

Russia felt it had fought and won the war but had been robbed by Germany of its due spoils and the Czar's conciliatory attitude to Germany. Dagmar subscribed to that view and so did her husband, and he said so. There is usually a feeling of disillusion after a war, when people recognise the inordinate cost of inadequate gain. Populations seek a scapegoat, someone who made unfulfilled promises or someone who asked for more than should have been given. The spotlight fell on Czar Alexander II and it was in this atmosphere that the revolutionaries gathered in groups. Some wanted peaceful, rational revolution. Others called for bloody overthrow. These tried the Czar in absentia, found him guilty and pronounced the death sentence.

Alexander knew about the sentence so he took precautions. When he moved about the country he had two identical liveried trains that travelled more or less in tandem, but the secret of which contained the Czar and which carried servants with all his baggage and paraphernalia was known to very few people. Revolutionaries laid their plans but they could not obtain that last fragment of intelligence; they tossed a coin, planted dynamite and blew up his luggage. Some servants died too.

Chapter 6

The following year the travails of the Czaritsa were clearly coming to an end and the family started to gather. The train bringing her brother Prince Alexander to Petersburg was delayed, putting the evening's arrangements back. The party finally arrived and the preliminaries were hastily dealt with, so that the Czar was barely half an hour late escorting his guests towards his personal dining room in the Winter Palace. As they walked, talking and laughing, down the corridor, the floor of the room ahead erupted with a roar and chaos, darkness, dust, and debris enveloped them.

A slow but accurate fuse had reached dynamite, smuggled in by workmen and assembled in the basement under the guardroom, which lay under the dining room. Forty guards were killed or maimed; the dining room floor had hurtled up with the dining table on it, then shattered and fallen, bringing down the massive chandelier to crush dying men. The terrorists were caught, satisfactorily interrogated and strung up, but they and their kind were becoming too bold and too effective.

Mikhail Loris-Melikov, a statesman and general who had distinguished himself against the Turks, was given absolute authority to root out and destroy terrorists, but also to seek and resolve abrasive issues between the people and the government. To the alarm of many aristocrats, he did not recruit police, make mass arrests, interrogate and punish. Inside a few weeks he had rescinded draconian measures, liberalised the membership of the Council of Ministers, calmed political disturbances, and relinquished his emergency powers. Revolutionaries feared men like Loris-Melikov. Their understanding could sterilise soil where discontent and revolution would otherwise germinate and grow. As it happened, enlightened men of influence were rare in a land where society was polarised and the political culture was almost entirely committed to repression. History would record eight serious attempts to kill Alexander. Seven failed.

The Empress died in her lonely bed. The formalities for the death of a Czaritsa – usually lasting four weeks with a year's mourning – were disposed of in a few days. Six weeks later the Czar married Catherine Dolgoruky. Dagmar and the Czarevitch were disgusted and said so.

Young Alexander believed his father had treated his mother disgracefully. So of course did a good many other people, but few dared speak. "Autocracy is autocracy so they can mind their own bloody business and so can you," was the Czar's response to one senior cleric who mentioned adverse public opinion.

And now the older man wanted nothing more than to sweep away the memory of his lady, replacing her by putting Catherine at his side in the Empress's role, the Empress's apartments, at the head of society.

While sharing her husband's disgust, Dagmar had a strong personal interest. There was a time in her youth when she might have had sympathy for the people involved, and sadness for the disappointment, love, and human frailty that had created the situation. Not now.

The Empress had treated her fairly, making her welcome, giving her guidance and opulent gifts, passing on those items of regalia she would need and warning her of the many pitfalls into which she could have fallen. Dagmar had been a receptive pupil. For fourteen years she had been high in the hierarchy of this strictest of stratified courts, obeyed without question, served with awed respect by virtually everyone including the richest and most powerful, but constantly required to be subservient to the Empress. Now, in this hothouse where position was everything, she was the dominant female.

Making Catherine Empress would give her precedence over Dagmar; when Alexander II died, Catherine would then become Dowager Empress, still with precedence over Dagmar, who would be the new Empress. The two women were almost the same age: if Catherine became Empress now, she would have precedence over Dagmar for the rest of their lives. Besides, Catherine had children by Alexander, sons who could compete for future honours, perhaps even for the throne. The Czar despised the Czarevitch's intellect and political philosophy, and made no secret of it. Under the influence of Catherine he was not above wrestling with the constitution to deprive his senior surviving son of his destiny. If ancestor Paul could establish the rules of succession then surely

Alexander could amend them.

Dagmar snapped that she would never curtsey to this upstart. If Catherine were crowned, she would go home to Denmark and stay there. "Not in the Imperial yacht you won't," replied the Czar. "I'd forbid your departure." Young Alexander yelled at old Alexander; old Alexander told young Alexander to behave himself. Catherine wept. Dagmar smashed priceless china. X refused to be in the same room as Y, Y declined to attend a party if X would be there. Russia saw the Imperial family behaving like spoiled children. It was an unimpressive spectacle and Russia was not impressed.

Then Loris-Melikoff presented the Czar with a strategy for reforming government and moving towards enfranchisement; it did not help that Catherine thought this was a good idea. Pobedonostseff, now procurator of the Orthodox Church, rushed to the Czarevitch, warning that this was the path to perdition. Young Alexander, supported by Dagmar, was convinced it was a step too far.

"If you loosen your grip they will pull us all down," he told his father.

"Go home and stay there," said the Czar.

"Am I under house arrest then?"

"Not if you go home and stay there."

One bright icy day in March 1881 Alexander II signed the Loris-Melikoff manifesto, went to Mass, reviewed a parade, and met destiny on the road.

Students, armed with crude bombs, had been hanging around the roads he travelled. The

Establishment knew the risks in theory but failed to recognise the reality. The Czar had several alternative routes back to the Winter Palace but his enemies had been watching; they knew them all. A lookout used a whistle to let the students know which he was following, and they ran across the snow between routes, scarves flying, carrying large snowballs, shouting to each other and laughing. The wind blew cold as a snowball rolled across the rutted ice under the Czar's carriage.

A horse, its belly split by the explosion, kicked and screamed in the bloody snow. Several Cossacks writhed on the ground and a boy lay huddled and still nearby. But the Czar, shaken and excited but undamaged, stepped from the wreckage. Guards gathered round him: was he sure he was unhurt? Would he like to see the man who would be condemned to die for throwing the bomb? Indeed he would. It had not occurred to the Cossacks that there might be a second bomber, a second bomb. They glanced with surprise at the snowball that rolled heavily between their feet.

Alexander was one of those dismembered by the second explosion. What remained of his legs was a mangled mass of cloth, flesh, and splintered bone. There seemed no part of him still undamaged and yet he lived, so he was carried into the palace where for forty minutes the Court watched him bleed him to death, treated by doctors who knew they could not save him but had to be seen to try. Nicholas was a sensitive boy of twelve. He was not clever but he loved his family and he did as he was told. He stood, sailor-suited, his teeth clenched and his stomach churning, staring between weeping adults at the bloody nightmare that had been his grandfather, and which still breathed and spoke. What in God's name could this mean? How could anyone on God's earth be so wicked, hate so much, be so beastly cruel?

Catherine had endured insult and humiliation for love of the Czar and now she was close to madness. Her shrieks as he died, his blood on her gown, her demented behaviour would haunt Nicholas for the rest of his life. But in the agate-hard world of ambition she was out of the running. Alexander III was Emperor, Dagmar was Empress, and Nicholas was Czarevitch. For better or worse, the Alexandrian Romanov line was back on course.

The new Czar gave Russia his response: reprisal, repression, and battening down of hatches. The noose mercifully followed thorough interrogation of the surviving assassins. Pobedonostseff rewrote the manifesto, vigorously excising any softening of autocratic conviction. Loris-Melikoff resigned along with other moderates; their spaces were promptly filled by hard-line supporters of autocracy. The police recruited extensively and no door was safe from the knock in the early hours. Arrest, interrogation, punishment, exile, and execution spread like a rash from Petersburg to Vladivostok. As the pseudo-Czar Joseph Stalin would one day say, "Russia deserves what is best for Russia and I am here to decide what that is." He would select the same solution as Czar Alexander III did: investigative social surgery, corrective social surgery, amputation as appropriate.

The coronation of Alexandra III, with his enchanting little Czaritsa in ivory silks, pearls and gold at his side, was everything that three centuries of developing grandeur, magnificent choirs and unlimited incense could make of it. In Moscow the Orthodox Church slipped into double harness with the new autocrat, while those who controlled the collective performances of communities across the Empire ensured that Russia rejoiced. Of course, good peasants would never disappoint their Czar; The Petersburg capella choir sang beautifully and Mikhail Galinka's opera, *A Life for the Czar*, drove home the message.

Chapter 7

Dagmar lacked neither intelligence nor compassion, but nor did she have second sight. She looked through the window of absolute privilege at Russia and saw a working system. Wealth that could have fed a multitude had been devoted to creating an environment from which she could not perceive the tragedies, hear the cries, feel the pain, or know the truth. When harvests failed she heard of difficulties, when arctic freezing killed thousands she received more furs, and when condemned prisoners emerged from interrogation physically incapable of taking the few steps to the gallows, she was told that Russia had been saved from wicked men. And she believed.

Her compassion for the less fortunate led her to the hospitals; she took gifts, talked to the sick and dying. Unlike others, she spent time with the derelicts and the spent. She sincerely cared for individual people whom she saw suffer but her vision seemed to go no further than sympathy for the immediate individual and a deep loathing of anyone or anything that threatened anyone she regarded as her own, most especially a loathing of Germany in general and Prussia in particular. The slogan of one of the greatest of Scottish clans was "Who hits mine, hits me." Dagmar would have been in harmony with those clansmen. Now the narcotic of autocracy had worked through her system, taken over from the simplicity of her youth. She would not now have considered baking a biscuit, nor comparing it to being a princess. She was Empress to the largest nation on Earth, answerable only to her husband and to God. She stood, imperious but unaware, at the mid-point of her real life: behind her, thirty-three years from birth in Copenhagen, in the future, thirty-six years from the murder of her son, the last Czar.

Nobody now could accuse her of being unglamorous. The carriage of those fine shoulders and alert head was unmistakably that of the Empress. Small, svelte and elegant, she dressed with the restrained excellence that can only be achieved by unrestrained extravagance. Her colours were rich: deep sea green, midnight blue or darkest plum, garnished with emeralds, sapphires, or rubies and always in impeccable taste. Now Dagmar could praise a lady of the Court with a glance, dismiss another with a lift of an eyebrow: she could do it and, whenever she chose, she did, without hesitation. She did not often now look at the portrait of a sensitive young man; in fact, she seldom saw it, because they moved from Petersburg to Gatchina.

Like Alexander himself, the Gatchina Palace was a structure that impressed those who valued bulk above style. Several eminent architects tried to improve it over the years but it retained the ambience of a huge barracks. This was an attraction to Alexander who fancied himself as a soldier, welcoming any excuse for a military parade on the vast area in front of the central façade. It was also moated and reasonably easy to make secure, provided there was a vast number of reliable sentries. This was achieved by careful recruiting; a local recruit might sympathise with local malcontents, so recruits were drawn from communities hated and feared by the local population. In so vast a land, riven by ignorance, superstition, and terror, this was not difficult.

The palace interior included the usual features beloved of Alexander's parents and, as would one day become evident, the woman Nicholas would marry. The Chintz Chambers were designed by architect Roman Kuzmin who, in each of the rooms, provided a single heavily patterned English flowered chintz for wallcoverings, furniture and ornately draped curtains. Kuzmin was also responsible for the Gothic Gallery, a long and extravagantly fan-vaulted corridor with stained glass, columns and arches in the nineteenth-century mock-medieval style that August Pugin was imposing on the British houses of parliament and churches from Land's End to John O'Groats.

Others had been equally unrestrained. Even the gilt and crimson velvet furniture of the Tapestry Room was overwhelmed by three immense tapestries illustrating the Adventures of Don Quixote, the great allegory written by Spain's Miguel de Cervantes Saavedra. Two of these would in the twentieth century be sold to hang in air-conditioned comfort in California but for the moment they contributed to the splendour of the state and parade rooms at Gatchina. Dagmar liked such things well enough – the grandeur of the Throne Room, the ornamentation of the flower garlanded Oak Chamber – but they were not important to her. Raised in relative austerity, her main concern was that her surroundings were appropriate to her status and her duties. Alexander cared even less for ornamentation, preferring quarters that sustained his self-perception of being an active soldier, with soldierly virtues. Which was why the Imperial family occupied cramped chambers in the Gatchina.

In the season they returned to Petersburg but there they lived at the Anitchkoff Palace. If they seemed obsessed by explosives, it was hardly surprising. Bombs, tunnels, and plots were alleged with terrifying frequency; many were the imaginary products of vainglorious students, avaricious informers, ambitious policemen and all the other parasitic vines that thrive where trust rots. The students and intellectuals who wanted vengeance for social injustice would have done better to recognise that revenge is a dish best eaten cold; when they allowed their anger to overheat they became indiscreet and indiscretion brought betrayal, interrogation and more pain than they had ever imagined. Or, viewed from another perspective, they simply disappeared.

In 1882 Olga, the plainest and the only one of Dagmar's children born to the purple, completed the family. By then, Nicholas was aged fourteen, gentle and diffident. His fine features would have suited a woman. In a man, in Russia, in the son of the hulking Alexander, they seemed weak. Fortunately for him his surviving siblings were also less sturdy than their father, so he did not stand out. The Czar still liked to straighten horseshoes and bend pokers to demonstrate his strength to his children but Nicholas now sensed a reproach in this and recoiled from these displays. So did Dagmar, who tried unsuccessfully to dissuade her husband from showing off.

Horseplay and practical jokes had seemed fun during her youth in Copenhagen but, as in so many things, Alexander approached humour with a heavy hand. He found turning a garden hose on visiting dignitaries or upending a bucket of water over people hugely satisfying. The children took him as a role model, tripping servants and embarrassing tutors from behind their impregnable social status. One tutor tried to make geography more interesting by describing his own experiences in faraway places; the scholars challenged him and were brutally contemptuous when he admitted that he had never been able to afford a visit to any of the places he described.

The Czar also liked routine. In August he always enjoyed army manoeuvres; the manliness, the camaraderie, the uniforms and the formal respect of inferior ranks all combined to provide a comforting traditional environment. After that, to Poland for some hunting, the fall visit to Denmark, back to the secure austerity of quarters in Gatchina and then into Petersburg for the season, followed by a trip to Peterhof. It was exhausting for him, he said, but the servants needed the exercise.

There was no shortage of servants, all of whom had plenty of exercise. Neither Alexander nor Dagmar lived luxuriously, preferring simple foods, plain clothing and undemanding pursuits when they were living informally. Still, at the Alexander Palace the family kitchen consisted of twenty-odd assorted rooms a general kitchen, store rooms, cold rooms lined with ice boxes, aquaria, hors d'oeuvres, candy, pastry, and biscuit rooms, even a kvass room with its own cold store, where the sweet liquor, quickly fermented from malted grain, bread and sometimes fruit, was brewed and stored for cooking and drinking. Tastes might be simple but Alexander would frequently descend into the kitchens, demanding kvass and a bowl of green vegetables stewed with crab and sturgeon, or a sturdy soup with soured cream. Much worse, he could declare the imminent arrival of substantial parties, when every luxury must be available. The demands of the Court and the government meant that vast resources had to be on call at any time. Palaces existed across Western Russia so that the full splendour of Imperial Russia could be invoked whenever the Czar thought it appropriate. Where the Czar went, the resources followed. The labour, involving over a thousand kitchen and serving staff, the cost, transportation and the waste were extraordinarily extravagant but Romanovs prided themselves in never asking the cost of anything.

Alexander was not a demonstrative man but he had grown hugely fond of the little lady who had given him six children and guided him through the minefields of human and political relationships. She was now in her mid-thirties and had told him that his five surviving children were enough. He would like, he thought, to mark nearly twenty years together with some gift, small and delightful, meticulously presented, just like her. Not another of those bloody ikons (God forgive, but even God must tire of those bloody ikons, and he had both given and received more crosses than he cared to bear). He had tried beautifully painted and glazed eggs from the Imperial Porcelain Factory; Dagmar had certainly liked those well enough but now Alexander wanted something really special. She had commented on a new goldsmith company whose brilliantly original work was making a mark in society. Alexander met Carl Fabergé.

Fabergé, skinny and bearded, listened, nodded his prematurely balding head and asked only for trust. Alexander smacked his shoulder, then thought no more about it until Easter was approaching. Russians make much of Easter and of Easter eggs too, with dyed eggs representing rebirth. Fabergé brought Dagmar's, Alexander gave him another buffet on the shoulder and told him to give the ornate package to her. Inside was a box, inside that there was an egg. A simple, white enamelled egg with a gold band round the middle. Puzzled, she picked it up; the egg was astonishingly heavy. She found the gold band opened; inside was a smaller facsimile in purest gold – a yolk perhaps. She laid the enamelled egg aside to see if the gold egg opened. It did, and inside was a gold hen with ruby eyes. She picked it up, delighted, but Alexander had been shown the full complexity; he stepped forward, took the hen and opened it. Inside was another egg – a single flawless ruby – surmounted by a tiny replica of the Imperial crown.

Dagmar was astonished. The highest echelons of Russian society were astounded. Those who had seen the miraculous egg boasted of having seen it; those who had not seen it, pretended they had. Fabergé's reputation soared into the stratosphere. From now on there would be an egg every year for the Empress, each with the blend of whimsy, brilliant craftsmanship, and disregard for cost that distinguished the work of the House of Fabergé in the service of the House of Romanov. When the Imperial eggs went on display in Petersburg's Derviz Palace in 1902, the aristocracy of Europe was amazed, while Fabergé could name his price for whatever he made.

One youthful aristocrat was manhandled out of the exhibition yelling: "The children of Russia go without bread to pay for these accursed baubles." His family ceased to receive invitations to anything at all and his brother's commission in the army was rescinded.

Chapter 8

Just as Dagmar's father found, the peaceful years did not last long. Six years to the day after his father was blown up, the family was traveling by carriage through Petersburg when five students who had been betrayed by an informer were arrested nearby. They were carrying carved out books packed with explosives. After robust interrogation they eventually confessed that they had intended to kill the Czar, so they were interrogated some more, just for the sake of satisfaction. This was not the only assassination plot but it earns a corner in history because one of those young people was Alexander Ulyanov.

A young man, unshaven and poorly dressed, raced up five flights of stairs and burst open a door. He stood, breathless, staring at the man who sat, hunched over a large and empty table. The young man breathed deeply. "Vladimir Ulyanov, we have the message. They have begun hanging them all. They are hanging your brother," he said.

There was a long silence before the figure at the table stirred. "They have begun to hang my brother. The way they hang people, it takes longer than a few minutes."

"We are with you. We are with him and with you.

Is there anything – anything at all – I can do?"

"There is only one thing to be done. Alexander is dying for trying to kill a tyrant. We must find another way. It is for us to exterminate the tyrant and the tyranny."

"He will be dead now, and at peace. That at least is something."

"No. He and I, we wrestled when we were younger. He has a strong neck." The bearded man at the table pulled out a watch. "He will writhe on the end of the rope for a while yet before he dies."

The man at the door twisted his cap in frustration. "Someone must pay for this atrocity. Come out with me Vladimir Ulyanov. We shall find someone…"

For the first time the gleaming head, prematurely bald, turned towards the door. "Finding someone is the old way. Go home and wait. The time will come when nobody will escape."

"I cannot leave you alone."

"I am not alone," said the man the world would come to know as Lenin. "I am with my brother."

Having completed a visit to the Caucasus in 1888, the Czar and his family sailed to Sevastopol where they boarded one of the twin Imperial trains. Both were due to trundle across the landscape, closely guarded by security along the line. In the dining car the Czar and Czaritsa sat, cheerful at lunch with twenty people. The Czar was in a hurry; he sent an order to the driver: go faster.

With respect, the speed was regulated; the line could not take such a heavy train at speed. The messenger explained but the Czar did not request, the Czar instructed. The Czar wished the train to go faster so the train would go faster. This was not open to debate.

The train went faster.

The train was certainly travelling swiftly now, rocking and with an occasional jolt… then the coach lurched, reared up, fell back and buckled as coaches ploughed into one another. The crashing ended as huge impacts gave way to small noises. The little sounds of fracture and escaping pressure followed, then they too ceased. From all around, the screaming started. Dagmar was bruised, bleeding from a crushed hand. The carriage walls were pushed in, the roof split and hanging across the compartment. Gradually the family gathered; they were all damaged but not seriously. The Czar's leg was trapped but attendants released it so that he could join them, limping, pale and drawn with pain as he rubbed his heavily bruised back. He gritted his teeth and joked that brother Vladimir would not after all be the third Czar in seven years. Dagmar organised help and tended the thirty-five maimed; twenty-two corpses were laid out on the embankment beside the shattered carriages.

Investigation confirmed that the heavy train was going too quickly on an old line with light rails. The driver was dismissed, and counted himself fortunate to have escaped with nothing worse than destitution. There was a rumour that the Czar displayed Herculean strength and heroic courage in rescuing his trapped family; another that there was a suicide bomber aboard the train. Both were fantasy but the accident reminded the Royal household how vulnerable it was. The incident might also have been recognised as the consequence of stupid, irresponsible autocratic behaviour, but that was unthinkable.

Terrorism and disasters were not all that threatened the dynasty. Nicholas had fallen in love. Alexandra of Hesse and By Rhine was in many ways an ideal candidate; she had a fine-featured, heart-shaped face, a beautiful translucence to her skin, reddish-gold hair and sea-grey eyes. Perhaps a little thin in the lips, with a dreariness about the eyes, but almost certainly capable of conceiving and bearing attractive children. Though she was not incisively intelligent, that was no drawback. She was said to be a melancholy hypochondriac; certainly she was preoccupied with leg injuries she had sustained during a childhood game, when she fell through a gardener's glass cold frame. Sometimes she affected the use of an invalid chair, and learned not to jump out of it when something excited her attention. If she seemed diffident it was hardly surprising; life had not been kind and she had fallen under the influence of incurable melancholics, not least Victoria, the Queen of England.

Victoria had mourned her dead husband with a durable devotion that far exceeded her affection for him. Before he died she knew he had enjoyed an active sex life with various men throughout their marriage, while he fathered their children with scant and diminishing enthusiasm. She was aware that he regarded her as intellectually inadequate, that he had investigated the possibility of divorce and had built Balmoral Castle so he could set up an alternative Court where gaiety, art, and intellectual debate could thrive. The relationship that had developed between them was not the sort that could possibly be followed by forty years of mourning, not unless the surviving partner carried unimaginable guilt. Victoria carried just such a burden.

She had watched her husband die a miserable and premature death to save her throne, and spent the rest of her long life in mourning, craving his forgiveness. She could not be sure what killed him but was sure he had died by human hand, and she in her confusion had been complicit.

Victoria's daughter Alice, who was Alexandra's mother, did all she could to help her inconsolable mother after Albert died in December 1872. Seven months later Alice married Prince Louis of Hesse Darmstadt in a ceremony where Victoria, entirely in black with a widow's cap, did everything in her power to turn the summer ceremony into a wake. "More like a funeral," she said with grim satisfaction.

Alice briskly set about creating a dynasty but she lost one son to haemophilia. This is a condition that prevents blood clotting naturally, so that any slight injury can continue bleeding until it is life-threatening. Slight damage that most people never notice – internal bleeding or leakage into joints – can become immensely painful and very dangerous. Aspirin, which works by penetrating the gut wall, can kill a haemophiliac. The condition is transferred by heredity through women, though it usually afflicts only males. Victoria had passed it to Alice who passed it to her son, who died painfully.

Another child went down with diphtheria, then four more in quick succession, followed by her husband. Gradually they all recovered but Alice had let maternal love triumph over caution: she had kissed and cuddled her sole remaining son when he was very ill. Six years to the day after Albert died, Victoria's Scottish personal attendant John Brown brought her a telegram. Alice, the daughter who had comforted her mother then, was with her father now. Victoria's grief manifested itself in increasingly theatrical mourning.

Into Victoria's sombre Court limped one of Alice's bereaved children, the shy, melancholy Alexandra. Immobilised by ailments both real and imaginary, Alexandra spent long hours reading greedily, and so it was she discovered and embraced the philosophy of the depressive Soren Kierkegaard, Denmark's theological philosopher who embraced suffering, guilt, and the expiation of sin. Years before, Kierkegaard had duelled with less melancholic spiritual guides for influence over the Danish Church, and had lost. But still some Danes read his essays and yearned for the catharsis of martyrdom. As she grew towards womanhood Alexandra would sit in her unnecessary wheelchair, absorbed by the penance of guilt and remorse that Kierkegaard's relentless god exacted from the thinker's family, reflecting on the suffering of her own family and drawing solace from empathy with him.

Victoria, dubbed the Widow of Windsor by an impatient English public, provided an excellent environment for her dark feelings to flourish: perpetual mourning with drawn curtains, portraits of a dead man gazing down on rooms unchanged since he lived in them; mawkish mementos everywhere:

gloves, alabaster hands and feet, locks of hair, tributes, poems, weeping muses, and an all-pervading hush, disturbed only by the rustle of the grieving widow in her stiff black gowns: short, fat, and inconsolable.

As Alexandra's femininity blossomed, Victoria nurtured her. Here was potential breeding stock for the future. The Queen would keep her son from the throne as long as she could – he was after all a libertine and a bully whom Albert had understandably despised. Victoria had done well to marry him to Dagmar's sister Alexander but poor Alexander had endured his brutishness, rather than rectifying it. Once Victoria died, Bertie's reign would, God willing, be mercifully short and then his son would rule the British Empire, with this sad beauty of Hesse at his side.

Unfortunately, the Prince of Wales' eldest son, the Duke of Clarence, was less than his grandmother would have wished and much less than Alexandra was prepared to marry. A mother-fixated child, he tried the fleshpots that continued to gratify his father but found them inadequate for his needs. The company of other males of his own age had seemed to suit him best but as he grew older, he seemed to have ever younger companions.

Many other girls, enjoying the privileged position of much-favoured granddaughter of the Queen, would have accepted the inadequate heir to so much privilege. Alexandra was not as other girls. She was adamant that she would never marry this odd and repellent youth. Also, during a visit to Russia, she had developed a childhood crush on the delicate Nicholas. In the exotic surroundings of Petersburg he shone for her like a sensitive angel amongst the broad-chested Romanov males. She had decided he would be her bridegroom and her determination was obsessive.

Refusing the English heir was revealed as an immensely lucky move for Alexandra when scandal ripped open the seamiest side of London's society life. Rich young men had been using a club to procure telegraph boys for their sexual delectation and one of the most enthusiastic customers had been Edward, Duke of Clarence. All the weapons of privilege, from blackmail and bribery to promises of preferment, were rushed to protect the young heir to the throne but men whose reputations were destroyed were too resentful to allow him to escape. If they were doomed to endure heavy sentences, then he would come too. It looked as though the court case would destroy him and with him, very possibly his father's insecure throne. Those in the know started speculating whether Edward might be Jack the Ripper. Quite why a man who lusted after prepubescent boys should hack prostitutes to death was never clear but even then England's chattering classes were reluctant to let facts interfere with a good scandal. Once again the unpopular English monarchy tottered. Then, in a suspiciously convenient twist of fate reminiscent of Prince Albert's propitious demise when he wanted to part from Victoria, Edward fell victim to an influenza epidemic and died at the age of twenty-eight. Brother George, a self-consciously inadequate man with more conventional appetites, became heir, to the relief of British monarchists.

Nicholas had returned Alexandra's childhood infatuation and had renewed his enthusiasm whenever they met but that had not stopped him gaining the usual experiences of a future Czar. While Alexandra was an adolescent, maundering over photographs and yearning for the romance of the opera, the ballet, and the young man she idolised, he was also close to the footlights, roistering in theatre dressing rooms. Dagmar and Alexander were appalled when they heard that Alexandra had set her sights on their son. They had it on good authority that she was melancholy, devoid of dress sense or style, preoccupied with her own ailments and, when roused, hysterically obsessive. Red blotches would appear on her neck, her voice would rise, and all control would disappear. Hardly the thing for the Nevski Prospekt.

They sent Nicholas on a world tour to forget. With his tubercular brother George, his gay cousin George of Greece, and a group of high-born Russian officers, he left Trieste in 1890 to see the sights, grow up, and sow such wild oats as he needed to get out of his system. In Kyoto, Japan, they caused offence by boisterously confusing female prostitutes with male transvestites. Next day as they returned in rickshaws from lunch in Otsu, a policeman chased them and lashed at Nicholas with a sword, slashing open his scalp. The Czarevitch leapt from the two-wheeled chair and fled, pursued by the swordsman. Brother George brought the attacker down by thrusting his walking cane between his running legs, then the rickshaw drivers gave the fallen man a sound beating before binding and dragging him away.

Although not life-threatening, Nicholas's injury was a serious blow to relations with a powerful neighbouring state. The Japanese Emperor Meiji, regarded as a god by his own nation, scurried with his entourage to Kyoto to express his devastation, through an interpreter, to the bandage-turbaned Czarevitch.

The Emperor and his princes sat inscrutable as his spokesman said: "The Emperor is appalled that this crime has been committed in our country. The scoundrel who did this was a policeman but he dishonoured himself by enforcing the predations of immoral people. Perhaps they wanted to rob you, Majesty. The assailant is not Japanese, not all Japanese – his blood is contaminated with that of one of the inferior races of the Orient. We have arranged for him to be chastised just now, at this moment."

Nicholas was startled. "Chastised?" Chastisement hardly seemed adequate for a murderous attack on the visiting heir to the Russian Empire.

The spokesman nodded vigorously. "Oh yes, Majesty, very chastised. He is being chastised by four men beating him with bamboo poles. He is being chastised to death."

The Emperor smiled and nodded at the Czarevitch. All the Japanese courtiers smiled and nodded, so Nicholas smiled and nodded. So that, he supposed, was that and everything was all right.

The hazardous tour solved nothing. Nicholas came home suffering from occasional headaches – he would blame the superficial wound for headaches for the rest of his life – and a desire to settle down with the lovely and, he thought, undemanding Alexandra. Many European and Russian aristocrats were covertly gay but Nicholas had enjoyed enough of the shaved masculine pleasures of Japan. He became exclusively heterosexual, amusing himself with mistresses, as much from boredom and for the look of the thing; really he wanted Alexandra. Queen Victoria continued to find inappropriate suitors for the girl and she continued to vigorously rebuff them. Then in early 1892 Alexandra's father Louis collapsed and died. Not yet twenty, neurotic and in an agony of grief, she desperately needed a man beside her, a family to depend upon.

This was a bad year for Russia – one of several. A drought dried the land like a bone so that crops withered where they stood. Stock stood gaunt, heads down, until they fell and, after a little struggle, lay still. Fish floundered, suffocating in shallows, mud dried into fissured cakes. Russians starved while crows, rats, and the other eaters of carrion feasted. Nothing like this had occurred in living memory. Some food supplies were distributed, with the result that Ministers congratulated themselves on keeping the official death toll to under half a million people. Though some thought more could have been done, it was a considerable achievement, greatly assisted by the custom amongst ordinary people of circulating subscription lists for voluntary contributions to support public endeavour. Churches, roads, public buildings, and now famine relief benefited from personal donations for communal purposes.

The Czar was preoccupied with the sufferings of his people but wanted nothing to do with anyone fostered by Queen Victoria, that interfering old imbecile of England. Empress of India, by God, what did dumpy frumpy Victoria know of Empire?

For Dagmar the problem of Nicholas's future

remained paramount. Alexandra could bring neither glamour nor prestige to the Romanovs. The Empress was amongst her godparents but remained adamantly opposed to this melancholic German of dubious health becoming Czarevna. She did not yet know that Alexandra was a genetic time bomb that could contaminate the sacred blood Imperial. The Princess of Hesse would do it through no fault of her own, but she would do it.

Time passed and the rains came. The Crimea flowered again, wind rippled ripening grain across undulating landscapes. Many Russians raised a toast to another catastrophe survived and wondered when the next would come. They did not have long to wait. With the water came plague diseases, so that multitudes of famine survivors died in agony. In every community the cry of "Throw out your dead!" was heard and burial parties again reached for their spades.

Dagmar, cushioned from the harsh realities of Russian life, reflected that Nicholas was still young; perhaps they could wait until a more promising candidate was available to him, although there was little enough on the horizon.

It was time for destiny to stir the pot. Alexander had not been himself lately. He loved the military reviews at Krasnoe Selo but this year he faltered as he took the salute. He ate his lunch, went ash-white and fainted. He was exhausted. Relaxation and leisure pursuits were essential, said his doctor in a prescription he would soon regret. To Alexander, relaxation and leisure pursuits meant stalking deer in Poland. Within weeks the doctor was obliged to take a train to Warsaw and then a rustic carriage down rutted tracks into the pine forest to re-examine his patient, who had made straight for his favourite hunting lodge. Spala was a dank, dark, uninspiring lodge built by Alexander II. His son loved the remoteness, the rustic lodge itself, and the pleasures of the hunt. Here he was free of social pressures. A local Polish taxidermist had grown rich, stuffing the heads of red deer shot by Alexander to decorate its walls.

The doctor, relieved of hat and coat, went straight to his patient. The Czar grumbled because his shoes no longer fitted him. He had been feeling unwell and his shoes no longer fitted. After an examination the medic diagnosed oedema.

"What the devil's oedema?"

"Fluid retention and consequent swelling, Your Majesty," said the doctor.

"I could have diagnosed that myself, Zakharin. What's causing it?"

"We shall need to investigate further, Your Majesty. Any recent infections?"

"Not really. I've been feeling awful and my face has got puffy."

"I'll call a consultant."

"My bootmaker could solve it. Bigger boots."

Dr Zakharin looked reproachfully at his master. "This could be a very grave condition, sir. I want you to know that I am deeply concerned. I shall consult with an authority of international renown."

Even the Czar recognised the signals but he gave no sign. "I'll have you know, Zakharin, that the skills of my bootmaker are envied by the cobblers of Milan."

Doctor Leyden, a renal specialist in Berlin, took the call, cancelled all his appointments, caught the Warsaw train and, once ensconced in the horse-drawn carriage, wondered what the jolting over that cart track was doing to his own kidneys. The two medical men knew what to look for and they found it: Alexander was a dedicated member of the Officer's Mess, with all its prejudices and absurdities; promiscuity was tolerated, even encouraged, but venereal infection was regarded as degrading. The patient feared the humiliation apparent infection might bring but eventually he admitted there was dark matter in his urine; it was blood and it was not new to him.

He had inflammation in the kidneys, they told him. The cause? Perhaps it was an infection? No? Then possibly it was the result of an injury. Had he sustained a severe blow in the lower back in the last few years?

"I took one hell of a smack in that train accident, but that was long ago."

Glances were exchanged.

"Have you felt pains there since?"

"It was sore enough for a while, especially on horseback, but I got over it. It's just that there seems to be a weight there, pain pulling inside, and sometimes... Well, what's to be done?"

More glances, the two medical men left the room and then returned. Leyden spoke. "It seems probably you injured one kidney, put excessive demands onto the other, and that probably both are damaged."

"How long will they take to heal?"

A pause. "Kidneys do not repair themselves in the way other tissues can. It seems probable that they will continue to pass matter that they ought not while retaining toxins that they ought to pass. By giving your system as little work as possible we may improve your expectations but I very much regret having to tell Your Majesty that the prognosis is not good."

Courtiers often smirked among themselves at Alexander's military posturing but he took this information with soldierly stoicism. "How long?"

"We can't tell, sir. There is no treatment except rest and cautious diet. Absolutely no alcohol. A warm climate, limited protein, minimum fats…"

"Stop it man, stop it. How long? Weeks, months, years?"

"Perhaps a year."

"Perhaps two years?"

"No, sir, not two years. Perhaps not one."

"Then I shall not live to launch the new Imperial yacht," he said thoughtfully. "We're going to name her *Standart*, you know. I laid the keel in a Danish downpour last October. Bloody silly time of year to be out in the rain. I'd have liked to sail in her though."

The Czar sat on the bed edge and gazed down at his bloated ankles. "Right gentlemen, you will join me in a glass of vodka, then off you go while I tell the little lady."

Zakharin stammered. "No, no Your Majesty. You must not drink vodka."

"Why not Zakharin? What harm is it going to do to me?"

Chapter 9

To her own astonishment, Dagmar collapsed when she was told her husband was dying. She had married a man she did not love on the instructions of the man she did. She had accepted the life, the marriage bed, the childbirth, the Court and the reconstruction of herself; she had grown accustomed to Alexander's boorishness and his lack of sophistication. Now the prospect of his early death was more than she could tolerate and she was amazed at the strength of her feelings. She loved her husband.

As soon as she felt strong enough and could get away she went with only two companions to Warsaw railway station, there to be locked into a first-class compartment with all the blinds drawn as the train trundled across the Russian landscape. A horse-drawn carriage carried the Empress up the Nevski Prospekt, where she had come as a bride to be, where she had first been recognised by everyone as the First Lady. Elegant, formidable, and entirely self-possessed, she walked the familiar staircase, the well-known chambers. She stood again before the portrait of Nicholas. Gazing into his eyes, she waited. She felt a great tenderness, a sense of infinite loss. Suddenly her large eyes were dancing again, full of emotional excitement and then, filled with tears.

She was deep in thought as she returned to Alexander. Now she knew that the girl who had come from Copenhagen had not metamorphosed into someone else. Now she was a wife, a mother, an autocratic Empress, with total commitment to Alexander, his empire, and their marriage. But still somewhere inside was a girl who had long ago given her heart and could never take it back. Whoever she was, she was going to have to be strong.

What had she done to deserve all this? Her husband, the father of her children, the man she had learned to love, was dying. George, the most intelligent of her sons, had joined them in Spala; she had looked into his eyes and saw there too the melancholy of resignation. Xenia, the finest of all her children, was marrying against Alexander's wishes. Now Nicholas, weak, loveable Nicholas was to become Czar, so breeding was an urgent necessity, and what had he done? God help them all, he wanted to marry an unrepentant Lutheran hysteric.

The tears came. They were not for her dead betrothed, not even for her dying husband, her dying son, or her inadequate son, she told herself. They were her last opportunity for weakness before she braced herself for what lay ahead. She had squared up to tragedy in Nice; now she would take her husband to Livadia in the Crimea and there, at their favourite palace, she would do it again.

She took pen and paper, then sat back and reflected. This was not now a matter of bereavement; this was a matter for judgement and she felt very alone. Better Alexandra than let the Alexandrian dynasty head hell-for-leather down a cul-de-sac.

Alexandra and Nicholas had already been cavorting in Germany and Windsor, exchanging promises, presents, and childish endearments. Reversing the romance would have taken a father's heavy hand and Alexander's hand had lost its strength; in any case, the succession needed consolidation. Alexandra would have to do but she must change; it was unthinkable that the lady of the Emperor could be anything but Russian Orthodox and ludicrous to suggest she could be a follower of the heretic Luther. Nicholas had done his best, summoning converts to try to convince Alexandra that God was just as much God from an expedient Orthodox perspective as he was from a Lutheran angle. She had been intransigent.

Dagmar's letter left nothing unsaid. The man Alexandra loved, she wrote, would soon be absolute ruler of the greatest Empire on Earth. Alexandra would stand beside him as Empress, with the blessings of his father and all the Czars that had gone before, the blessings and adulation of all the Russias, the glory of the Russian Court, the friendship of all and the encouragement of the woman who would then be Maria Feodorovna, Dowager Empress.

The Russian Orthodox Church had stood proud for a millennium, defending Russian unity through Tartar domination, feudal conflict, foreign invasions, and the doubts of sceptics. Orthodoxy and the Romanovs were the two inseparable rocks that formed the foundation of the Empire, so she said.

Destiny held precedence over dogma. A true Christian could worship God at any altar. This was the destiny of the Romanovs, ruling dynasty of all the Russias. There was no question because there could be no question. It was essential, so it would be done: Alexandra would become Alexandra Feodorovna and would stand beside Nicholas in the appropriate place when they became master and mistress of the greatest private estate the world had ever known.

Come to Livadia no later than October, she wrote; it will be time.

Everyone in Livadia was subdued that fall, except the Czar. Arriving unannounced amongst the kitchen staff, he demanded: "Whose kitchen is this?"

"It… it's the Czar's kitchen, Your Majesty."

"Well there's a stroke of luck," he cried, "for I am the Czar and I'm hungry. The Czar wants vodka and a bowl of golden ikra. The Czar wants it here and the Czar wants it now." Neither vodka nor caviar, even the beautiful golden eggs from the Volga reserved for the Emperor's family, was on his diet. Another time he bellowed for vodka and zakuska, mixed hors d'oeuvres with fish, shellfish, cheese, stuffed dumplings, and more of his favourite ikra.

He insisted on Ministers continuing to bring him cabinet reports, telling them they must smuggle vodka to him. He proposed mischievous toasts to his own cunning, raising glasses with eminent and eminently embarrassed grandees. Dagmar stayed in bed one morning when lumbago was troubling her but, after a draught of laudanum and some sleep, she felt well enough to see how Alexander was.

It took her some time to find him. He had bullied the kitchen into making kallalaatiko, a dish he had discovered in Finland and liked inordinately. "I found him sitting in a corner with a bowl of the most extraordinary mixture of fish and meat in some kind of custard," she told Xenia. "He was eating the disgusting concoction as though terrified it would be taken from him, and swilling it down with kvass. I cried: 'Don't you care that you are killing yourself?'

"He looked at me like a scolded dog. 'Don't you care that I am enjoying myself?'

"We stared at each other for a long time and then I left him to enjoy his little luxury. Why in God's name should he not? Next day the doctor told me Sasha had kept it down for less than an hour."

Gradually his bellowing laughter weakened. His complexion discoloured and his yellowing eyes gazed out from dark hollows. Ministers came less often, bringing no bottles. He would sneak into the kitchens and call for sousi stew, chicken Tamara served cold in a rich walnut sauce, Hungarian porkolt, grilled venison with tkemali, the plum sauce of Georgia. But when the food was brought, he could not eat it. Even the gentle foods he was permitted remained untouched. Each day he fought to rise, to be a part of life and movement, but each day he spent longer in bed, exhausted. Soon he could no longer walk and Dagmar spent days and nights beside his bed.

Booked with little ceremony on a train from Wolfsgarten to the Crimea, Alexandra had an uncomfortable journey. Trains covered long distances in Russia, but slowly. There were first class, second class, and third class compartments, none memorably comfortable. In the East there was a fourth class but travellers on such trains needed strong stomachs.

An end section of a first-class carriage, with one of

the few lavatories, was locked off for Alexandra and her two companions. The lavatories were valued only because there was nothing else available. Washbasins had no plugs and no taps; pressing a spring-loaded stud released a trickle of tainted water. A uniformed official repelled curious and indignant fellow passengers, grudgingly providing Alexandra's attendants with tepid drinking water when they demanded it.

At Warsaw Alexandra alighted in icy rain while the crew took on coal and water. Passengers jumped out to fill their tin kettles from a vast samovar, steaming under a platform canopy. Others bustled to buy roast chickens, stew, soup, fruit, vegetables, and slabs of black bread at the local peasants' vending stalls. They would return laden to their compartments to brew black, sweet tea and then picnic amongst the bones, crusts, and wrappers of previous repasts.

Inside the station's spacious buffet, similar food was served with slightly more finesse, with bottles of wine on linen-covered tables. As her companions tried to assemble dainty refreshment for her, Alexandra read again a letter in female handwriting, then she tore it in pieces, which she dropped into a wastebasket. A clerk was summoned and agreed to wire ahead – not to Dagmar but to Nicholas. If he could spare time from his father's bedside, please would he arrange for a ceremony of conversion for her. She would embrace Russian Orthodoxy but, she said, under no circumstances would she repudiate the faith with which she had grown up. They had no choice, she thought; she was mistress of the situation now. She was right and Dagmar, who had bitten the insides of her cheeks as she had herself been forced to insult the decent faith of her fathers, would remain silent. But she would remember.

At Simferopol she was met by Nicholas, pale with stress but in full dress uniform. "We must go straight to Papa," he said.

She looked down at her crumpled traveling clothes. "Once I have changed…"

"There is no time. He will bless us immediately."

"But surely he is not… not yet."

Nicholas took her arm and hurried her to the Czar's room. All her life she would remember the smell. Alexander too wore full uniform, hanging loose upon him but resplendent with gaudy medals. He was gaunt and hollow-eyed; often he had to turn aside to take deep breaths from an oxygen mask. He embraced her, blessed her, blessed them, and then they were ushered away as he leaned on his tiny lady. Alexandra let her breath go with relief as the door closed; his mind, she thought, had decayed faster than his body, but she was wrong. He spoke softly and clearly. "An hysterical, hypochondriac, heretical and horrible Hun. God help us all."

Ten days later it was over. He was not yet fifty years old when he died in Dagmar's arms, murmuring: "We were the last Olympians, weren't we?"

When his father died, Nicholas disintegrated. "What is to become of us all? What is to become of Russia?" Dagmar looked at him. He was her son and she loved him, but he was no Olympian. He had asked two good questions; she believed they would both be answered before her little body lay again beside that of the

Olympian bear she had learned to love.

Gales ripped at the formal gardens, thrashed the sea into a torment as chaotic as the emotions inside the imperial mansion. But there was work to be done; the succession must be assured. Alexander's rapidly degenerating body was taken to Moscow for three days and then to Petersburg to be interred on 19 November. Dagmar kissed the decaying cheek of the man she loved, as did all the family including Alexandra. It was required.

Nicholas called after his soldier cousin in a corridor, caught up with him, turned with him into an empty chamber. "How in God's name can I aspire to be the most powerful Emperor on Earth, Nikolai?"

"You don't have to aspire, Nicholas. You are the man, you are the ikon. You are the Czar, by the grace of God."

"But I cannot fill the position. I cannot take the role of those who went before."

Nikolai reached out both hands, took his cousin's shoulders and stared into his eyes. "They too had their doubts. Your father, all our forefathers knew that, no matter how glorious the throne, there is nothing to be put upon it except a human arse. But each time a new arse is placed on it, that arse is the arse of the Czar. It is easier for us, people like me, who have already learnt to serve the Czar. You will find that God will strengthen you to wear the crown Nicholas. Only be patient. He will not ask you to play the role of any of those who went before. He will require only that you are Emperor Nicholas II."

"Will you serve me, Nikolai?"

"To the grave if need be, Nicholas."

"Thank you."

"No thanks are needed, cousin. It is my destiny and I am content with that."

A week after the burial of Alexander, mourning was lifted so that Nicholas could marry his Alexandra. Throughout the ceremonies Dagmar, pale and hobbling with lumbago, was the centre of attention. Everyone knew her, knew she wanted none of this, especially not this stiff German woman. Everyone respected her, knew she would do her duty. She looked frail but she took her place – always first, even before the bridal couple. The Emperor is dead. Long live the Dowager Empress. Long live the Emperor. Long live the new Empress – the Russian Orthodox Empress.

On her wedding night Alexandra had a headache.

Chapter 10

In those early months of Czar Nicholas, Dagmar behaved as if she were Regent, taking counsel and making decisions on behalf of the Czar. Just as she had when her husband was away, she deputised for him. If anything needed authority, she gave it. The word of the Dowager Empress was law. She had authority and she took precedence over the Empress. She also took, whether she was entitled to it or not, precedence over Nicholas; she was, after all, his mother.

During the eighteenth century Emperor Paul, who detested his daughter-in-law almost as much as he had his mother, Catherine the Great, had established the principles of male Romanov succession and the precedence of a Dowager Empress over an Empress. So, when he was murdered in his bedchamber by ambitious officials and bitter aristocrats, his widow Maria Feodorovna was dominant and remained so for decades. Dagmar – also named Maria Feodorovna – would be the next to benefit from this subsection of the Pauline principles of succession. Alexandra resented this, complained about it to Nicholas, but what could he do? Mama knew what to do, how to do it. She had authority.

Alexandra demanded: "Who is the Emperor?"

"Well, I am of course but Mama is Dowager Empress. She has so much experience and she has her grief to live through, and she is so very determined."

Alexandra's mouth set in an even thinner line. Stuck here in a few cramped rooms of the Anitchkoff palace, under the hostile eye of her mother-in-law, she could not even yell at her husband. Things were going to have to change. She was going to have to change them with the only tool she had available: this weak, diffident little man. She would just have to wait a little, until everything was secure, and then things would change. She would begin to develop a technique for dominating Nicholas more effectively than Dagmar could and then she would operate through him. If Nicholas was weak, she would exploit his weakness. The older woman used steely authority, strength of personality, irresistible determination. Alexandra would use terror. She had seen the look in her husband's eyes when she became hysterically frenzied and she knew it was an unbeatable weapon. She would win.

Although the court had come out of mourning for the wedding, it was still a time of deep grief, especially for Dagmar. She wanted her son close to her so Nicholas and Alexandra joined her for meals, when she took the head of the table. After dinner, Dagmar and Nicholas discussed court gossip, the state of the nation, how to be Czar. Dagmar had profoundly influenced decisions taken by Alexander; now she took as of right the same control over Nicholas. On one occasion when Nicholas was absent Alexandra fitted a cigarette into her amber holder, lit it, and said to Dagmar: "You wrote to me promising that you would guide me in the role of Empress."

Dagmar, who chain-smoked at times of stress, dropped her cigarette into a malachite ashtray, taking another from a matching box but lighting it with her own little gold petrol lighter. "When you need guidance I shall give it you, my dear. So far you are doing very well indeed. And so is Nicholas; there is so much for him to learn, we must not mind if it takes him a little time. I am here to guide you both when necessary and I am happy to do so. It is my function as Dowager Empress."

Alexandra braced herself. "It seems to me that Nicholas would do better if he were more free to exercise his own judgement and make his own decisions."

Dagmar smiled benignly and said: "I shall be very glad to guide you in being Empress whenever you need guidance, because I was Empress myself. I know how easy it is to make embarrassing errors of judgement in the early days. As to how I perform my duties, I was guided by my late husband's mother, who was also very experienced. Perhaps one day you will have the experience to guide your son's bride."

Alexandra's cheeks coloured. For a moment she met the older woman's unwavering gaze; then she looked away. She knew that she could not win over this adversary, not on Dagmar's home ground. Any new bride sharing her husband's family home could have told her that she would inevitably lose any conflict with her husband's mother. Dagmar was not her friend but nor was she her enemy; both could benefit if they worked together. But Alexandra was the Czaritsa, Alexandra was her husband's champion, Alexandra was determined.

She knew that her husband kept some matters from her, convinced she would resent his mother's involvement. Nicholas, having heard a Minister's reasoned arguments and then reflected for a while, would frequently announce that he would need to consult his mother on this issue. When he dithered, as he often did, bolder Ministers might suggest consulting his mother, and he usually agreed. That was enough to make the Czaritsa see the Dowager Empress as her rival.

Dagmar had the Court on her side. The Court ran on precedent and precedence; Dagmar understood the system, so everyone knew how they stood with her. She was socially skilled and meticulous in her courtesies. Alexandra had no knowledge, sought no advice from Dagmar, rejected guidance from anyone else, was awkward and uncomfortable. And she believed her every move was reported back to Dagmar. She showed no social skills, usually leaving any function early, to many ladies' relief. When she saw the guest list for a Court ball, she deleted all those names that had been linked with others in court scandals; as a result, the event was a disaster. Alexandra loathed these occasions so she gave in when Nicholas carefully suggested that guest lists could in future be left to keep his mother occupied. But Alexandra thirsted for a victory.

She inspected the clothing Dagmar had selected to stock her dressing room and decided the Dowager Empress wanted her to look dowdy. She ordered in the fashion houses, took her own counsel and set out to impress the Court. Her selections were a series of errors. Dagmar, with an unerring eye for understated elegance, had set out to introduce Alexandra as a lady of sophistication; certainly she felt no affection for this daughter of Hesse but the dynasty needed the Czaritsa to be worthy of respect. Instead, Alexandra's ostentation was immediately identified as provincial ineptitude. Those who knew what had happened accused her of ingratitude.

Her own servants had been sent back, as Dagmar's had been when she came to Russia. She forbade her new servants, appointed by Dagmar, to carry tittle-tattle about her. She might as well have told the tide not to turn.

Having made one faux pas after another, Alexandra would have difficulty establishing her status, but it must be done. She chose her ground: it would be the crown jewels. She subjected Nicholas to an intense campaign until eventually he gave in, sending his mother a note saying that the crown jewels must be available for and convenient to the Czar and his Empress so he would be arranging for them to be taken from the Anitchkoff to the Winter Palace. This jewellery was beyond price and immensely symbolic, with specific items linked with official engagements; some had become official regalia. Dagmar summoned her son, loftily explaining that Nicholas's father had bequeathed guardianship of the jewels to her and she assumed that Nicholas shared her desire to implement the late Czar's wishes. Nicholas went home and suffered the storm. He had to insist, he told his mother. She sent the least desirable pieces. No, all of it, he demanded. She sent a few more.

Gradually, as events required that Alexandra wear the appropriate pieces of jewellery, Dagmar issued them on loan, knowing they would not return. "It's not losing the jewellery that hurts," she told her sister, "it's the letting go." Eventually Alexandra had the pieces she needed while Dagmar had many of the pieces she liked, so there was no clear victory. Alexandra remained frustrated.

Then Dagmar made a careless move. She mentioned to a clerical friend that, having precedence in Court, she would of course expect to retain precedence in the liturgy. Alexandra, seizing her opportunity, explained her position to Nicholas in her unusually emphatic way, so Nicholas asked the synod, the ruling body of the Russian Orthodox Church, for a ruling. This was a tough decision for career clerics, for they wanted to have no enemies in high places. Eventually they ruled that the Emperor came first and the Dowager Empress second but the Emperor could not be separated from his Empress so he would be accompanied by her – before the Dowager Empress. Here at last was a victory. So far, she had borne Nicholas a daughter but a son would surely come, and the coronation would finally set matters in stone.

The coronation, in the ancient city of Moscow, was a sad and bitter experience for Dagmar. In magnificent ceremonies surrounded by the full glory of nearly three centuries of unbridled autocratic rule, she saw others take the roles of herself and her young husband, roles they made their own in those days when everything was new and exciting, when there were no limits to their opportunities. So little time seemed to have passed and now she had interred her husband's remains. Since then, she had spent a few weeks in Nice with her more intelligent son, George, whose weak lungs continued to threaten his life. Her favourite daughter had made a questionable marriage and Nicholas, God help him, had married a woman who was even more inadequate at filling her position than he was at his. Dagmar withdrew from as much of the celebrations as she could – let Alexandra have the limelight, in her gaudy gowns. Immediately there was a crisis, a test for Czar Nicholas, an opportunity to show his monarchic instinct, an opportunity he threw away.

Hundreds of thousands of peasants had gathered in the huge Khodynka meadow for the coronation; it was a proud tradition, recognised by the authorities and welcomed by the Czar. These peasants would represent the people of all the Russias. All night long they celebrated with music, dancing, singing. They became eager for refreshment and stimulants; when wagons arrived with kvass and food, they surged forward.

The meadow was frequently used for military training; it was cut across with earthworks. When half a million people surged, some fell, then more tripped and fell on top of them. People panicked and surges became rushes, peasants climbing over each other, falling, screaming, dying as bodies piled up. As daylight bleached streaks across the sky, the Khodynka looked like a battlefield. Official estimates were around 3,000 dead and injured but eyewitnesses put the total at more than 5,000. The Czar's uncle, Grand Duke Sergei, was Governor General of

Moscow; he argued that any change in the programme would indicate that he was blamed for this misfortune, which was, of course, the direct result of brutish behaviour amongst the lower orders. "It was not," he told his nephew, "as if anyone of note was lost or was even present when it occurred." Disastrously, Nicholas decided the celebrations would not be cancelled.

When Dagmar demanded cancellation of that evening's ball, Alexandra told Nicholas that his mother was trying to minimise the impact of the coronation. "This is the Russian Empire's greatest event and she wants to extinguish it because a side show has collapsed." Nicholas set his jaw and announced that the ball was to go ahead. Worse, he attended with Alexandra on his arm. The spotlight was on the new Czar to see how he reacted to his people's suffering. What the people saw was the Czar and Czaritsa enjoying a festive ball. The Dowager Empress, white with anger and frustration, spent hours that day in the hospitals, comforting, helping, arranging relief. The people of Russia saw that what she did, she did alone.

After that, the performance of Galinka's patriotic opera *A Life for the Czar* seemed threadbare and cynical. It is all about a noble-spirited peasant heroically sacrificing his life to save his beloved Czar; when a catcall of "Only one? There were thousands at Khodynka," received spontaneous applause, Dagmar rose and stalked out.

Nicholas' reign was doomed to be troubled at home and abroad. Well aware of his own inadequacies, he tried to continue with his father's reactionary policies and was delighted to find that these were in harmony with the views of his Empress. Unfortunately the times were rapidly changing so that what was a blinkered domestic policy after the middle of the nineteenth century was blind folly as he stumbled towards the twentieth. And meanwhile he had to try to satisfy competing domestic pressures. The old Czar had given Dagmar a Fabergé egg every Easter. Nothing had changed that: she expected nothing less from the new Czar. Alexandra pointed out that the old Empress had received a Fabergé egg from the Czar every Easter. Nothing had changed that, so the new Empress required an annual Easter egg from the Czar. Fabergé said of course it could be done, and it was. Still the cost was never discussed; the eggs were designed, made, delivered and paid for.

Chapter 11

When, in 1896, Dagmar went to Nice to winter with her sister Alexandra, her brother-in-law Bertie, and his mother, Queen Victoria of Britain, she took her two younger sons, George and Mikhail. She thought twenty-seven year old George, poor, weak-chested George, could benefit from the climate; Mikhail was aged eighteen, and she wanted to keep an eye on Mikhail. Both were sexually active, George with the bright-eyed compulsion of the consumptive, Mikhail with the enthusiasm of youth. There would be less scandal if they disported themselves amongst the courtesans of Nice. In any case, Dagmar had listened long enough to discussions of memorials to Alexander.

There would be statues, perhaps one dominating Znamenskaya Square, so that everyone passing along the Nevski Prospekt would see it. Perhaps another here, perhaps another there. Alexander III had not been highly regarded but a dead man is given more respect than a living one; he cannot take advantage of it.

A bridge on the Seine would show how the people of France and Russia felt about each other. The name had caused debate. After all, the country of Napoleon could hardly celebrate the opening of the Moscow

Bridge. Now it could be named after the late Czar. He had died in 1894 and planning took a couple of years; in 1896 Nicholas laid the first stone of the Alexandre III Bridge.

It would be a triumphal bridge, an ornately magnificent bridge, reminiscent of the glories of Napoleonic France. To avoid spoiling splendid views, it would also have to be a technologically brilliant bridge, with a single span of nearly 110 metres arching no more than six metres at the centre. "That will show Germany," Dagmar exclaimed delightedly.

She could have had no idea how impressed Germany was, could never have guessed that within a few decades, soldiers of the Reich would be marching over the Alexandre Bridge.

The arch was made in prefabricated sections, then brought to the site for assembly. This guaranteed precision but factory prefabrication was in its infancy – the techniques took time to develop, and the project ran late. Final stages of construction were rushed so the bridge could be opened just in time for France's magnificent Universal Exhibition of 1900.

But the decision to dedicate the structure to Alexander had made Dagmar reflect on such matters. Throughout her marriage she had known Alexander felt he was her second choice, and so he was. She had lived and loved as his committed lady and Empress to his Emperor but she had never forgotten leaning on her brother and sobbing: "It should have been him." One of the Gospels says simply: "Mary kept all these things, and pondered them in her heart." So it was with Dagmar.

Of course Alexander should have such a memorial dedicated to him, and statues on the Nevski Prospekt too. God knows, England was littered with vainglorious memorials Victoria had erected to Albert, "the great and the good". The perverse and pathetic might have been more appropriate, she reflected, but that was a matter for the English and they, it seemed, would put up with any trash.

A magnificently martial bridge, signifying the joining of national purpose against the Germans: that was entirely consistent with Alexander's character and beliefs. It was no less than his due. Naming a Cannes boulevard after him, well, if they wanted to, she did not mind. But surely it was appropriate for his older brother, the Czarevitch robbed by fate of his destiny, to have a splendid spiritual sepulchre, reflecting his more sensitive soul. When he had died in Nice, there had been a Russian Orthodox church in the Rue Longchamp – where that dreadful funeral had been held. There was another in Cannes and Tersling had designed another for Menton that had not long been completed. But these were not places of pilgrimage, they did not reflect the immensity of the catastrophic loss.

One day of torrential rain, she went to the park in Nice of the Villa Bermond. What was called a villa then was in reality a community of mansions in parkland. Alexander II had bought part of it and had there erected an impressive Byzantine chapel of commemoration, on the site of the residence where his son had died. The Czar had given generously to help finance the project, as had many others. Amongst these were soldiers of the regiments in which Nicholas had held honorary command, who had a compulsory levy subtracted from their pay. They were commanded to greet the announcement of the levy by singing the anthem: 'God save the Czar'. Several were flogged for showing inadequate enthusiasm.

Consecrated two years after Nicholas died, the chapel displayed a pantheon of saints. The little lady walked from one ikon to the next. "I should have remembered. They are all painted by Neff," she said. "Where is the Czarevitch's own ikon of Saint Nicholas?"

"It is outside, Your Majesty," said the grey-bearded archpriest. "Perhaps we should wait to see it, until the rain stops."

"If Saint Nicholas can endure the rain, then so can we," she said.

Standing on the massive steps in front of that ponderous façade, the cleric pointed upwards and Dagmar turned her face into the stinging downpour. In an ornate niche directly above the doorway, there was a panel, uniformly black. "That is not the representation of Saint Nicholas," she said.

"The sunshine, Majesty. It is so strong here, it has darkened the varnish."

"When it is not raining," she said tartly. "Why is it exposed to the elements?"

"The Czar, Your Majesty. He said it must be placed there. That is, Czar Alexander II."

"Take it down," she said. "Show it reverence. It is sacred to the memory of St Nicholas the miracle worker." Then more softly: "It is sacred to the memory of the Czarevitch. It was at his deathbed. I touched it then and prayed for intercession, but there was no miracle."

Archpriest Serge Lubimoff could not be sure, but there seemed to be more than rain on her cheeks.

Dagmar sat alone that evening. In her imagination great onion-shaped cupolas, surmounted by gleaming crosses, stood high amongst the palm trees, brilliant against the dense azure of the Mediterranean sky. A more fitting tribute than that lumpen chapel, a cathedral more splendid than any bridge, would be erected in Nice. Its ikons, stonework, woodcarving and frescos would show those belle époque artists what Russia could achieve. And its name would refer not to Czarevitch Nicholas, and not Czar or Emperor, for he had been neither. But he had been an Olympian. It would be called the Cathedral of Saint Nicholas. She had thought often of erecting a proper memorial to the greatest Czar Russia never had, but her husband had been deeply jealous of the memory of his dead brother; he glowered at her on those rare occasions that the name of her young suitor was mentioned. Well, now Alexander could have a bridge over the Seine while Nicholas would be remembered for all time with a glorious cathedral in the sun.

Even in death, Alexander could only ever come second.

Dagmar returned to Petersburg, where she casually raised with Nicholas the proposal of building a church in Nice; a cathedral, she told herself, is only an important church. Initially he liked the idea but once he had discussed it with Alexandra, his enthusiasm withered. Undeterred, Dagmar lobbied. She had developed powerful contacts throughout the higher levels of Russian society, and she used them.

To an ecclesiastic she might say: "The Church's message is not just for Russia; Russians abroad have even greater need of spiritual succour." Or to a politician: "Our bond with France needs cultural cement to demonstrate our unity." Or to the great, the good, and the travelled: "Where Russians are, there is the church."

There were problems in Greece, where the Turks were thrashing brother William's forces. Queen Victoria wanted Russia to calm things – she had relatives at risk there – and together the Great Powers imposed a kind of peace on the area. At home, Alexandra gave birth again – a second daughter. Dagmar made no effort to conceal her impatience but she had other concerns: her mother was dying so she returned that summer to Bernstorff, staying on after Queen Louise died, to comfort King Christian.

Alexandra brought forth a third daughter and yet again, death gave Dagmar emotional turmoil that blocked the birth out of her mind. Her second son George, living in health exile in the Caucasus, had found the rush of air he experienced on a motorcycle relieved his tubercular breathlessness. He rode out frequently and the day came when a peasant woman found him lying beside the machine, his mouth and chin bloody.

He was crumpled like an unstrung marionette. She moved him a little so he lay like a man resting, then used her scarf to wipe the worst of the mess from his face. There was blood, bright and red, and there was clear sputum, not stained or marbled but streaked with blood.

She jumped back when his eyes opened. She had never before made eye contact with one of these great ones. She knew who he was – he had killed one of her hens on his noisy stinking machine, which now lay leaking on the roadside. By sight she knew the women who went to his house to requite the urges that his affliction laid upon him. They were not women she would speak with – she crossed herself when they passed her – but they must have been well paid for their ministrations; the older women who washed clothes at the riverbank said their tables never lacked bread and meat. But until now she had never looked him in the eyes. Now here he was, badly, dangerously injured, looking her straight in the eyes. "I shall fetch a doctor, sir," she said. His head moved slightly, a slow negative.

"A priest then, sir, you're hurt. You're ill. Your mother…" Another gentle refusal.

"What would you ask of me, sir?" No answer. "Shall I sit with you and say a prayer?" Perhaps she imagined it but days later – when she had been summoned, taken to the mysterious railway station, transported in huge clattering trains, in leather-upholstered carriages and God knows what, driven through towering cities to immense palaces, led into gilt chambers greater and more glorious than any church she had ever entered, more magnificent even than the heaven of her dreams – she told this man's little mother that his eyes seemed to smile.

Did he seem frightened? She thought, then said: "No, lady. He seemed surprised that he was lying there but he was not afraid. He seemed peaceful, like a child who has been busy and wants not to be busy any more." And Dagmar locked into her heart an image like an ikon, of George, a gentle martyr resting in soft sunlight, the peasant's incantations merging with the humming of insects amongst the myrtle and wild thyme. In her imagination he slipped from tranquillity into sleep and from there into eternity while bees and the woman murmured their timeless litanies.

The hacking cough, the bloody spray, the gulping for air, the shawl she spread across him that she later had to burn, and that final vermilion outpouring relentlessly from his nose and mouth so that when he slumped she did not know whether he had drowned or bled to death – these things the woman alone would remember. She was a mother too; she told this little lady only that her son had been at peace, and that was true, his mild surprise and resignation were a lasting memory. The woman ate well and went home, where life returned to normal. Still she crossed herself when the cheap women passed but now she also smiled; she too had earned the gold coins, but she had done it without soiling her body or her immortal soul. Dagmar watched as another of her own joined the growing number of those she loved best, lying in the tombs of Petersburg.

This death precipitated a constitutional crisis. Nicholas's daughters could not inherit the throne so, unless Alexandra produced a son, there would be disruption in the line. With George dead, the first line of inheritance was gone; Mikhail was recognised as heir but he recoiled from the prospect; Nicholas refused to declare him Czarevitch.

Alexandra announced that she was indeed pregnant. Dagmar and Mikhail breathed more easily and there, it seemed, the matter could wait, but abruptly Nicholas collapsed. He had typhoid – his survival was not assured. Dagmar implored him to declare Mikhail Czarevitch, to act as regent until the Czar recovered. Alexandra was shrill in her response: until Nicholas was well again, she would rule. She was Czaritsa, with the priceless benefit of guidance from God. She was inspired by God and would prove equal to the task.

She could have forgiven argument but they did not argue with her. They ignored her. Nicholas placated his lady as best he could and did nothing. He slowly recovered, the process seeming to allow him to slip more comfortably into the role of head of state. Dagmar increasingly found herself having no role but to watch while Nicholas's judgement and decisions were evidently influenced by his lady's opinions. The Dowager Empress visited the recuperating Czar and told him she was to sponsor the design and construction of a new Russian Orthodox church in Nice. All places of orthodox worship are churches, she told herself, even cathedrals. Reluctantly, Nicholas agreed to give it his Imperial blessing. "But I'm not paying for the damn thing," he said unwisely.

Dagmar glared, then denounced his ingratitude, his errors, his disrespect for the memory of his forefathers.

"I show no disrespect to Papa's memory," complained Nicholas.

"You ignore me! He would have found that unforgivable. Now I hear you plan to tear down the villa where he died. Have you no heart?"

"That's where I caught typhoid. God knows the place is decayed enough and the sanitation is a nightmare. Anyway, the Maly Palace still stands and you haven't been back there since Papa died there, so what do you care?"

"I am the one who knows what he would have wished you to do, not like that narrow-minded daughter of Germany. What does she know? Your father would never have agreed to your marrying her but that he was dying. No more would I. She is there simply to give you a son and she can't even do that."

In the following months Dagmar saw Nicholas only on those formal occasions he could not avoid. Gradually the relationship mellowed and relaxed but Nicholas would never again accept his mother as the power behind the throne. Alexandra had her hand on the reins; she was desperate to be the gateway to the future, and her belly held the key. In June 1901 she gave birth to a fourth girl.

Chapter 12

Alexandra remained desperately unsure of herself, subconsciously convinced of her own inadequacy, obsessed with a desire to succeed. Now, under intense pressure to bring forth a son, she began dabbling with people she regarded as mystics. Philippe Nizier-Vachot, a fairground charlatan from Eastern France, claimed to be able to identify and, if he chose, change the gender of an unborn child. Alexandra said she was pregnant again and the glib Frenchman, introduced by two princesses, the daughters of Nicholas of Mentenegro, announced that no control was necessary – this would be a boy. Nicholas and Alexandra treated him like an Old Testament prophet. Estranged from his mother by frequent disagreements with her, Nicholas began to consult the little man on matters of state.

Dagmar called upon Russian intelligence and confirmed that Nizier-Vachot was a fraud, with a string of convictions for deceit. Alexandra and Nicholas were indifferent to this information, continuing to see him and to take his advice with gratitude, and imperial gratitude meant wealth. Nature came to Dagmar's aid when Alexandra had a phantom miscarriage and medical examination revealed the truth. She had been suffering from anaemia caused by inadequate eating; she had not been pregnant at all. This was followed by a public outcry against the French mountebank and at last the Czar sent Nizier-Vachot away. Alexandra continued to correspond with him, sending money and receiving guidance.

She also began questioning officials about the rules of succession. Catherine had been Emperor – what prevented another woman sitting where she had sat? A woman of the blood Imperial? Well yes, of course a woman of the blood Imperial. That woman's husband – yes, that could be a problem, for he would also be at the head of the Empire... what if she were a daughter of the Czar, of the blood Imperial, and married to a man of the blood Imperial, perhaps a cousin, could she then take her place in the succession?

The rules? What rules? Who made such rules? If a Czar had made these rules then surely a Czar could amend them? He could not? And who was it then, who would have the task of telling the Emperor that he could not do as previous Emperors had done? Alexandra locked her notebooks away, saying nothing to Dagmar. But the Dowager Empress's network was established and infallible. Years ago, even as the young Alexandra had crept with her book into corners of Windsor Castle, luxuriating in the shadows and the melancholy and her dreams of love with a Russian Czar, Dagmar had developed her sources.

The succession remained as precarious as ever, nor was that the only threat. Bad harvests and low prices brought increasing poverty to the vast tracts of Russian land. In remote areas starving peasants murdered landowners and looted their properties. Destitute families invaded industrial communities where work was already declining. Borrowers turned on moneylenders and that developed into a new wave of murder, riots, and pogroms.

Meanwhile, revolution continued to ferment in hidden cellars. Being based upon polemics, the revolutionary organisations suffered more than most from schism: Social Democrats would have nothing to do with Social Revolutionaries; when the Democrats gained ascendancy they split into Bolsheviks and Mensheviks. So they snarled and snapped at each other, each betraying any rival group that tried to take direct action, and bickering over what they intended to do to the old order, thus giving the old order more time to carry on as though the storm clouds were not gathering.

The world had been devoured by great powers – now the Empire buffet was over and nations like Great Britain had digested the delicacies they had grabbed so greedily. Prospectors, merchant venturers and evangelists had toured subjugated regions to identify investment opportunities; soldiers had deployed logistical strategies, engineers were installing communications, delving for minerals, farmers were ploughing up ancestral lands and publicity seekers were 'discovering' new miracles of nature that were history to indigenous populations. The earth's landmasses had been comprehensively carved up. But still there were territorial ambitions. Even then, in the early years of the twentieth century, many reasonable people had difficulty understanding the competition between powerful nations for control of lesser nations but in some locations the aggressions and aspirations were so deep rooted that both reason and compassion had ceased to have influence.

Nicholas had continued with his father's magnificently blinkered policy of Russification. The nation that covered one sixth of the world's land surfaces had never been homogenous, nor could it be. It embraced peoples of different cultures, different religious beliefs, different languages; fewer than half were Russians. But Nicholas was convinced, as his father had been, that strength lay in suppressing minorities, imposing a single culture, a single religion, a single language – all under a single autocratic ruler. Alexander III had pursued the policy with vigour, alienating such amiable people as the Finns by trying to substitute Russian ways for their own, imposing Russian troops upon an independent people. Armenians, Belorussians, Ukranians, had all been subjected to the unwelcome process. Nicholas continued with the task, unaware of the festering resentment.

In the summer of 1900, leaders in Peking lost patience with the insolence of invaders and directed mobs to lay siege to the European legations there. A massacre appeared imminent so people became excited; around the world communities where Chinese and Europeans coexisted became stressed. On the Russian bank of the River Amur the people of Blagoveshchensk heard Manchurians on the other side of the river letting off fireworks, firing guns and beating drums.

Blagoveshchensk, with a population of more than 200,000, was a substantial port where the Rivers

Amur and Yeya met. It had been annexed by Russia and returned to China in the seventeenth century, but it had been occupied again since 1856. A stop on the trans-Siberian route, it would one day soon have a railway station with troop trains and munitions for the Russo-Japanese War. Its agricultural hinterland, together with goldmines and thriving trade into and out of Manchuria, brought prosperity. The waters were wide but excellent trade had been maintained by boat. Thousands of Chinese coolies provided the port's labour force so that both Russian and Chinese merchants grew rich there. One of these merchants was the governor, who recognised the rumours of war from beyond the far distant bank. It would be best, he said, if all Chinese returned to their own country within twenty-four hours. That would avoid abrasive confrontations.

The Chinese people readily agreed and asked if the Russian boat owners would ferry them. The boat owners would not. Next day the Chinese were still in town. Leading Chinese citizens came to explain that they would have gone but were unable to do so. The Cossack garrison, bayonets fixed, surrounded the group, marched them out of town to the river and forced them into the water. Some tried to clamber out downstream but Russians hurled them back into the water. Other Russians surrounded the town's Chinese quarter. Men, women, children, old people, mothers with babies, all were driven out, spat on, beaten, gathered in groups and marched to the river. Stores and houses were looted.

Those who resisted were bayoneted and thrown into the water with the rest. Yelling mobs flung stones at struggling swimmers, boys with rakes and hoes raced up and down the bank, thrusting at the flailing arms. Manchurian fishermen, attracted by the noise, sailed closer, then tried to rescue the stronger swimmers. Rifle fire from the Cossacks sent two of them tumbling and the boats sailed out of range.

There were too many to be marched down in one day. That night bonfires were lit by gangs of intruders into the Chinese quarter. There was vodka and singing. A few Chinese were dragged out of hiding and knouted to raucous applause. Cheers greeted the screams of women being violated. At first light the weary Cossacks roused themselves and resumed their work. By late afternoon only looters occupied the Chinese quarter. Not a single Chinese man, woman or child remained.

After two days of solitary prayer in hiding, priests came apologetically into the evening light. A strange quiet hung over the town, where some people found it hard to meet one another's eyes. In distant fishing boats, silent Manchurians stood watching, their broad faces expressionless.

The authorities conceded a death toll of nearly 5,000 people. When news reached Czarskoe Selo, Dagmar asked: "How could a few dozen soldiers kill so many Chinese?"

"Oh, you can always rely on the Cossacks," said Nicholas. A chuckle ran round the dinner table.

Chapter 13

In Nice, a site had been found for the church. An eminent engineer was consulted and he approved, so the land was bought at the intersection of the rues Rivoli, Berlioz, and Verdi. The head of architecture at Petersburg Academy of Fine Arts, MT Preobrajensky, had been responsible for the cathedral at Reval and had recently completed a church in Florence. When Dagmar explained her vision to him, he realised this was not another church. He was already very successful, hugely respected, but this was a project that could set him unassailably at the head of his profession. He dedicated day and night to developing a design that reflected the very best of Russian ecclesiastical design from the late sixteenth and early seventeenth centuries.

A high central cupola would be surrounded by four lower ones, all in black and green-blue tiles; a fifth cupola, on the bell tower, would be gilded, and all five would be surmounted with golden crosses. Twin porches would each have a green and gold spire and on top of each, wings outspread, would perch a golden, twin-headed Imperial eagle. The design owed much to the Moscow cathedral of Saint Basil the Blessed but Nice provided a very different environment: Professor Preobrajensky elected to put terracotta-coloured brickwork and grey-white stone against the strong sky of Mediterranean France. The same green-blue of the cupolas would be repeated in decorative ceramics. In strict order of precedence, Dagmar recognised the excellence of the proposal and she loved it; her committee approved it, and the church technical committee gave it their blessing.

Then the architect appointed to oversee construction submitted a report. He had found the site was incapable of supporting so massive a structure. Icily, Damar asked: "Did we not consult an eminent engineer on this very subject?"

"Indeed yes, Your Majesty," said the Chairman of the Committee. "A former vice-president of the Institution of Civil Engineers in London has retired to live in Nice. He assured us that the site was suitable."

"Did he indeed? And what does he say now?"

"He says that previously undetectable flaws are present but that the consultancy of which he was senior partner is perfectly capable of organising the piling of the site to provide a solid foundation."

"Would that work be carried out by way of an apology?"

"Well no, Your Majesty. In fact, it would immensely increase the cost of construction. The site would cost almost as much as we expected to pay for the building work."

"I do not discuss costs but listen to me very carefully. That man and his organisation are never to work on that site. Never. Neither are they to work in Russia."

"I do not have that authority, Majesty."

"I have. Tell those who may have to make such decisions, and ensure that it is so. I hold you personally responsible."

Bermond Park, where the commemorative chapel was built, had been bequeathed by Czar Alexander II to Alexander III, who bequeathed it to Nicholas II. This, close to the chapel, was an appropriate site. Dagmar spoke to Nicholas. Russia's reputation with an essential ally was at stake. When a prestige project falls on its face, humiliation replaces prestige, she told him. Dreading what Alexandra would say when she got to hear of it, Nicholas agreed.

"We can build on your land then," said Dagmar.

"Oh no," said the Czar. "I don't want to be involved. I have no use for the Bermond Park land. I'd like you to find an appropriate cause to donate it to, Mama, to dispose of for the benefit of Russia."

His mother smiled. "Don't blush, Nicholas," she said. "Guile can earn more peace than courage can." He blushed deeper, but now work could begin. Funds were collected and spent; the site came alive.

Czar Nicholas had no more regard for the Japanese than he had for the Chinese. He preferred not to remember the pleasures of oriental concubinage and the youthful excitement of watching a bewitching figure removing female garments to reveal shaved and rampant manhood. When he thought of Japan he often ran his hand along the scar on his scalp; Japan was responsible for his headaches.

Japan objected to Russia's territorial ambitions in Manchuria. China had been disabled in war and now

Japan shared the contempt for Peking that Russia had already displayed in Blagoveshchensk. Japan had wanted to dip its bread in the gravy but had been thwarted by Russia. Now Russia was developing its hold in Manchuria and Korea.

Dagmar and others called for negotiation with Japan. Hardliners reasoned that Japan was no real threat – the Russian army was so much larger and more powerful: Russian combatants outnumbered Japanese five to one. In any case, if the Japanese pushed their luck, giving them a spanking would divert attention from troubles at home. That appealed to Nicholas, who instructed that Japan would be ignored.

In February 1904 Japan attacked Port Arthur, Russia's ice-free port on the Pacific Ocean, with formidable force. Only then did it occur to Russian Ministers that most of their troops were 4,000 miles away from where they were needed.

Blockaded in port, the Russian Fleet was trapped. Admiral Makaroff, a hugely respected figure, was sent out to bolster morale, to show Russia that Port Arthur was well defended. Once there, Makaroff's ships sailed out daily but usually scuttled for cover under the own shore batteries. One night of drizzling rain, Russian searchlights showed there were ships sailing back and forth on the fringes of visibility but, in the obscuring drizzle, nobody could see what they were doing.

Next day a few Japanese ships tempted the Russian ships out, only to be joined by a larger force to drive them back. The mysterious boats in the night were forgotten until the cruiser *Petropavlovsk* hit a mine, and then another. The boilers burst, the ship submerged, and then the magazine exploded so that the sinking hulk erupted in flame through the water. Within minutes the Petropavlovsk took Makaroff and 700 of his men to the bottom. The admiral had been in Port Arthur no more than a month.

Fanatical troops, of the Empire of the Rising Sun, landed to stand between Port Arthur and Russia's troops in Manchuria, shattered Russian regiments. As war and humiliation reverberated through Russia, Alexandra gave birth to a son. It was what the Romanovs needed, what Russia needed – the birth of Alexei could not have come at a better time. He was a fine, golden-haired baby, everything they could have asked for, except...

His navel seemed unwilling to heal. A month after birth, it still bled. Tests were conducted and the problem was identified. Haemophilia, brought into the blood Royal by Queen Victoria and spread throughout European royalty by her progeny, was surfacing once more. It had passed genetically, mother to daughter, from Victoria to Alice – who had lost a son to it – and from Alice to Alexandra. At the very moment she believed she had established her authority by providing the dynasty and the nation with its glorious future, Alexandra had to recognise that her genetic flaw was the curse that could end everything. Alexei's health became shrouded in secrecy; the people must not know. Above all, the Dowager Empress must not know.

Alexandra would devote her life to ensuring that he became strong and remained healthy. The hand that rocked his cradle would rule his world, his father, and Russia. By whatever means, she would be mistress of all the Russias.

The Trans-Siberian Railway, capable of taking the immense Russian war machine to the East, had been developing for a dozen years but was still incomplete at the outbreak of war. The largest freshwater lake in Asia, Lake Baikal, measuring 400 miles by fifty-five, could be crossed only by boat in summer. In winter the ice froze deep, cracking and rearing up into a nightmare landscape of cliffs and fissures that the locals believed were infested by demons. A light and hazardous railway was laid but there had been no hurry – until now.

Japan relied on Russia being unable to deliver its troops and armaments where they were needed; the Japanese Minister of War was appalled when massed labour, laying simultaneous sections, completed the 5,500 mile line and brought men and munitions pouring through. By October the railway was bringing troops and supplies to the Russian front to reinforce those facing the Japanese at Mukden.

Hurling suicidal troops against machine guns was all very well, Japanese field officers reported, but an ammunition belt was more readily replaced than a dead soldier. Still they repeatedly launched advances through wind-driven rain. There was the infinite noise of conflict, single shots, machine gun bursts, explosions, cries of command, yells of aggression, screams of agony, the neighing of terrified and dying horses. Machine guns chattered and men fell. Poorly fused grenades killed indiscriminately – exploding prematurely, maiming the men who threw; going astray to blast shrapnel into friend and foe; being picked up and tossed back. There was no opportunity for daring, and courage earned no respite; there was nowhere to escape to. Rifle fire constantly hacked and slashed at living flesh and bone. Artillery shells hurtled overhead, ignored until the blast sent scything fragments to blind, dismember, and amputate. Hand to hand combat, men fighting eye to demented eye, driven by the adrenalin of terror, bludgeoning with rifle butts, driving bayonets into bellies, firing into fear-filled faces at point blank range. Splattered by the blood, brains, and bowels of comrades and enemies. Slipping, falling, taking the shot, the bayonet, the shrapnel. Crying out as they felt their bodies being smashed. Falling to die amongst the already dead.

Faced by absolute and unrelenting conflict from overwhelming numbers, the Japanese fell back. The Russian front remained where it was.

In January the Port Stanley commander listened to his officers, who reported that they had enough provisions and munitions to withhold a siege until the spring. He retired to his quarters and then, without further consultation, he surrendered the garrison to the Japanese. Petersburg was as appalled as his officers. Japan's forces no longer had to face both ways: their 270,000 men turned their concentrated attention on Russia's force of 330,000 at Mukden. The Russians formed a line to face them; full frontal assault was a bloody business but there were seasoned troops here now. They dug with their bayonets, working down into the earth. In this kind of warfare, Russian stoicism was indomitable; they would endure.

The flaw in their strategy was that this would be a different kind of warfare. In February an army of Japanese moved swiftly round to drive into the Russian

Eastern flank while another, which had marched undetected through the flanking mountains, smashed into them on the West. Then Japan struck full force in the centre. Caught unawares and in imminent danger of being outflanked and surrounded, Russia fell back in what began as organised retreat. It swiftly developed into a rout as Japanese riflemen and artillery poured shot and shell into the confusion. The Russian army lost its dignity and nearly 100,000 men to a numerically inferior force.

Nobody, apart perhaps from the adversaries of Pyrrhus, ever enjoyed defeat but Russians found it intolerable. This was an enemy they did not respect, invading them in a war they did not want, and beating them. There were protest marches, riots, and violence in the streets. Nicholas needed a scapegoat so he relieved the popular General Kuropatkin of command. Then in the heart of Russia, his own uncle, Grand Duke Sergei, was blown to pieces by an assassin's bomb. A scapegoat was not enough to counter public disaffection on this scale: Nicholas complained to his Empress that he must have a victory.

Alexandra was inspired. She had always thought Nikolai Nicholaevitch was too good a soldier, too clever, too popular, looking and behaving far more like a Czar than Nicholas. And he always did what was manifestly decent and right. Alexandra relied on inspiration and, if others chose to mistake that for spite or petulance, it simply showed their lack of vision. There was something disconcerting about Nikolai; if it ever came to rivalry, he could so easily be a candidate to topple Nicholas.

Then the Okhrana, the secret police, reported a plot to Nicholas and he carelessly told Alexandra. "The police report that some of the senior military want to depose me and establish Nikolai as military dictator to sort out all the unrest. They are identifying those responsible."

"My God," she cried, "I knew it. He has command of the Petersburg military and the Imperial Guard. He will have our throats slit in the night. He must be got rid of!"

"I can't just get rid of a Grand Duke, even if I wanted to, and there's no evidence yet that he is part of this conspiracy."

"Make him Commander in Chief over this war, that will keep him out of the way. And if the war were to be a fiasco, let Nikolai take the blame." Nicholas began to think deeply about his cousin.

"It would be a grave mistake to make Nikolai Commander in Chief against Japan," Dagmar said casually to her son the following afternoon. His cup rattled in its saucer; how could she have known? Alex had only yesterday nominated Nikolai as the best potential leader for Russian forces, and since then he had discussed it with only two people.

"Why, do you doubt his abilities?"

"Quite the contrary, I share your high esteem for his qualities, both as a soldier and as a Romanov. And that is why he should be here in the East. In these troubled times, when the future and the succession are so obscured, we need to keep our most able cousins close to us. In any case, we shall lose this absurd and degrading war, a war that we should never have provoked in the first place. A degrading compromise is the best we can hope for and then Nikolai, if he were commanding officer, would be disgraced, and the Imperial family along with him. Surely that can't be what Alexandra wants? Or is it?"

Nicholas set down his cup and saucer, spilling tea. "For the first time in many years, the succession is assured. You need have no anxiety on that front, Mama. We have a son, or had you forgotten?"

There was a silence. It stretched until he looked at her, suddenly alarmed. Slowly, she spoke. "Alex is misguided in believing that I am in ignorance of the Czarevitch's condition. Hers is an error you would be ill advised to share. If you order Nikolai to command, I shall instruct him to refuse your commission. He is more loyal to you than those whose judgement you so foolishly rely upon."

Nicholas had sent the Baltic Fleet to relieve Port Arthur and on the way they noticed some ships, so they turned their guns, blasting what turned out to be the British fishing fleet on the Dogger Bank. Britain, which was neutral but had a treaty with Japan, was furious, making the most of the faux pas. Russia looked callous, incompetent, and ridiculous. Faced with the possibility of Britain declaring war, it grovelled and promised generous compensation.

The Baltic Fleet had been at sea for seven months and Port Arthur was no longer in a position to be relieved. So the fleet, with twenty cruisers and battleships plus twenty-five other ships, headed for Vladivostok. The Japanese, who had thirty cruisers and battleships, took up a parallel line, three or four miles distant. The exchange of gunfire began.

The Japanese had been constantly practicing their gunnery, firing high-temperature incendiary shells primed to explode on impact. Fired with textbook accuracy, these shattered and set fire to superstructures, burning and dismembering men on deck, where their comrades could see the carnage. Survivors spoke of masses on decks and in companionways, heaps of something that must once have been people. Russian shells, on the other hand, were designed to penetrate armour and then explode out of sight, inside the target vessel.

Rear Admiral Heihahiro Togo's fleet sailed apparently untouched while flame belched from Russian ships, smoke pluming and billowing over the water. While disaster burned and exploded on an epic scale with ships blazing, exploding and sinking, individual Russian sailors fought on, stoking boilers, firing crippled guns, staunching the flames, dragging maimed comrades from the wreckage.

It was all for nothing.

Of the Russian fleet, only a light cruiser and a couple of destroyers made it through to Vladivostok. During the next few days a dozen of Russia's lesser vessels were captured by Japan or staggered into neutral ports; the rest went to the bottom in the Straits of Tsushima. Japan lost only three torpedo boats. Russia's dead and wounded numbered 10,000; Japan suffered fewer than 700. The battle of Tsushima had been catastrophically lost.

Mutiny fired by frustration and anger swept through the remaining Russian ships in European waters, strikes and riots shattered communities across the land. As ever, secret grievances were satisfied, old debts paid. In the chaos, many people fled to the United States or wherever they could find refuge.

Russia's intelligence organisations were powerful at home and improving in Europe, but they were virtually non-existent in Japan, so Russia had misjudged the Japanese position before war broke out, it had misjudged Japan's military and naval resources during the war and now it misjudged the Japanese position again. It knew its own wounds were grievous but was oblivious to the cost of warfare to Japan: its adversary was exhausted and virtually bankrupt. It did not have Russia's ability to soak up punishment but, since Russia didn't know that, it would not need to.

The United States stepped in as mediator, with President Roosevelt in control. The war was, after all, not so far from US soil that it could be ignored and neutral ships had already been sunk. Russia had to make concessions, scuttling out of Port Arthur and other possessions, and recognising Japan's domination in Korea. The humiliation could have been far worse, Dagmar told her son. "We have identified our weak links; now we can build our strength. Turn your eyes to the West; Germany is arming herself again. You have a son, Nicki. You could not pass on your health and strength but at least bequeath him a strong Empire, as your father did for you."

The Dowager Empress's efforts to comfort her son did not reflect the public mood. Across Russia, widows, families, communities counted the cost. They had lost a war that, but for mismanagement, they should not have had to fight. If it were fought, it was a war that, but for mismanagement, they should have won. The reckoning was counted by the unforgiving, who intended that it would be paid in full.

Others counted their profits. With a Government culture that regarded balancing costs against benefits as socially demeaning, corruption was everywhere. Worse than that, befriending industrialists, accepting bribes and giving benefits in return was not regarded as corruption, it was a way of life. And Russia had just lost a war it should have won; that must never happen again. The government needed ships, guns – armaments of every kind. Russian-built ships had performed poorly against Japanese vessels, poorly even compared with Russia's imported ships. Its communications had failed until late in the day, so more roads and railways needed to be built. This could all be achieved on time by organisations represented at the dinner tables of the great and the good, and at agreed prices. Very high prices but that didn't matter. What mattered was that each contract cost at least what a Minister had said it would cost. Ministers had their reputations to consider.

And others, comfortable in Potsdam, watched and waited.

Chapter 14

Dissence and disillusion were widespread. Neglected discontent hardened. Shadowy figures moved amongst the gullible, the half-committed and the spear carriers of revolution.

One such was Yevno Ahzeff. As a young man his contact with radical students and his thieving from his employer attracted the attention of the secret police, the Okhrana. They noticed that he was ambitious, cunning, grasping and unscrupulous so they would have arrested him. But he had no principles so instead, they recruited him. His qualities, if that was what they were, were also recognised by the radicals. His adopted creed of revolution by terror, terror by assassination, attracted followers.

Ahzeff found a kindred spirit in Sergei Zubatoff, who had taken a similar route to become Moscow chief of the Okhrana. Together they devised a strategy for their joint prosperity. Ahzeff would arrange for a crime to be committed, then he would give Zubatoff details of the perpetrators so that they could be arrested.

They tried it on bank robberies and it worked; the world was their oyster. Ahzeff could dispose of rivals among the revolutionaries while Zubatoff could have his political enemies killed and they were both rewarded for their diligence. They even decided that those arrested did not have to be the actual perpetrators: interrogation techniques had reached a sophistication that could virtually guarantee a confession from anyone and, even if a confession could not quite guarantee an execution, there was always the involuntary suicide option.

Ahzeff instructed and then surreptitiously denounced a student who shot and killed the Minister of Education, Nicolai Bogolepoff. More murders followed and terrorists came to recognise Ahzeff as the reliable organiser of assassinations. If police spies later tracked down the killers, well they had taken their chances; nobody could blame the brilliant planner. He even had troublesome colleagues done away with, accusing them of his own betrayals. The assassination of a minor governor in Kiev, of the brutish Russian governor of Finland, of the Minister of the Interior Dimitri Sipiagin – and the name of Ahzeff seemed always to rustle amongst the whispers. Sipiagin was shot in the Maryinsky Palace and his insolently executed killing opened a vacancy for Viakesloff Plehve at the Ministry.

Plehve was an ideal enemy for any radical. He had hunted down and harvested the assassins of Alexander II. He loathed Jews, having provided weapons for pogroms and ordered local police to look the other way when Jewish families were being slaughtered. He had persecuted Finns and others who resisted Russification. He expanded the numbers of police, interrogation centres and prisoners beyond anything the Czar could comprehend, he made exquisite torture a basic tool of interrogation and he promoted paranoia throughout Russia. The Czar's habit of saying, when someone had displeased the Czarina, "I never want to see that man again," sometimes became a far more terrible indictment than the transfer or dismissal that had been customary. Plehve's plans for eradicating revolutionaries would have wiped out a generation of intellectuals.

Plehve was publicly recognised as the instigator of new levels of autocratic brutality. Ordinary people, raised to love the Czar, said Nicholas was a simple man who did not know what was going on. The Czar was demanding the prevention of persecution and massacres while his Minister was supporting these persecutions. People shook their heads over Nicholas's shortcomings, as they so often do over hereditary rulers. He was not a bad man, they said. Plehve was the dark power behind the throne, using and abusing the Emperor's authority.

He enthusiastically supported Probedonostev, who had been the subject of repeated assassination attempts, one of which injured him severely. But Plehve was convinced that his own defences were impregnable; wherever he went his entourage of police vehicles guaranteed his safety; he did not consider the possibility of assassins acting with information and support from his immediate junior, Okhrana chief Gerassimoff, and his valued agent Ahzeff.

Every terrorist in Russia prized the Minister's scalp more highly than the Czar's. One came close to success but Ahzeff heard of it and betrayed the organisers. This was a trophy that he wanted for himself; it could make him a clandestine legend amongst those who mattered. It would raise Gerassimoff to the highest position, and give Ahzeff power over him.

One summer day Plehve's cavalcade drove down the Nevski Prospect in Petersburg. There may be safety in numbers but not if large numbers slow the potential target down. Figures ran from the pavements and rolled their bombs under the carriage. Again a street was strewn with carriage panels shattered into matchboard, broken horses kicking in their own blood and pedestrians lying huddled and still. Plehve's stocky body was torn to pieces.

Ahzeff gave Gerassimov names, the nominated people were arrested and, after interrogation, they confessed. They may even have been responsible. Ahzeff received sufficient gratitude in return to deposit in overseas banks, while the killings and the betrayals went on. Not all were masterminded by Ahzeff but he had a hand in most, one way or another, and he usually got the credit.

People became jittery. On the appropriate day the Emperor went in procession with the great and good of the church, out onto the ice of the River Neva to bless the waters. Guns on the Peter and Paul Fortress fired a salute. The steady dull rhythm of timed artillery was broken by a bang and a crash: one gun had been mischarged and fired part of a casing through a window of the Winter Palace. The panic was comic, the investigation and repercussions disproportionate. Nicholas, who would in a few years make himself Commander-in-Chief of armed forces, was so ignorant of artillery that he believed terrorists had mixed live shells with blanks. Cashiered officers licked their wounds while knouted gun crews hoped to heal, but terrorists gratefully accepted a propaganda gift. Paranoia was working for them.

This was a time for the opportunist and Ahzeff was one of a number of consummate double agents with a keen insight. A man who runs with the hare and hunts with the hounds develops an intense understanding of how things fit together. He became aware that Father George Gapon, leader of the Russian Workingmen's Assembly, had something in common with himself. The association was a primitive trade union, seeking a better deal for thousands of workers. Plehve had known someone would set it up so he did it himself, paying the idealist Gapon to head it. Gapon was above reproach, everyone knew he was a simple, straightforward, good man. But he steered all the union's energy towards the employers; the Czar was Little Father of all the Russias; the Czar loved his people. Gapon would not hear a word against the autocracy.

This extraordinary synergy between the oppressor and the oppressed was invented by Czar Paul and it had taken root. Soldiers went into battle with the Czar's picture close to their hearts. Peasants died of oppression, clutching Czarist symbols. Gapon subscribed to this and, without any feeling of guilt, fed Czarist propaganda to the multitude. He was a union leader because he wanted to improve the lives of workers, a police collaborator because he was a genuine patriot. And because he was not a complete fool, he divulged less than everything to either the workers or the police. Ahzeff observed, like a wolf watching the exile road.

During the war with Japan, a steelworkers' strike, complaining against the industry's management by steel barons, had seemed to Gapon to be a golden opportunity for the greatest demonstration of all, the grand gesture.

He would lead a multitude of workers to the Winter Palace and there explain to the Little Father of all the Russias that an eight-hour day, a democratic assembly, a minimum wage, universal suffrage, and a clear divide between the state and the Orthodox Church were essential to the people, the narod, in a just Russia. The Czar would listen and understand; then all would be well. The police never worried about Gapon's demonstrations against employers because they were well controlled, peaceful, even dignified. Gapon always told them in advance what was happening.

Chapter 15

Wind skirled through the frozen streets that January Sunday as more than 100,000 workers gathered in the early morning light to take a just message to a loving Czar.

He wasn't there but nobody had told Gapon. They raised the national flag, religious ikons, a huge portrait of the Czar; this was no demonstration – it was a crusade. They were loyal, respectful patriots singing the national anthem, *God Save the Czar*, as they approached the palace. Gapon, at the head of one of the long columns making their ways through several streets, turned a corner and hesitated, amazed. A few hundred yards ahead the way was blocked by infantry in formation, backed by mounted Hussars. The singing faltered, then rallied; the marchers wanted their loyal sentiments to be understood.

All singing ceased with the first volley of shots.

There were no screams at first, just people scattering, running, dodging for cover, and sometimes falling to twist and kick where they lay. Soldiers fired on the fleeing figures like boys shooting rats in a barrel.

Only a few hundred died that day, with many more seriously injured: a mere blood spot on the history of

Russian massacres but for an appalled people, things would never be the same again. One for whom there was no return was the Emperor. The authorities blamed a frightened conscript, a nervous officer, a misunderstood order. But for the 100,000 who marched off in good faith only to return terrified and appalled, and for the multitude who watched silently from Finland to Vladivostok, this man could never again be the Little Father of all the Russias.

Many believed that at last the scales had fallen from their eyes; now they could see who was their enemy. Faith is suspended disbelief and when the thread of delusion snaps, reality is unforgiving. The revulsion was obvious in the villages and the streets. It was apparent where the merchant classes met to drink and talk. It was discernible in the corridors of power. But in the palaces of autocracy, on the highest plateau of privilege, it seemed to be little more than a nasty smell.

The Dowager Empress wrinkled her nose; the Emperor must be detached from involvement in this unpleasantness. She demanded that Nicholas denounce the massacre, name and punish those responsible, make an example of them, on the gibbet if need be. Above all the dynasty must be absolved of complicity in this betrayal.

It could not be. The Emperor had instructed that the marchers were to be stopped, by force of arms if necessary. Nicholas could hardly plead that the Czaritsa had been incoherent with fear – the troops knew, the police knew, and the surviving marchers knew. Above all, Russia knew. She was putting all her trust in a spirit guide called Rasputin. He had told her about the danger of the march; he could see blood, hear screams. So she told Nicholas to stop the march. The Czar's uncle, Grand Duke Sergei, Governor General of Moscow, had been in Petersburg, had reported the build-up of demonstrators to Nicholas, had stirred up his paranoia. They had called in the commanding officer of the garrison and told him that not a single demonstrator was to get as far as the palace. Gerassimoff had rushed to the Winter Palace, begged for an audience with the Czar. He was told to wait. He had still been there waiting when dawn broke; he heard the distant singing, he heard the shots. Sitting on a gilt and red velvet couch, he held his head in his hands. "Go now," said the secretary. "He is not here. I was forbidden from telling you last night in case you thought he had run away."

Gerassimoff stood up and smoothed his coat. "Why would I think such a thing? Until now there was nothing for the Emperor to run from."

He was close to being right. Now the extremists had their martyrs; they knew whose finger had been on the trigger and they demanded retribution. It was then that a bomb exploded under the coach of the Czar's uncle Sergei, Governor General of Moscow. Explosives had improved since one had fatally maimed Alexander II; this new generation bomb killed the Grand Duke, leaving him with no time for reflection, and half-killed his driver. Ahzeff divulged that it had been thrown by a young man called Kalieff.

Sergei's lady Elizabeth was close by at the time and was quickly on the scene, arranging for his remains to be taken to a consecrated building.

She visited Kalieff in Moscow's Boutirki prison

where he told her that protesters had no alternative to the bomb if they were to be heard; she told him he was forgiven. He said he regretted the injury he had done her but, when she subsequently declared that he had shown remorse, he denied it. She would have a memorial erected beside the spot where Sergei died, engraved with the Mercy of Golgotha: "Father forgive them for they know not what they do." Elizabeth, known as Ella, was the sister of the Empress. Kaiser William had, in his youth, fallen deeply in love with this beautiful princess of Hesse but she had chosen to marry Sergei. She found herself wedded to an active homosexual when both society and her own profound religious beliefs recoiled from such inclinations. She wanted children, both for herself and for their families but this would never happen in this marriage. Sergei was also a cold, unpleasant man. She prayed deeply, in the Lutheran manner, and she came to the conclusion that God was testing her, as he tested Job.

Three months after the assassination Kalieff was hanged: not dropped with the knot behind his ear to break the neck, but hauled into the air with the knot under his chin, to avoid blocking the throat. A fit young man could take some time to die that way. The executioner waited thirty minutes before the squirming had given way to twitching and then until the twitching had ceased. Only then could the body, soiled by the final agonies, be cut down.

Ella, who had endured her unhappy marriage to Sergei with patience and dignity, relinquished rank and wealth to take a nun's habit and commit the rest of her life to her faith. She built a convent in

Moscow, became its abbess and distributed the rest of her property to the needy. She stayed out of controversy until her sister fell under Rasputin's influence. Ella believed she knew how God worked and it was not through mountebanks like Rasputin; she denounced him as a charlatan. Her sister Alexandra would never forgive her.

Many Establishment figures received formal notice from secret radical cells that they had been tried in their absence and condemned to death. Most made light of the threat but none attended Sergei's funeral; their safety could no longer be guaranteed by the rule of law.

Not until valued advisors spoke of life and death – Nikolai Nicholaevitch said unless there was reform he would shoot himself, and Nikolai was never known to make empty threats – would Nicholas agree to the creation of an elected assembly, the Duma. It was an obvious development, following the reforms begun by his grandfather Alexander, but Nicholas was incapable of the intellectual leap from absolute autocracy to autocratically controlled democracy. He hated and despised reform – it led towards chaos. Having freed the serfs, his grandfather had been blown to pieces by a revolutionary's bomb. "You can tell me nothing," he said bitterly. "I was there. I saw what bloody wickedness comes of giving them freedom. They see it as weakness and use it against us."

Allowing necessity to erode his autocracy caused Nicholas immense pain. He believed they still loved him as he did them. They understood that he must correct those who went astray and threatened the system that sustained everyone. There were subversives trying to mislead them and those traitors would not be forgiven. From the refined perspective of his palace, the Czar's unpleasant duty was clear: feed the Russian bear those freedoms that would make him content and then, once he was calm, cut out the cancer that had driven him to wound his master.

He issued a manifesto declaring his recognition that people had freedom of conscience, freedom of speech, and freedom of assembly. This would be made manifest through an elected, two-tier authority, the elected Duma and the Council. It would be weak enough but it was the beginning of the end of autocracy, and perhaps of much more.

This was not welcomed by everyone. There were many who shared Nicholas's conviction that the key to the future lay in the past. Pre-Petrine intellectuals were plentiful – they believed that change had begun contaminating civilization during the reign of Peter the Great, when control had started moving away from the ancient Orthodox capital of Moscow, and the church had lost most of its minority share of the Czar's autocracy. Opposed to them were the Modernisers, those who pointed to the progress of Western Europe and the United States; they challenged the autocracy, the church, and tradition. The introduction of the assembly was a triumph for the Modernisers; they also laid the track down which the locomotive of revolution would steam.

The Winter Palace saw the early green shoots of Russian democracy on a bright day in April 1906. The new Duma, made up of deputies with virtually no collective authority, was to meet Czar Nicholas, not in its own apportioned billet, the Tauride Palace, but on his home ground, the lavish Coronation Hall.

On the one side stood the grandly caparisoned Establishment; on the other, subdued and well-scrubbed representatives of at least some of the people of Russia. "The uniformed facing the uninformed," commented a British diplomat loftily and with a magnificent lack of understanding. Those who had run the gauntlet of becoming part of the Duma, with the inevitable security investigations, knew what the issues were. Some were toadies, hoping for privilege or benefit; some always are; some were puppets; some always are. But some were brave men prepared to stand up and be counted; they knew the risks and deemed them worthwhile if they could make a difference. Tears ran down Dagmar's face as she left the hall. She complained at having seen so many commoners inside the palace and to her astonishment, she believed she had seen hatred on some faces. She would not have needed to look hard.

Nicholas appointed Peter Stolypin Prime Minister. Stolypin was no toadie but he was a reactionary and he launched a new terror. Police arrested thousands, interrogated them and incarcerated them, awaiting trial. His traveling courts tried, condemned, and strung them up on gallows that were designed to be dismantled for swift transport between the buildings hastily requisitioned as prisons. Suitable houses were seized, sealed, and fortified; it was a technique with which Nicholas would one day become familiar. The gibbet became a new ikon for the people, a gift from Stolypin said many; from the Czar, said some, but quietly.

Immediately there was conflict in high places. The Czar had carelessly taken his lady's judgement on the administration of land. Nicholas was quite simply wrong and Stolypin had no choice but to tell him so. The Czar wept with humiliation but the sound advice of his mother prevailed and he compromised from an untenable position. For someone who had been raised to regard himself as the infallible appointee of God, this was a monstrous blow. He would not forgive his Prime Minister until it was too late to matter.

Throughout the winter, arrests and executions became commonplace and indiscriminate. Neighbours denounced one another and were denounced in their turn; villages denounced villages and everyone denounced Jews. And it was all in the name of the new democracy.

Troops, acting on the flimsiest evidence, burnt barns, houses, villages; they raped, slaughtered, and stole. The rope was slow and bullets were in short supply so execution was increasingly by bayonet and bludgeon. The provincial military approved the educational value of mass execution. Nothing concentrated the minds of neighbouring communities better than a village burnt, with its occupants' bodies heaped in the ruins, dogs and distracted infants whining amongst the embers.

Nicholas grieved at having conceded a degree of government but he limited the Duma in every way he could. And he consoled himself that he had taught the revolutionaries a lesson they would never forget.

Indeed he had. He had done much more than allow people to glimpse liberty, more even than make certain that they would feel no gratitude for it. He had established that reprieve was not an option that opponents of autocracy could take. Next time, once the people had brought the colossus to its knees, the revolutionaries would cut out its heart.

The workers grew disheartened and hungry; many would have settled for trying to survive in a harsh world, but the Czar was told to be angry. Alexandra glared at him, demanding: "What of your sacred autocracy that they spurned? What of retribution for the fifteen hundred officials, officers and soldiers slaughtered by demonstrators?"

Stolypin closed down the Duma, marking this step with an enormous reception at his villa near Petersburg. A small group of men arrived but their names were not on the guest list. Guards prevented their admittance so they walked slowly away, then turned suddenly to hurl their bombs into the villa entrance. Bombers, guards, and guests were among the thirty dead.

Now Stolypin knew they were coming for him. Perhaps he had some time but not much. He would end an evening at the theatre with a weeping Czar beside his bed and a bullet in his liver. Gapon was found tortured and hanged but nobody ever answered for the crime. Ahzeff slipped out of Russia to live quietly and in fear, moving frequently and leaving no forwarding address. He would one night die in Berlin of natural causes at around the time that Nicholas and Alexandra Romanov were setting out from Tobolsk on their journey to Ekaterinberg. A lone companion mourned his passing, but not for long.

Chapter 16

Work ceased on the church site in Nice. Immense sums had been poured into the project as zealous attention to detail forced costs to escalate. Brick manufacturers in Italy, France, Germany, and Russia – but not England – were commissioned to create bricks of the right dimensions, colour, and quality and then to conduct experiments to ensure they possessed the correct qualities. Limestone of great strength and hardness was sought, quarried, and delivered; stonemasons were summoned from Italy; roof tiles and floor tiles were designed, fired, and tested; engineers experimented with new techniques that would enable them to create the cupolas from reinforced concrete. Artists who were to paint the majolicas – elaborately enamelled ceramic panels on the facades – were taken to see the portrait of Nicholas in the Winter Palace. "The Dowager Empress is immensely impressed by the spirituality of that portrait," they were told. "She wants that spirituality to be reflected in all the faces of angels and, most especially, in any representation of the sacred face of Our Lord. Pay special attention to the eyes and the shape of the face." Easels were erected and copies made.

And the money ran out. Dagmar spoke to

Nicholas. "I am sorry, Mama," he said, trying without much success to meet her eyes. "This is just a bag with the bottom dropped out of it. The more money we put in, the more we are going to have to put in. I have done as much as I can. I made a gift of the site and the rest is a matter of raising donations."

"I regret the discomfort you suffered for giving the land to God," said Dagmar. He knew she must have heard how Alexandra had harangued him for the gift, just as he knew she was now trying to embarrass him into giving money. He squared his shoulders.

"I am sorry Mama, but the cost of this project is no concern of mine and I can do nothing to help."

She smiled. "You are quite right, Nicki. We are Romanovs, who have never considered the cost of anything, and it would be wrong to begin now. I shall direct my administrative people to pay whatever is necessary."

That afternoon, Prince Alexander Shervadshidze begged an audience of the Dowager Empress. Dagmar knew and liked him; his face reminded her of someone else. She had considered him for a position in her household, though she could not imagine what he could want with her now. "His Majesty has instructed me to help administer your finances, Empress," he said.

She was astounded. "What do you mean?"

"I myself don't mean anything, Your Majesty," said the miserable young man. "His Majesty told me that his Ministers believe your state income, paid every year, is anachronistic and out of keeping with the dignity of your position. It is to be discontinued. I am to collect all receipts for expenditure, validate them, and forward them to the Ministry of the Imperial Court. There they will be paid."

"You are to collect and validate all receipts so that some civil servant can decide whether or not they are to be paid?"

He knew as he blurted out the words that he could not have chosen a worse phrase to use. Appalled, he heard himself say: "If it pleases Your Majesty." He had said it – there was nothing he could do now. He brushed his unruly hair back and gazed desperately at her, waiting for the storm.

Fury rising in her, Dagmar glared at this wretched lackey of her spineless son and... it seemed to her that a face she had never thought to see again gazed back into her eyes. The tear-filled eyes, the youthful despair. "We are not to have our happiness," she heard an echo say. "It is not to be."

The terrified prince could not believe what happened. The Empress had risen with a face like thunder and... burst into tears. He stepped forward to stop her falling but she steadied herself, stretched out an imperious hand. "You do not touch the Dowager Empress," she said. "You administer my finances, that is all. You have seen me weep, and few have had that privilege. Leave me."

Dagmar would deal with this in her own way.

The Montenegrin Grand Duchesses Anastasia and Militza had added style, elegance, and mischief to the Russian Court. Montenegro was a small state on the Adriatic coast, which held strategic significance because of its sea access to the Mediterranean. Many of Russia's problems arose from inadequate access to the seas and oceans.

The name meant black mountain. It was distinguished by an intensely proud Court of its own where nobody who lacked the skills of Machiavelli would have felt comfortable; deviousness and intrigue were de rigueur. Anastasia and Militza were worth daughters of that Court.

Prince George Romanovsky, sixth Duke of Leuchtenberg had married Anastasia and Grand Duke Peter Nicholaiovitch married Militza, so both were firm family members. Unfortunately Anastasia's marriage did not last and the scandal of divorce shocked the Court. People who have reluctantly accepted compromise to keep their own marriages intact are sometimes inclined to criticise those who don't; both Dagmar and Alexandra showed their disapproval.

One relaxed evening, the ladies had left a dozen gentlemen gathered in cheerful mood at table. Cigar smoke swirled and glasses clinked. Two or three conversations were going on amongst groups around the table. Even Nicholas was comfortable after a good dinner and more wine than he usually drank. He had turned to Nikolai and said: "I hear you're seeing a fair bit of a certain Montenegrin lady these days."

His cousin grinned. "I doubt if that unnamed lady has any bit that is not fair, Nicki, so I hope you don't object to my seeing her."

"Not at all, old chap," said the Czar. "Your private life is your own affair."

"Well that is a relief, Nicki," said Nikolai, "because

you see, I've decided I should like to marry her. If that's all right with you, of course."

Nicholas painstakingly set down his glass and tried to focus his mind. "Now we do need to give her a name," he said. "I believe we are talking about Anastasia, and she is divorced from George…"

"A cousin, the Duke of Leuchtenberg, yes. But it's 1907, Nicki, and these things aren't as taboo as they used to be. She's a splendid lady, I like her very much and she misses being at Court with her sister. If we married, she'd be back there where she belongs."

Nicholas turned to him. "Damn it, man. Her sister is married to your brother! Isn't there a law against that sort of thing?"

It took all Nikolai's sangfroid to raise a careless laugh. "Not at all, Nicki. Two brothers can marry two sisters, there's nothing wrong with that. They just can't mount each other, or their own sisters, not this side of the Urals, anyway."

Nicholas laughed. "You're a coarse bastard, Nikolai. Alex wouldn't like it you know. Nor would Mama. They don't approve of divorcees remarrying and you're in the inner circle."

Nikolai steeled himself to drink slowly before he said as casually as he knew how: "Yes, and of course, the female's point of view is perfectly understandable. But, as I was saying to someone only today, the one important thing you must never ever lose sight of is, Nicholas is the Czar. Nobody else is the Czar. Nicholas is!"

Nicholas nodded vigorously. "Bloody right," he said. "Bloody right. I'm the Czar and if I say you can marry your Montenegrin then you can marry your Montenegrin and nobody can say you can't!"

He staggered to his feet, raising his glass. "Gentlemen, my cousin and beloved friend Nikolai Nicholaiovitch is going to marry Anastasia of Montenegro and they have their Czar's blessing on their union. We drink to Nikolai and Anastasia." He spilt more than he drank but it did not matter. Nikolai had his blessing and there could be no going back.

Dagmar took tranquillisers while Alexandra took vengeance on Nicholas, but the deal was done. Dagmar was immensely fond of Nikolai, so before long she forgave him, but not Nicholas. After the discreet wedding, Anastasia rapidly re-established her position at Court. Even Alexandra overcame her reservations. Fascinated by the strange and occult, she again befriended both the exotic sisters and spent time with them. And so it was that she called one day on Anastasia at home.

She was shown into the salon, where she had expected to see the tall figure of Anastasia. For a moment she thought there was nobody else there but then she noticed the straight-backed little figure, sitting on a chair as though she sat a horse side-saddle. Dagmar's eyes were fixed upon her; there was no escape.

"Come over here and sit down, my dear," said the Dowager Empress.

Alexandra did as she was told. "I had not expected to meet you here."

"No indeed," said Dagmar. "We are so busy, we spend so little time together and never seem to have any time to talk to one another. That was why, when I called on Anastasia and realised you were expected, I requested a few minutes with you when you arrived."

Alexandra did not know what to say but did her best. "How agreeable… was there anything you wished to discuss, in particular?" That was inexcusably rude but for God's sake, she thought, let's get to the point.

Dagmar was unperturbed. "Well yes, my dear, there is something. As you know, there is a church under construction in Nice. Archpriest Lubimoff persuaded a number of influential people that the religious resources of the area were inadequate for the many Russians who have homes there. And of course, others too. There are so many Romanians, Serbians, Bulgarians, Greeks in the region. You should spend more time there yourself you know. The climate is so invigorating."

"I find the heat oppressive," said Alexandra.

"Yes, nowhere is perfect, but so many devout people do like Nice and many have business there – Villefranche is so important to the Imperial Navy of course. It seemed a very good idea to build a church that could accommodate them. So many, many people have put a great deal of effort into the project. Unfortunately they have simply run out of money, without having completed the church. Of course I should be delighted to help them but I have never been involved in money matters, you see. It's one of those household, administrative things. I have it all done for me. Now the whole thing is in an embarrassing muddle. I really think Nicki should sort it out."

"Then perhaps you should ask him."

The reply was brutal. "I have, but you stopped him doing anything to help."

Alexandra could hear her own heart thudding. She faced Dagmar's direct gaze and felt she was on trial. She could deny it of course, but Dagmar knew everything: it was impossible. Alexandra gazed at her hands. "I thought the project was excessive. I know you have tragic memories of Nice but I'm not sure a memorial to someone who has not even been your husband…"

Dagmar's face paled but she retained her composure. "Even now Froloff is creating mosaic ikons of Saint Alexander Nevski and Saint Mary Magdalene to grace the church façade in memory of the late Czar and my love for him. When he is finished, there will be no money to pay for them. Already Vassilieff has asked for payment for the marvellous sketches he made to guide Froloff. But there is nothing for him either. The honour of Russia is being compromised."

The silence stretched unbearably and Alexandra knew Dagmar was content to let it stretch. She tried to sit it out but could not bear the awful emptiness. "It seems ostentatious to have what is really a cathedral in a mere provincial city in a foreign country."

Dagmar was in no hurry but eventually she spoke.

"A provincial city? It was in Nice that destiny took a hand in a way that put Nicholas on the throne he occupies today. A foreign country? It is with France that we are maintaining peace in Europe. They are increasingly becoming our allies and without that alliance Europe will tear itself to pieces. And only Holy Synod can bestow the title of cathedral on a church. It has not to my knowledge done so."

She stood now, her voice rising and her little fists clenched. "Ostentatious? Is it ostentation to state unequivocally that we stand proud for Russia, devout in our religion and loyal to our alliances?" Dagmar usually spoke to Alexandra in English, though she often slipped into French and even Russian to express herself; now she was using occasional German expressions.

Alexandra did not dare look up. She sat, downcast and waiting. Dagmar spoke again, quietly and evenly. "I want nothing of you except an answer. When I ask Nicki to resolve the humiliation that the Empire and the Church are enduring in full sight of the entire international community, will you encourage him to agree, or shall I have to take whatever measures are necessary?"

Alexandra wondered what on earth she was threatening, but she felt leaden dread as she listened to her heart thudding, thudding. Perhaps she could win herself a little time to think. She said: "What will happen if he agrees?"

"Professor Preobrajensky is conducting a detailed and fully costed audit of all the work that remains to complete the structure of the building, with its exterior finishes. Within two weeks, this can be submitted to Nicki. There are several ways the Czar could deal with it; he will achieve credit and recognition if he authorises payment from his private chancery. There are of course ways that he can subsequently replenish his chancery if he wishes."

Alexandra saw a chink of light. "That is the exterior but there are rumours of lavish interior decorations, magnificent ikons, an iconostas to match Moscow's. What of all that?"

Dagmar, seeming to relax, almost smiled as she concluded that the unrepentant Lutheran was working the strings on this Russian Orthodox marionette, but Alexandra had raised no objection to Nicki paying to complete the exterior. "Once the Czar has made the house of God secure, God will provide, my dear. Trust in Him and His congregation will equip His place of worship.

"Nicki is coming to me for tea this afternoon, when I shall raise the subject. Perhaps you would like to be there and join in the discussion."

Alexandra raised her face and looked directly into the large and unrelenting eyes of her husband's mother. "Thank you but I doubt if I shall be able to come. I feel an enlargement of my heart, so I shall need to rest.

"I have heard what you have said and I must say I agree with you. Nicki needs to ensure that the building is made secure and complete. Of course, the decision is his, but I shall certainly tell him that I should like him to do what you ask."

That afternoon a message was brought to Alexandra. She lifted the cold compress from her eyes and, sitting up, took the slip of folded card from the proffered tray. It was from Anastasia. "I am so sorry," she had written. "There was nothing I could do – you must know the feeling. Stana."

The Empress slowly tore the message into pieces and dropped it back onto the tray. Then she lay down again, covering her eyes. She knew the feeling only too well. She called it defeat.

Chapter 17

Dagmar tried to suppress the giggle that rose in her throat. Prince Paul Trubetskoy heard the strangled noise and thought he recognised choking emotion. He turned solicitously towards her but Dagmar, still choking and clutching a handkerchief to her face, turned away.

The statue Trubetskoy had toiled to create was always going to be absurd. Nicholas was determined that his father would be presented as at least the peer of pseudo-sophisticated Western European heads of state, so of course that meant an equestrian statue. But Czar Alexander III must be seen as a totalitarian Russian warlord. So the massive figure, dressed in traditional Russian uniform, sat astride the cow-like body of a small horse that looked very unhappy about it. Dagmar had casually approved a small model but now, at a private viewing before the unveiling, she saw how ludicrous it was. Next day she would stand inscrutable with Nicholas and Alexandra as the Nevski Prospekt came alive with crowds and pageantry for the unveiling.

Locked out of government processes, Dagmar had meetings, discussed details, approved drawings for her great project, which was rapidly approaching completion. Of course the cathedral in Nice was for Nicholas and for Russia, not for her. And yet she derived great comfort from it, the satisfaction of doing what needed to be done. Ikon authority Nicholas Globa had brought Pianovsky, a highly-regarded artist from Moscow's Stroganoff school of art, and they too were shown the portrait of Nicholas. The spirituality of those eyes, the expression, the very facial features – all epitomised for Dagmar the essence of Jesus.

Pianovsky was a romantic, he understood. He had toured churches in Moscow and Iaroslav, studiously copying and developing the concepts of long-dead masters. Then he had sent sketches to Italy, where Designori developed proposals for magnificently ornate and stylised frescoes while Pianovsky had joined forces with the ornate metalworking brothers Kliebnikov of Moscow, to create the elaborate ikons that would screen the altar. Her involvement encouraged donations, so that work progressed to plan. For a time, she was happy. Nicholas gave her a crystal Fabergé egg containing a gold replica of the statue she knew as 'the bear on a cow statue'.

Easter 1911 brought the Fabergé egg of the fifteenth anniversary. As fine as any that Fabergé's craftsmen had made before, it bore immaculate miniatures of the Czar, his Empress and their five beautiful children, with tiny scenes of the most important events of their lives so far. Their date with destiny was six Easters away, but first the valkyries must have their day.

Germany had gained less in the Empire Stakes than seemed appropriate to Kaiser William, a man whose monstrous self-esteem was supported by all those Germans who had no choice in the matter. Britain had an extended and profitable Empire and so did Russia, in its peculiarly Russian way. The French and the Austrians hadn't done too badly either, but Germany had been rather left out. It didn't seem fair, somehow.

It wasn't as if Germany lacked efficient services and administration, or trained soldiers or modern weapons and technology. It had just not been in the right place at the right time. Of course, the Kaiser had built magnificent palaces and done everything he could to turn Potsdam into a latter-day Versailles. He had acquired ever more splendid uniforms, struck poses for increasing numbers of cameras, waxed his moustache into more unlikely spikes, but somehow no other emperor quite took him seriously. At Bertie's funeral in England, he had not been given the deference that was his due. Nicholas had avoided him, while Nikolai – his banter had just the hint of insolence about it. But perhaps all was not yet lost for the empire. Other countries were re-examining the map of Europe, speculating on how redrawing national frontiers might improve the whole equation; perhaps it was time for Germany to rethink its boundaries.

For decades Europe's major countries had been manoeuvring around one another, each seeking the best alliances for long-term advantage. Bismarck, the midwife of twentieth-century Germany, had perceived the perils of having to face both East and West simultaneously if Russia and France joined forces to become belligerent, so diplomatic alliances were created, strained, broken, reassembled. Gradually Europe had divided into two adversarial groups: on the one hand, Russia, France, and Britain began solving their differences in private, while Germany, Austria-Hungary, and Italy tended to dine together.

Britain was not entirely comfortable sharing interests with the Russian bear it had distrusted for so long but France and Russia forgot Napoleon in their opposition to German ambitions. Dagmar found this eminently satisfactory. French bankers rode up the Nevski Prospekt, dined well and did business. Leaders in Paris purred with pleasure when Russians visited

Others had been building too. The cathedral in Nice was completed, dedicated and in need of inauguration. Dagmar set out happily with a compliant Nicholas and Alexandra. The event would be spoiled for her by Mikhail.

Her son Grand Duke Mikhail Alexandrovitch had some reason to regard himself as an unfortunate man. His romantic life had been unhappy, with brother Nicholas quashing his hopes of a morganatic marriage in 1906. Dagmar might have tolerated Mikhail's marrying a commoner – the woman was after all a lady in waiting – but Nicholas, driven on by Alexandra, would have none of it. If Mikhail married the woman Dina Kossikofsky he would be thrown out of the army, the country, and the succession. Mikhail and the unfortunate Dina planned to marry secretly in Russia and were thwarted by the secret police. They tried to leave separately so they could meet and marry in Italy but Nicholas again sent the Okhrana after them. Eventually Mikhail despaired; they drifted apart and the family breathed more freely.

There was worse to come.

Mikhail began to visit the home of Vladimir Wulfert, a lieutenant in his regiment, the Blue Cuirassiers, and his lady Natasha. She was young and lovely; she was unfortunately divorced, but that was not a serious problem for a lieutenant. But gradually an understanding developed between the lady and Mikhail; it was the husband who began to feel that he was an intruder. Vladimir confronted Natasha, she told him exactly how she felt before she left him, so he challenged Mikhail, his commanding officer, to a duel. Dagmar, honorary Colonel-in-Chief of the regiment, heard of it and laid down the law.

Mikhail was promoted with immediate effect to the command of a distant cavalry regiment, while Vladimir was forced out of the regiment in disgrace. There was no duel and Dagmar, who could not entirely condemn her son's colourful life, felt duty had been done.

Mikhail did not recognise he had been dealt with sympathetically; he had seen his family snatch happiness from him before and had no intention of allowing that to happen again. Gradually, from clandestine meetings, he and Natasha built their relationship. There was gossip and scandal, a child, divorce, wrangling over paternity, acrimony, recriminations, financial compensation and every possible obstruction put in the way of marriage. But their bond endured.

Now, with his mother and brother in Nice for the inauguration, Mikhail made his move.

Mikhail was very well aware of the pleasures of the

Cote d'Azure, having spent so long there that he had even founded a golf course – based upon the course at Saint Andrews in Scotland – years before at Mandelieu. He had become comfortable with the palaces, the socially aspiring, the courtesans, and the climate; above all, he luxuriated in the distance from the restraints, the constraints and the sheer bloody cold of the Baltic region. Now he enjoyed the irony of sending a message to the Palais Romanov in Nice, advising his brother that he had slipped away while on holiday and married. Mikhail believed it was a done deal and that his brother could do nothing more, but he had badly miscalculated.

Nicholas was aghast. Only weeks before, Alexei had been screaming with the agony of internal haemorrhaging, while Alexandra had been in a frenzy as she tended the suffering child. She had sent telegraph messages to her mystic guide Rasputin, who was in faraway Siberia but he did not reply until after the boy had received the sacrament. Alexei would not die, he said. Alexandra relaxed. Perhaps this enabled her son to relax too; in any case, the bleeding ceased. With one leg crippled – temporarily the doctors thought – Alexei gradually recovered. And still Nicholas, his lady and his mother had kept the terrible truth concealed from Russia – and from Mikhail. Knowing what they did, Mikhail's action in marrying this tainted woman was beyond comprehension or forgiveness; to him, ignorant of how precariously the succession hung, he thought he was simply behaving honourably to the woman he loved.

Having got through the inauguration, Nicholas hurried to confront his brother. With his lady's fury reverberating in his mind, he issued his ultimatum: renounce either the marriage or his place in the succession. Exhausted and stressed beyond endurance, Nicholas yelled, his voice rising as his rationality disintegrated. Mikhail turned and walked out.

Nicholas had his brother dismissed from the army, deprived of his own fortune, removed from the succession and banished from Russia. When the greatest of all crises struck and war was declared, Mikhail would be in exile. Dagmar, furious with Mikhail for having precipitated the crisis, simultaneously blamed Alexandra's domination of Nicholas for his excessive reaction. "I have lost one son from God's will and another from a hypochondriac's hysteria. Now," she told the Czar, "the dynasty is one bullet and a nosebleed away from obliteration."

Nicholas glared back, his jaw muscles working. "You are talking about the death of your son and of your grandchild."

"I am talking about the destruction of the Romanovs, you imbecile! The fall of the Russian Empire. Is that what you want? Is that what she wants? Perhaps in her German heart, it is. Is she past childbearing age, that she cannot bear a son capable of shouldering the burden?"

Nicholas stared at her miserably. "Did you do any better?"

For once there was good news from Potsdam: the Kaiser's daughter was to marry. William invited the crowned heads of Europe to luxuriate in his magnificence and they came, but still he was dissatisfied. Georgie of England – "He's married to a German lady, in God's name!" – came only in a private capacity because the British Government wanted to treat him, Kaiser William, as a diplomatic pariah. And Nicholas seemed to be avoiding being alone with him, while spending a lot of time hobnobbing seriously with Georgie. Perhaps they despised him because he had a withered arm. He knew Edward VII of England had called him Silly Willy, while Dagmar freely referred to him as a silly ass. Perhaps the others all thought their empires were so much grander than his. Well, let them hear the sound of gunfire and see where the frontiers lay after that; that would show them just who was silly. It was easy in the soft Crimea to believe that these were difficult times that would settle down so that they would all once again drive up the Nevski Prospekt, attend balls and dinner parties, go to the ballet and the opera. Paranoia and megalomania corroded his sanity.

Hungary armed, the Serbs suffered, Bosnia and Herzegovina festered, Bulgaria attacked and withdrew, Austria menaced, a wounded Turkey growled. Tensions in Europe were becoming impossibly complex. In England, parliamentarians spoke of the powder keg of Europe; a single spark could so easily ignite the entire continent.

Chapter 18

It is a peaceful summer Sunday in picturesque Sarajevo, and the Bosnian capital is in carnival mood. Archduke Franz Ferdinand, heir to the Austrian Empire, is visiting in his splendid red uniform with his charming lady, Sophie Duchess of Hohenberg. Her pregnancy can still be discreetly concealed by an immaculately tailored white dress. Of course, the Serbs are inclined to resent Austrian domination but surely they too are enjoying today; it is after all Serbia's national day.

A missile curves through the air, hits the Archduke's open car and bounces towards the following vehicle. At the explosion the leading driver accelerates away, straight to the Town Hall, as planned. The waiting officials know nothing of the bomb. They look at their watches. Excellent! He's right on time. One steps forward to open the car door, behind him another clears his throat to say welcome. The Archduke jumps up, red with fury. "I come to visit Sarajevo and somebody hurls explosives at me!" he bellows.

Bosnian student Gavrilo Princip is left standing nonplussed in a crowd on the pavement. He grips the automatic handgun under his worn jacket and bites his lip. He had known nothing of the bomb until he saw it thrown. Now it had missed but still it has deprived him of his opportunity of glory. He had not planned to be available to do anything afterwards – he had supposed that he would have been either killed or arrested by now – so he has nothing to do. Like many of the crowd he is still standing there when he sees the cars returning. He slips the safety catch off again but then, as he steels himself, the first car turns aside and the Archduke's follows it. Serbs have some powerful oaths and Gavrilo Princip mutters to himself. But something is happening, something entirely unexpected… the Archduke's car is coming back.

Gavrilo Princip steps forward, aims wildly at the Archduke and fires twice. Bright arterial blood spreads across the white dress. Blood spills too from the Archduke's mouth as he turns to his pregnant lady and begs: "Don't die, Sopherl."

The stricken couple are carried into the reception hall to die. Nobody has told the servants; the priest performs his melancholy duties for the dying, to the distant clatter of luncheon being prepared to honour them.

Onlookers have grabbed the assassin, tearing at him. The police rush forward; he must be saved for interrogation. The teenage student, too frail to make a success of his moustache, too young to hang, smiles. He may be weak, tubercular like his siblings, who were already buried in a communal grave. He would never walk free and would be dead of consumption within four years, but nobody will ever again ignore Gavrilo Princip the postman's son. He smiles again at his first interrogator. "I am Gavrilo Princip the freedom fighter," he says.

The fuse is lit.

Within a month of the shots on the streets of Sarajevo, an Austro-Hungarian alliance had declared war on Serbia. With discretion and diplomacy, all might yet have been well. The declaration was a ferocious bluff, mandatory chest thumping. Everyone needed to stay their hand, remain calm so that negotiation could gradually dissolve the bitterness while tempers cooled. The world held its breath and waited.

A generation of men who were to die in horror might have lived their natural spans, multitudes that suffered could have been spared. But Czar Nicholas was called from swimming to be told that the alliance had declared war on Serbia. Red-cheeked from exertion, he listened attentively. "Very well," he cried, accepting a towel and drying himself vigorously. "Mobilise our armed forces. Mobilise immediately!"

He had never felt better. Exhilarated by swimming in cold water, he had grasped the situation at a glance, knew instantly what to do and did it without hesitation. For once Nicholas believed he was truly Father of all the Russias – now surely, he was an Olympian. Mercifully he would never face the fact that it was he who loosed the dogs of war.

Germany embraced his irresistible invitation to declare war on Russia and France, then invaded Belgium. Rapidly they engaged the French. Italians could see no attraction in dying for the Kaiser so, to his intense annoyance, they declined to join in.

The technology of warfare had advanced so that many traditional techniques had become obsolete. Never again would European infantry stand in massed blocks as enemy artillery cut down swathes of them, as they had in years gone by, or march towards the enemy in full sight and order of rank and file. The Crimean War, with its thin red line and its charge of the Light Brigade, its elegant uniforms and cucumber sandwiches for the well-born observers, was history. Histrionic heroism was dead; only the agony remained. On the Western Front they dug in for trench warfare, heads down under artillery fire. Then, as soon as the big guns fell silent, they advanced through entangled barbed wire towards the machine guns. Our turn today, theirs tomorrow. Casualties by the tens of thousands, and nothing gained. The firing squad for those who hesitated. Lunacy on an epic scale, with no escape for the sane.

The Eastern Front was even more different. Russia opened it to divert German attention from the West, where the French were immediately enduring heavy punishment. For Nicholas, this promised to be payback time, and he relished it. On the Prussian border he had two Russian soldiers for every German. Perhaps their armament could have been better but Britain had more or less promised arms and munitions – and Britain had that magnificent Lee Enfield 303 rifle; it was said to be the first personal weapon since the Battle of Agincourt that could match the firepower and killing potential of the English longbow. The promise had been rather more from Windsor Castle than from Whitehall but surely the purple could trust the purple?

Unfortunately for Russia, the Eastern Front was of no interest to the British Government, who had more than enough problems without having to honour damnfool promises given by the precariously perched King George V. People in England had not been deceived when their Royal house of Saxe-Coburg und Gotha changed its name to Windsor to disguise its German origins. The political scene there was undergoing earthquake and eruption as both the monarchy and the House of Lords tottered, one major political party headed for extinction and a new one struggled to fill the vacuum. Society was in turmoil, with the aristocracy sending its heirs off to die at the head of the troops, women demanding equality at the ballot box if not in the trenches, massive unemployment, and almost universal unrest. The unemployment had its useful side though: hungry men, no matter how disenchanted, could be easily and cheaply recruited into uniform. They took the King's shilling – the traditional expression for signing away their civilian rights – just to have an occupation and a tiny income to send back to their families. "Nothing could be worse than watching the kids go hungry," they told each other. Then they arrived on the Somme and realised they had been wrong.

By then it was too late.

The promise from England was not honoured; the munitions never arrived, but that was not the only shortfall in the East. The Russian Commander-in-Chief was the Czar's cousin, Nikolai Nicholaevitch, now in his forties and at the height of his powers. Throughout the Russian armies and beyond, he was recognised as a capable leader. He looked like the soldier he was, straight, level eyed, accurately smart without ostentation, courteous, concise, and expert. Unfortunately his armies had inadequate communications, porous security, and scanty supplies. His senior officers were politically appointed, selected for him by the Czar and by the system: he had only nominal control over the men who held the power to win or lose. The best he could do was brief his commanders and send them into the field with their men. After that they did whatever they thought was appropriate. Sometimes they told him by messenger and sometimes they left him to find out from events. The CinC lived in logistical turmoil where few supplies were available and no services worked effectively. He did all he could but resources of everything were inadequate – except for cannon fodder: he had plenty of men to suffer hardship and death. To an intelligent and compassionate Commander-in-Chief like Grand Duke Nikolai Nikolaevich, it was an endless nightmare where everything he tried to achieve was thwarted.

In August 1914 two Russian armies invaded East Prussia, skirting lakes and marshlands to engage Germany on two fronts. Within a week General Paul von Rennenkampf's First Army had defeated the larger part of the Prussian forces while the Second Army, under General Alexander Samsonoff, was threatening the weak rear of the German army. Nicholas was jubilant and told them so. Nikolai's problem now was that he could give them further orders only by messenger or telegraph and, given the ego of each of the commanding officers, plus their mutual distrust and loathing, they were likely to ignore them anyway.

Telegraph technology had been around for a while but somehow, although educated Russians sent each other messages from time to time, the military had never really dealt with its flaws. There was no cipher available so any messages were sent as they were.

Only the very brave or the very stupid try to intercept telegraphy in a war zone, because doing it effectively means shinning up a pole, attaching wires to the wires at the top, and getting down again, without having been shot. Sometimes though, it is well worth the risk. Rennenkampf, in charge of the First Army, having already achieved the adulation of his Czar, was disinclined to do much more for the time being and he said so – in an unscrambled telegraph message. He wanted to regroup at Gumbinnen and give his men some well-earned rest and regrouping before he did anything else.

Reading the message, the German General Erich von Ludendorff recognised it might be a trap but if it were not, what a stroke of luck. And a trap seemed unlikely. After all, this was Rennenkampf. Crinkly-haired and with an extravagant handlebar moustache, Rennenkampf had been in the army for more than forty years. *The Times* newspaper correspondent reported during Russia's war with Japan that he was 'a poor leader of men' and he had no detectable subtlety. By the time he marched into Prussia he had recovered some reputation by his merciless pursuit and destruction of revolutionaries in Siberia.

Samsonoff had engaged the Germans at Orlau Frankenau and now intended to press home a heavier attack. His detailed battle plan was described in a message that, through the nimble work of agents clambering up and down telegraph poles, fascinated Ludendorff.

Leaving his forward infantry, artillery, and cavalry ostentatiously facing Rennenkampf, Ludendorff surreptitiously withdrew most of his troops from that confrontation to face Samsonoff frontally and on both wings. An entire corps was transported by train from north of Samsonoff to face his southern wing, without Samsonoff getting wind of it.

Rennenkampf and Samsonoff were of the old school. They were both graduates of the Nikolaevsky military academy and both ran their commands as they ran their estates. They detested each other, having disputed which of them had cost Russia most dearly in the war with Japan. When Samsonoff publicly accused Rennenkampf of failing to support him during the battle of Mukden, they started a fist fight. Nikolai had walked in and separated them, then stared from one to the other. "Show contempt for fellow officers if you must," he said, "but don't disgrace the men who serve you." Junior officers speculated on whether there would be a duel but neither seemed inclined to revive such traditions of the past. Whenever they did meet they fell to yelling insults and usually tried to punch one another. Each gave the other nothing, especially intelligence, which was what they needed most.

Samsonoff had fought against the Turks, the Chinese, and the Japanese when he was revealed as energetic, quarrelsome, and strategically unimaginative. He disliked being anywhere but on horseback and regarded himself as the personal servant of the Czar and of God, from whom he took his inspiration. He thumped his field desk with his fist when his officers said they must send for support from Rennenkampf. "Over my dead body!" he roared. Why humiliate himself to that posturing halfwit when he was confident that the other army was already on its way anyway? It wasn't and, what was very much worse, while Samsonoff thought it was, Ludendorff knew it wasn't.

"Remember the lesson of Mukden," said a message from Nikolai, deliberately cryptic to confuse German agents. Samsonoff's staff officers said the Commander-in-Chief clearly meant that he must be vigilant for an outflanking manoeuvre that could leave his army surrounded. But Samsonoff roared that the lesson of Mukden was that nobody in their right mind would trust that moustached moron Rennenkampf to do the proper thing, and that nobody needed to remind him, Samsonoff, of that.

Chapter 19

Stretched across a slowly advancing front of more than fifty miles, the Second Army was vulnerable. Ludendorff waited for the right moment, then struck. German artillery hit Samsonoff's wing, forced a retreat, and opened the way for German troops to break through, circle round, and close on the Russian rear. Nikolai's warning had been ignored and his fears justified.

Samsonoff's messages, calling too late for support, reported heavy losses but they could never describe the carnage and the incompetence. Ill-equipped, starving soldiers were ordered about aimlessly as supplies, command, and communications failed. In some units there was one rifle to every ten men. They would fight each other for possession of one of the magazine-loading Mosin-Nagant rifles. Any man who had a few cartridges for an MN kept them close – he might get a rifle from someone who had run out of luck or ammunition, and a man who held a loaded rifle when the Germans charged might survive a little longer. Otherwise he had to face the enemy, slack bellied, using stones and sticks against trained, well-fed infantry with rifles and machine guns.

Though there were few rifles, there were plenty of

bayonets. Most soldiers carried one of the scabbardless stabbing swords at his waist; they were useless for anything but the one purpose: they could be driven into someone. More than one possessor of a rifle took from behind a surprise bayonet thrust in the kidney and lay dying in the mud, too agonised to scream, as his precious MN was pilfered by a comrade. A few men carried ancient Berdan rifles. The only advantage of a Berdan was that nobody else wanted it, said the veterans. If you could steal an MN or plunder one from a corpse, even if you didn't have any ammunition, chances were there were a few cartridges in the magazine. But a Berdan was a single shot, black powder weapon. The Berdan barked deep and belched an impressive plume of smoke with a spurt of fire. One shot was enough to tell the Germans where you were so a sniper could home in with the optical sight on his Mauser rifle, wait while you reloaded, then take you as you peered out for a target. And even if he missed, you had one round before you needed to reload; the sniper had five rounds in his Mauser magazine, and they were smokeless cordite. The best anyone could hope for from a German sniper was to hear the crack as he fired. If he aimed true, you didn't even hear that. Against modern weapons a Berdan wasn't worth stealing; that was what the seasoned soldiers said. But there wasn't one of them would not have thrown aside his stick to pick up a rifle – any rifle.

The chances were that the swine of a sniper still had the tastes of beef, bread, and beer in his mouth too. Just one chance to put a bullet through his full belly, please God, and leave the rest to destiny. That was the way they thought and that was the way they died.

The German troops were ordered to sight in on the officers first. Officers were usually armed only with pistols but they knew what they should be doing. Once they were gone, untrained, unfed, mostly unarmed men could be cut down like cattle, and they were. They had no answer as they faced the thunder of artillery, the cackle of automatic fire and the sharp crack of rifles. Their tormentors increasingly found they could with impunity run forward to toss grenades amongst the despairing Russians.

By the dozen, the score, the hundred they fell, bearded peasants kicking disembowelled in the blood-smeared mud beside boys who would never now grow beards. "It is the harvest season. We must make such slaughter that they will never dare march into our territory again," said Kaiser William. That was asking more than they could achieve but they made such slaughter that when Russians marched again on German territory, thirty years later and in another war, they carved a more terrible vengeance than William could have dreamed in his foulest nightmare.

A Russian recoil attack opened a gap for a few to escape, so Samsonoff, with a few thousand men, managed to break out through the German lines, leaving behind 140,000 of his 150,000 soldiers dead, dying, or about to be captured. Becoming a prisoner of war, one in tens of thousands, in East Prussia in early September was a dreadful fate; few would see the spring.

Gangrene, that will be the end of the line. They all knew it was coming. A wound, a scratch, any part left exposed to the frost. A man turned in his sleep, leaving his ear uncovered, white in the moonlight. A grimy hand relaxed out of the rags. The silent frost bit the rim of a wound, froze unguarded skin, crept through drenched cloth and sodden boots. Thaw in the morning, scream as feeling returned to ruined flesh, watch black stains invade. Men with rotting noses, their faces turning black. Men hacking their own toes away to cut out the gangrene, slashing at fingers to amputate pain.

General Winter was not particular, he harvested without preference. Prisoners or guards, winners or losers. The land was his and they came uninvited. Now they would stay, rotting from the extremities inward. This will be the season that recalls Napoleon's retreat from Moscow; was it a century ago? Then too, the General reaped men like wheat.

For every man who came away with Samsonoff, fourteen remained. There were tens of thousands, fearful in the starving nightmare, waiting for Winter. A captured officer called for *God Save the Czar* and began to sing. A couple of his own men clubbed him to the ground while others looked on. As the blows fell and his cries did away in a gurgle, some became aware: maybe he was the lucky one.

Samsonoff surveyed the ragged ranks of his muddy survivors – the walking wounded with their black-encrusted bandages, almost indistinguishable from the able-bodied: filthy, starving, demoralised, and exhausted. Kaiser William had called the first British forces on the Western Front 'this contemptible little army'. What would he have made of this wrecked remnant of the immense horde that Samsonoff had marched to destruction?

Samsonoff looked to his aides but somehow, none

was facing in his direction; almost as if by accident, they all had their backs to him. The General dismounted, walked calmly into a clump of trees, put his revolver to his temple and fired. His aides came there to stare at his body: stocky and heavily bearded, with a raft of medals across his chest and half his cropped head pulped. They moved on; the enemy were close behind. He had ignored their opinions when it mattered, now they were all paying the price.

Germans found the body next day. They knew from his uniform who he was, which was as well because a badger had gnawed his face. They aspired to gallantry so they gave him a soldier's funeral – more than his comrades were inclined to do.

The Czar was with the Commander-in-Chief, Grand Duke Nikolai Nikolaevich, when an aide burst in. "They have confirmed that what remains of the Second Army has broken out, Your Majesty."

Nicholas gazed at the man. So the humiliation was massive but not total.

"How many?"

"Perhaps eight thousand men, sir."

"No more than that?"

"It seems not, sir."

"Was Samsonoff with them?"

"Yes sir. But he… he has blown his brains out."

Nikolai stretched back in his chair. "Must have been a damn fine shot," he said.

Nicholas guffawed spontaneously but his laughter shrivelled. Of course the stiff-necked Samsonoff was right to have fallen on his sword, for he carried responsibility for this catastrophe. The commander on that front, Yakob Zhilinsky, would also be held responsible. Nikolai would escape blame, but he was still on borrowed time. He was a distinguished and enlightened soldier, a far better CinC than he, Nicholas, could ever be. Yet Nicholas was going to have to take from him the poisoned chalice of command.

The trouble was that Nikolai thought too much. He implemented military reforms and made them work. He proposed political reform too, so Alexandra distrusted him, thought he had ambitions – a general who wanted to become Caesar. "Let your people see their Czar lead them in battle," she urged. Bloody nonsense, Nicholas reflected; what did he know about warfare? Still, she was only at the wheedling stage so it could wait a while. He could probably wait until she got to the flaring nostrils, the melodramatics in shrieked German, then the tortured silences, the white knuckles and the sudden bursts of hellfire. He shuddered.

"Why in God's name did you give that stable hand Samsonoff the Second Army?"

"Because you told me to, Your Majesty."

"Did I? Well why the hell didn't you ignore me? Everyone else does."

"I must admit I wondered what an inflexible cavalry man was going to make of marshland but someone or other questioned your decision, so of course I gave Your Majesty's judgement my unwavering support."

"Stop mocking me, Nikolai. You have a weakness for horses too."

"I'm not mocking you, Nicholas. I know you have the worst job in Russia and I have the second. And Samsonoff's horses certainly brought a bit of style to the whole affair. Imagine what a vulgar massacre it would have been without the cavalry."

Nicholas laughed. "You're a bastard, Nikolai, but I'm glad you're on my side. Samsonoff wasn't married was he? I don't want to have to write to some hawk-faced harpy and tell her what a splendid fellow he was."

"Speaking of wives, how is Alexandra?" The question was totally unexpected. Nicholas stared at his cousin in an effort to understand why he asked. The older man looked straight back. "What have I done to offend her Nicholas?"

There was no point in evasion. Nicholas gathered himself. "The problem is that she's afraid you'd make a better Czar than I am, Nikolai. I know it's daft but she's scared. You have the same blood, you look like you're the Czar, you never doubt the system, you never doubt yourself. And the men worship you. Nikolai, you know as I do there are plenty of people who want me out of it and into exile – people in our own family too. They say I'm so bloody useless I'll drag the whole dynasty down." He paused. "The truth is she's afraid of you, Nikolai. Years ago we heard there was a military plan to depose me and establish you as military dictator. She believes the plotters could invite you to be Regent in my place and you'd do the job better than I do."

"And what do you think?"

Nicholas sighed. "Well, it would make sense, Nikolai. You know it would."

The older man walked to a cupboard, returning with two neat little glasses of clear spirit. He handed one to his cousin. "The Czar and the Czaritsa are right about some things and wrong about others," he said. "The Czar and the Czaritsa are right that there was a proposal in 1905, and I told them to go to hell. I rather believe the Okhrana made sure some of them did.

"The Czar and Czaritsa are correct in believing there are now people who want to move them to one side. They are right that some of them have suggested I become Regent. They are wrong in supposing that I could ever accept. I serve the Czar as long as I can be of service to the Czar."

He smiled at his friend and shrugged. "You are the Czar." He raised his glass.

Nicholas looked at the soldier, raised his glass and they both drank. "Thank you Nikolai. I did not realise they were so close on my heels. I have only one question: was my mother implicated?"

"They spoke to me in confidence, Nicholas. If I were to break my word to them, what value would my word have for you or anyone? I know this about your mother though: she has the best interests of you and of Russia at her heart. I believe she may be a little anxious about some of the counsel you take."

"So am I, Nikolai, so am I. God alone knows how anxious I am."

For weeks trains loaded with hundreds of Russian

guns trundled away into Germany. The battlefront that was opened to alleviate pressure on France had given their adversary a magnificent gift of ordnance. Trains played a major part in the early days of the war but ironically, the more Germany succeeded, the less successful it became, partly because of the railways. German trains ran on a different gauge from Russian trains so, once they were on Russian soil, the Germans could use only captured rolling stock. And Russia was immense. Huge distances, climate, and terrain soaked up endeavour as they had for Napoleon. And always, when soldiers had faced the terrain, endured the climate and covered the distance, they were confronted with limitless numbers of the enemy. These were not well trained, or armed or supplied, but they were there and they wanted to kill Germans. They suffered in winter but not like Germans suffered. As temperatures fell, these indomitable Russians could endure. They came through the ice and snow to die but on the way, they killed.

It did not matter to a German soldier that the workforce of the largest agricultural nation on Earth was being herded into battle, leaving farming to manage however it could, that essential industry was being turned to armaments, that scarce reserves were being squandered on war supplies. What mattered to him was that the Russians that he faced wanted to kill him and, no matter how many fell, no matter how bitterly cold the wind, they would be replaced. Meanwhile distances seemed to become greater, conditions more daunting.

Russian forces had more success invading Galicia but Hindenburg faced them and Hindenburg, who had already played a major part in Russia's humiliation, was a thinking commander. Using hundreds of trains and rapid response, he mounted a bloody but brilliant defence. By the time Russia was driven out the following year, its military losses were already estimated at two million men, many claimed by General Winter, the name sardonic troops gave to the cold so intense that a weary man who leant against a tree to rest might never march on.

For the record, Rennenkampf survived criticism for his failure to support Samsonoff but was eventually dismissed for ineptitude. Four years later he would be shot by the Bolsheviks.

Chapter 20

Nicholas and Alexandra visited Dagmar for lunch in September 1915. It was the first time in a year that the two women had met and for once the Czaritsa was in high good humour. Dagmar was courteous but restrained throughout the meal. Afterwards she rose and said: "There are matters of state that may not wait for me to discuss with you, Nicholas. We shall not burden Alex with them but shall return shortly." She then led her son out of the room.

Once alone, she stood before him, her chin high and her eyes large with emotion. "I begged you not to do this thing."

Nicholas shuffled his feet and looked down at them, as if wondering what they were doing. He would take a chance – after all he had nothing to lose.

"Yours is not the only opinion I hear. I had to make my decision on all the information I received and as Czar I have made my decision. I shall take command. I have written to Nikolai and as soon as I can get to headquarters I shall confirm it to him, man to man." He wished he could have sounded more authoritative; Nikolai would have done it better.

Dagmar stamped with frustration, her tiny hands clenched. "Man to man! This war will go from disaster to catastrophe," she cried. "Even Nikolai cannot prevent that happening but he can sacrifice himself for the dynasty and for Russia, and he will too, taking the blame and the disgrace, if you let him. What can you do that he cannot? You are not half the soldier that he is. Will you take the blame and the recriminations? They will not blame you as Nicholas, you fool. They will blame the Czar. They already say the Czar is pulled by the nose by an hysterical German woman and a treacherous peasant – and they will be correct. They will not pull one man down in disgrace; they will destroy us all.

"You do not have the right!"

Nicholas looked at her. She had never screamed at him before, never really frightened him. She was not far short of seventy; she should be living a peaceful life and so, oh God, so should he.

"I see it as my duty."

"And so it is, if your duty is to obey a German lunatic when Russia is brought to its knees in war with Germany."

"Why have you never been kind to Alex?"

"When did she ever give me cause?"

A fire flickered deep in Nicholas's soul. "She is the mother of the Czarevitch."

He stepped back as she reared towards him, flaring with fury. "How can he ever be Czar when she has given him a disease which will kill him and she has driven you insane with her preposterous delusions? She has made the throne untenable for him and made him unfit to sit in it. What should I do? Take bread and salt with her? May she live to see the devastation her madness has brought to Alexander's Empire. Get out of my sight."

"I leave for Moghileff in the morning," he said.

"Then go, for God's sake. If you will wreck the Empire you had best get started." He stared miserably at the back of her head, waiting, but she did not turn.

"Wait," she said. "While you are in Moghileff commanding your soldiers, who commands Russia? Does Vladimir know what to do?"

Nicholas, Czar and Emperor, moved his weight nervously from one foot to the other. "I have this morning written to Prince Vladimir Orloff telling him he is no longer part of my secretariat. He showed disloyalty and was no longer acceptable."

There was silence. After a long pause Dagmar spoke, quietly and conversationally. Still without turning, she said: "Vladimir is as true a friend as you have. He is as true and loyal as Nikolai, whom you also intend to dismiss. And you dismiss him for the same reason: so that you and Alex can fulfil the destiny that your charlatan guide Rasputin has predicted for you. Even Nikolai's lady Stana and her sister have come to recognise what a fraud that degenerate Siberian is. He tells you that you will lead our soldiers while she leads Russia, glorious and magnificent, genuinely admired for your great virtues, as a Czar and his Czaritsa should be."

Now she turned, walked to him, and gazed straight into his face. "The glory that dissipated drunkard Rasputin speaks of is not of this earth Nicholas. You will lead our armies to defeat while Alex… may God help us all."

Nicholas tried desperately to bluster. "What I do, I do for the best," he spluttered.

"All you have done is to set Russia and our dynasty on the road to destruction. Here in reality you will always be recognised for what you are and we shall all suffer for what you are. There is no earthly glory for you. What happens on Rasputin's higher plain I do not know. Perhaps he will be there himself soon but none of us will be far behind him. Not after what you have done.

"May God forgive you, for I never shall. Russia began to die when Alexander died."

The following day, as the Commander-in-Chief left by train for his headquarters nearly 500 miles away, Dagmar seized her opportunity. She let it be known that the use of the German tongue would henceforth be regarded as unpatriotic; she, the Dowager Empress, did not expect to hear German spoken in Court, where French was usual, or anywhere else; should anyone have the temerity to address her in the abominable language, she would behave as though they had never spoken. She thought it appropriate that every lady of quality should do the same.

The restraint was more insulting than restricting because the Czaritsa usually spoke English. She had never become comfortable with the Russian language, in which she could express herself adequately but not well. Still, Dagmar congratulated herself, believing that she had wrong-footed her son's lady, scoring over her in full view of the Court.

It was petty and largely ineffective but it gave the

Dowager Empress the hollow satisfaction of spite. Petersburg changed its name to Petrograd in the general repudiation of anything that might be thought Germanic. Within a fortnight of Nicholas's departure he suspended meetings of the Duma. There were no proposals for meetings of the cabinet of Ministers: Alexandra simply commanded those that she summoned for instruction or dismissal. She had won: now she was in control.

Dagmar sadly instructed her people to pack her train; if this was the command centre for the Empire, she wanted no part in it. Traveling south towards Kiev, she watched the endless panorama of Russian countryside unroll before her. It never seemed to change. Dear God, if only it never had.

She spent a couple of weeks with Olga, displaying unexpected tolerance when her daughter talked of annulling her marriage. Fifteen years before, when she was nineteen, Olga was persuaded by her mother to marry Prince Peter of Oldenburg. The advantage was that his mother was Princess Eugenie of Leuchtenburg, a close and influential friend of Dagmar's. Unfortunately Peter was in his mid-thirties, an effeminate and self-indulgent hypochondriac who devoted his days to gentlemen's clubs but preferred rougher trade at night. Olga explained to her mother that she was now thirty-four and wanted to bear children; that would never happen while she was married to Peter. Dagmar nodded. "I did what I thought was best," she said. Olga was astonished to see that she was crying.

Nicholas, his mother's contempt still corroding his waking hours, puzzled over her reference to Rasputin.

Perhaps he would soon be on his higher plain? What did she mean?

He dismissed Nikolai as soon as he arrived at his headquarters. They shook hands and embraced; Nikolai knew what demons drove his friend and cousin. He would spend the rest of the war commanding Russian troops in the Caucasus. He accepted his demotion with grace and courtesy.

Nicholas had defied his mother and every advisor he had, apart from Alexandra and Rasputin, in taking command himself. "You will have at least one loyal soldier as long as I live, Nicholas," said Nikolai. "But may God help you."

The Czar stared into space. "He never has," he said. "I doubt if he's going to start now, whatever Our Friend tells Alex."

Chapter 21

Dagmar – along with most of the Imperial family, Government Ministers, the diplomatic community – had been convinced as pressure grew that revolution might be delayed, could even perhaps be avoided, if Alexandra could be separated entirely from political influence. But now the Czaritsa was in rampant control.

Dagmar described her son's lady as "an hysterical hypochondriac blessed with ill-health," pointing out Alexandra's uncontrolled rages if thwarted. They would hardly have mattered if Nicholas had shown the same indifference to his lady's opinions that his father and his grandfather both exhibited towards theirs, but Nicholas was a more tender plant. Appalled and horrified by his lady's frenzied outbursts, he became a terrified puppet whenever the storm broke, capable only of trying to restore the comforting support of her mellow moods. Intelligent enough to recognise his own inadequacy, he simply could not cope with adversity when his essential supporter became his implacable assailant. Her frenzy was most intense when she heard rumour that Rasputin had been assassinated.

Educated Russians were almost entirely united in detesting Rasputin. Russia, rambling, shambling, starving Russia, was fighting territorially aggressive Germany the only way it knew how: with blood, sweat, toil, and more blood. Would Rasputin use his influence on Alexandra, and would she use her influence on Nicholas to fell the Empire? Many people believed the plot was already laid. The Czar must have known, they said, that the revered Nikolai was a capable CinC, and that Nicholas was incapable of filling his place. The story went round that when Nicholas was born his father had asked his doctor what he thought of the child. "Useless specimen, might as well shoot him now," the doctor was said to have replied. But the Czar shot the doctor instead, to try to keep the boy's inadequacy secret.

A peculiarly Russian joke but it illustrates what people thought of Nicholas in human terms. Many still thought of him as Little Father of all the Russias – more than eighty years later, some still do – but they knew what he knew: in truth, he wasn't up to the job.

He also knew that they regarded Rasputin as a dangerous, interfering, jumped up peasant, a one-name son of a one-name, time-served criminal. Utterly unsuitable to have anywhere near the Romanovs. Everyone except Alexandra and those with a political interest said so. And Nicholas was beginning to recognise that going along with Alexandra's fixation, far from solving his problems, was making them much worse. He began to think the unthinkable; was Alexandra's conviction of the starets' infallibility no more than wanton superstition?

Myths have developed around the man they called Father Grigori Rasputin, the Mad Monk. He was not a priest, nor was he mad, nor a monk, but he was an extraordinary man who deserves examination. He came from a basic community where one name was enough; his father's name was Efim, his was Grigori. Rasputin started as a nickname when he was a sexually active adolescent. Grigori Efimovich Rasputin simply meant Grigori, the debauched son of Efim, which was an accurate summary.

Rasputin was one of three children born to the former criminal Efim who had been exiled, served his sentence and settled down in Siberia with his woman. In childhood, Rasputin's sister Maria swam with him and died by drowning. When his brother Dimitri was also in danger in a mill pool, Rasputin claimed to have tried to save him. Both were rescued but Dimitri had inhaled fresh water; the lungs can absorb salt water but not fresh, and Dimitri died that night. There were no charges but from then on, few people in that community were prepared to take the risk of spending time alone with Rasputin and when he swam, he swam alone.

He married and had children but constantly searched for a faith that fitted his nightmares. He believed he could attune his mind to those of other people and – earning his kopeks as a carter – even of horses, adding the fear of witchcraft to his neighbours' suspicions of murderous derangement.

He was in his thirties when a follower of the Khlysty sect hired him as a guide to return to the Verkhoture monastery and on the journey explained the Khlysty convictions. These were the usual bundle of unreasonable obligations, excessive license, superstition and guarantees of precedence in an afterlife. To the mentally disturbed carter they were what the light on the road to Damascus was to Saul of Tarsus. By the time he reached Verkhoture, Rasputin was ready to become a convert. After brief instruction and vigorous self-flagellation he was a changed man. People were drawn by his rhetoric and the magnetism of his personality, but the local priest made accusations of heresy against this cellar-dweller who converted visitors. A church commission investigated but the devout bearing of the peasant and the devotion of those who followed him were impressive; the commission seemed to be overcome by the man's hypnotic personality. He was a natural celebrity.

Having abandoned home, wife, and children, Rasputin made a neatly stage-managed entrance into society, at a mass attended by many aristocrats, including the Grand Duchesses Anastasia and Militza. The two Princesses of Montenegro loved all things arcane and mystical. They were inevitably attracted by Rasputin's air of occult mystery and they knew the Empress would be fascinated by this extraordinary man. She was indeed intrigued by descriptions of the gloomy peasant, by the eulogies of the priest and those of the Montenegrin Grand Duchesses. The same priest would soon denounce Rasputin as a charlatan and a libertine but by then Alexandra would have become convinced. It would be the priest who trudged into exile.

Despite his haemophilia, Czarevitch Alexei had, with the petulance of childhood, tried to play as other children did, and had damaged his fragile body; he was haemorrhaging internally. His mother Alexandra lived with the immense burden of knowing he had inherited his haemophilia through her; she had brought this curse that could end the dynasty. Worse than that, this agony was her gift to her beautiful son. Alexandra was ready to grasp at straws, and here was one; she was sceptical but, like all desperate people, she could not throw away what might be the last chance. Within days Anastasia came with a cloaked companion, through a quiet rear entrance at Czarskoe Selo. The cloak shed, the guest was revealed as a peasant, tall, gaunt, carelessly unkempt in his homespun, but he walked, she thought, as Jesus must have walked, while his direct gaze seemed to pass through the trappings that were the Empress to engage a frightened girl who, having watched her mother die, now believed her son was also doomed. Without hesitating, Rasputin embraced both Nicholas and Alexandra. Then he prayed, and woke the sick child. He spoke to Alexei, moved his hands over him, murmured quietly, and gazed into the boy's eyes. Alexandra had seen charlatans before and remained sceptical. But the boy slept and, as he slept, he healed.

Alexandra saw the light. This was a man who would heal her son; by doing that, he would also secure the future of the Romanovs and her position as Little Mother of all the Russias. Both she and Nicholas found the man's bluntness, his unconventional dress and behaviour refreshing, just as Queen Victoria had embraced gruff John Brown and, when he died, employed even more incongruous familiars to alleviate the suffocation of court conventions. Rasputin's uninhibited way of looking at a problem seemed immensely helpful to them when they found complexities too much for them. "You must lead Russia and to do that you must do what is right," he would say. "If you do not trust a man, which makes it difficult for you to do what is right, that man must go. It matters not whether you want him to go, nor whether it is justice for him. It is your holy duty." More than all that, he looked deeper into her innermost self than anyone else could; he touched her only to embrace formally, but he was her lover in all but physical embrace.

Rasputin grew rich and influential with their patronage. He established himself and the stumbling procession of nervous, questing women who followed him, in a Petrograd apartment; from there he dispensed wisdom, and there he enthusiastically accepted gifts, bribes, dubious favours, and large quantities of alcohol. Asked to espouse the cause of one politician who provided sexual adventure for him over another who did not, he did not hesitate to commend the corrupt man to the Czaritsa. She recommended the candidate to the Czar and preferment was achieved. The result was that Rasputin had friends he could not trust and enemies who hated him implacably. Those at Court who were not involved in political intrigues detested the unwashed, whoring peasant who spoke to them as though he were at least their equal. The bourgeoisie were intolerant of a social inferior who had leapfrogged over them into the court of preferment and privilege. Rasputin did not care. "This man helped you to do what was right," he would say, "but now he makes it difficult for you to do what is right. It is your duty to rest him from your service. That other man will serve the needs of Russia better." The vigilant Okhrana opened a file, sent agents to keep watch. The name Rasputin was too distinctive – when written or spoken, it attracts attention. They gave the case a nickname: Tiomni.

To many peasants east of the Urals, Rasputin was a saint who by courage and spiritual strength had penetrated the degenerate court of the Czar, but in Petrograd the man had few friends and increasing numbers of enemies. In those febrile times everyone wanted someone to hate and Rasputin was an obvious target.

In truth, Rasputin was too concerned with carousing, sexual assignations, and his strange amalgam of mystic gifts and exotic convictions to care much about wars or politics, while Alexandra was convinced he was the wonderful faith healer who helped her son to live. She loved mysticism, superstition, arcane explanations for natural phenomena. But, just as Alexandra was unnaturally loyal to anyone she liked, she loathed anyone she disliked, and she disliked many politicians. She lacked the vision and the curiosity to indulge Machiavellian schemes but she would say to Nicholas: "I detest that loathsome little man and our friend agrees. I never want to see him again. Never, never."

And Nicholas, knowing that the woman he loved, when dissatisfied, could turn his life into a Bunyanesque vale of despair, would have a word with someone. "So-and-so rather upsets the Czaritsa. Couldn't we find something for him somewhere to avoid embarrassment… see he doesn't lose by it…?"

So-and-so would fade from the scene to some lucrative post where he would bother Alexandra no more and Whatsisname would gleefully step into his shoes. If Alexandra liked Whatsisname, he could do no wrong for several months; if not, the inevitable

arrived sooner and Whatsisname would follow So-
and-so into obscurity. Buggins would step forward
because it was now his turn, and so on. It began in
the church, where clergy who had thought Rasputin a
breath of freshness and had said so, changed their
minds, denounced him and promptly found
themselves exiled. The mystic had no influence over
them but he did not need to have; he could influence
someone who had. When Alexandra found she could
exercise this power she embraced it. From the
cathedral she took a small stride for the woman but a
giant stride for Russia, and started playing chess with
government Ministers as pawns. In a year and a half,
four Prime Ministers, five Ministers of the Interior
and ten assorted War, Agriculture, and Foreign
Affairs Ministers trudged into and out of office in a
ludicrous game of musical chairs. Given Alexandra's
temperament and Nicholas's shortcomings, all this
was inevitable but for many – including senior
officers of the Okhrana – it was intolerable.

Nobody could believe that the truth was sad, silly
and banal, a story of human inadequacy. Conspiracy
was much more credible, so it had to be a conspiracy.
And, if there was a conspiracy, there were
conspirators who had to be stopped, violently if
necessary. Alexandra, despite her Teutonic origins,
was high born and even higher married; Alexandra
was untouchable. But Rasputin was a peasant, son of
a liberated Siberian criminal. Rasputin's death would
cut the subversive tumour out of the brain of Russia.
Many would celebrate and who would grieve? Only
the Czaritsa and, without Rasputin, she would have
no motivating power of destruction.

The first attempt, Operation Tiomni, used the materials to hand. Rasputin, having made good in the big city, was visiting his people in Siberia. He continued to behave with the same vigour as ever, enabling a woman who had been handsomely paid twice, once to satisfy his desires and once to stab him in the heart, to reach a knife from under the mattress and push it into him. She told police that she wasn't sure where a man's heart was located. She had made a poor guess, because he became gravely ill with peritonitis, but he survived. Through the long, hot ominous summer of 1914 he wrote to Czarskoe Selo, begging Alexandra to prevent the Czar from going to war.

Rasputin recovered and returned to Petrograd. He was not now so mysteriously magnetic to women. The lean peasant body was becoming corpulent, while alcohol was blurring the haggard facial features women had found so fascinating. His nocturnal performances were no longer so athletic, nor so protracted. The homespun was gone; he wore silks and velvets. He was increasingly seen staggering drunkenly with friends down the Nevski Prospekt, urinating as he felt the need arise. He aroused public fury after asking three young women if they would like to see his impression of an elephant. They giggled uncertainly as his friends watched and laughed. Rasputin pulled his deep breeches side-pockets inside out and dragged out his unusually long penis. Laughing uncontrollably, he bellowed: "Look at his ears! Look at his trunk!" Police officers reluctantly intervened to rescue him from irate citizens, then politicians had to intervene to rescue him from prosecution. The Okhrana had been watching him for months and one Minister, Feodor Golovin, discovered from their reports that his own daughter Maria was an intimate friend. An angry Golovin dispatched his daughter to stay with friends in Moscow.

Still Alexandra depended on Rasputin, still she claimed power over Nicholas and the body politic and still she was seen to pass that authority to 'Our Friend'. Clearly, solving this problem demanded more than a bribed whore with a knife and a vague comprehension of anatomy.

Finally he played into the hands of the plotters with a clumsy attempt to blackmail young aristocratic men who were experimenting sexually. That was exactly what the plotters needed to steel the resolve of their appointed assassins. Nicholas's nephew Grand Duke Dimitri had grown close to the Czar and the Czaritsa. He was intelligent but not belligerent. Gentle and courteous, he was firm when he needed to be, and far-sighted for his age. Alexandra had told Nicholas that, if Alexei did not survive, Olga, married to her cousin Dimitri, could succeed to the throne with him. She cited Catherine the Great, she pointed out that a marriage between cousins was not a weakness but a strengthening of the Romanov blood. "I have spoken to Our Friend and he sees no impediment. If Alexei lives until he is seventeen, he will outlive his illness. Our Friend says so. That means that by 1921 we shall know. Olga will be twenty-six."

Nicholas nodded, then shook his head. "The rules of succession…"

"Previous Czars have changed the rules of succession. Please don't plead your inadequacy to me." Nicholas did not reply.

Young Dimitri knew nothing of this but he did know their patronage could be very valuable to him. Young men sometimes make mistakes. He and Prince Felix Youssoupoff had been introduced to some dubious clubs by Vladimir Purishkevitch, a reactionary member of the Duma. They were not specifically gay establishments but they did cater for a variety of tastes and, while Felix was varied in his preferences, Youssoupoff's gay reputation would damn them. Rasputin had advised Purishkevitch that he had evidence of their activities and that, if it were applied judiciously to acquaintances of his, it would send them all into the wilderness. Rasputin wanted money.

Felix had been aware of increasing desperation amongst Rasputin's enemies. He and Dimitri discussed it; they could rid themselves of this blackmailer while convincing everyone who mattered that they were being patriotic. Alexandra would be upset but even Nicholas, while pretending to hang on his every word, was clearly exasperated with the starets' arrogance. They did not know how acute Alexandra's hysteria could become – she and Nicholas kept it behind closed doors.

They took their thoughts to others and a plan evolved. These young aristocrats were so high born that they would be virtually untouchable. They would be assisted by various friends, politicians and, of course, servants. Purishkevitch had nothing in common politically with Golovin but they both wanted rid of the eccentric from Siberia and both had influence. Afterwards the Establishment would present a united front, protesting that they had never done more than express a vague wish to be rid of this turbulent priest; the young hotheads had simply overreacted out of excessive patriotism. The Empress might explode but once the man was dead, what was to be done? Nicholas was ineffectual – if he alone wanted to comply with his lady's desire for justice and vengeance, surely the united establishment could prevent prosecutions?

The strategy devised was sound, unofficially cleared with officers of the Okhrana, but clumsiness and stupidity repeatedly took the project to the brink of disaster. Firstly, although the volunteers who undertook the task were of high social rank, they were inexperienced in dealing with practical problems. Secondly, Rasputin's reputation for tenacity was justified. Thirdly, the doctor was out of his depth both socially and criminally – he did not want to hang. But worst of all, Nicholas's revulsion against wild hysteria and his willingness to appease his sometimes half-demented lady at any cost came close to causing calamity.

Nicholas left for the battlefront on 7 December 1917 and was not expected back until the New Year; Alexandra was visiting Stavka. The Germans were prepared to talk peace, and Dagmar, who detested Germany, was determined they would not have it. Rasputin's time had come.

The story of the murder is well-known if unedifying. Far from fearing death, Rasputin believed in reincarnation, so he accepted a dubious invitation to go at midnight to meet Prince Felix Youssoupoff in a basement room of the Moika Palace in Petrograd. Stark, vaulted, and stone-walled, it had been furnished and decorated that same day. In a society that officially denied homosexuality, perhaps Rasputin expected to enjoy some of the sexual experimentation for which the prince was well known, as well as being paid to keep quiet. He ate cake – cake allegedly laced with cyanide – and drank poisoned wine. He must, in more than 150 minutes of rambling conversation, have realised that Felix was in a state of high nervous excitement, so the only possible explanation for his staying is that he was curious. He wanted to know what came next.

What did happen was now inevitable. Felix had also been drinking to steady his nerves. Committed by having administered what he believed to have been enough poison to fell a jury but driven to desperation by the poison's failure to take rapid effect, Felix had to see the murder through. He had recently spent several evenings sat in the dark, watching the flickering magic lantern. He had in his blurred and excited mind a picture: one man fired and his adversary fell dead. He fetched Dimitri's Browning revolver, fired at Rasputin and watched his victim collapse.

The other volunteers had been drinking too. They rushed in and one, the doctor who had prepared the cyanide that failed to kill, declared Rasputin dead. The deed was done, the objective achieved, so they had another drink. Then they noticed that the wounded man had staggered up and lurched away. Gasping and drooling blood, he escaped from the cellar into a courtyard. There they caught up with their victim and Dimitri shot him down. They kicked and knifed him as he died, then wrapped his body in cloth and threw it through the ice on the River Neva. They congratulated themselves: the stinking peasant had violated a woman for the last time. The gunfire attracted attention from the local police station but Okhrana agents, keeping a watching brief, stepped out of a parked car to meet the officers who came to investigate. There was a muttered conversation, the agents showed their identification. The officers returned to their station, where they reported that nothing suspicious had occurred.

Two days later the corpse was discovered under the ice. When water was found in the lungs, further myths about the man blossomed. Poisoned, shot, stabbed, and finally drowned... a man of superhuman resilience. In truth, as the lungs cooled and shrank, they had drawn a little water in; he was strong but the difficulty he encountered dying was caused by ineptitude. Violence can make the body untenable but life does not depart willingly. Millions upon millions would die in the coming years. Very few would go swiftly or without suffering.

So Dagmar, shocked of course by the violence, thanked God for removing an unholy element, while the aristocracy and associates closed ranks, as planned. But to everyone's astonishment, no one heard from the Empress, who was by now in nearby Czarskoe Selo. No one, that is, but Nicholas.

Nicholas himself evinced shock at the crime of murder although he was clearly relieved that Rasputin, who had become one of his greatest causes of grief, would bother him no more. But Nicholas grew thin and ill. Rumour claimed that the Empress was giving him drugs, whether to control him or to avenge Rasputin's murder, nobody could be certain. The truth was that he was facing in private the hysterical and unrelenting tirade of a woman on the edge of insanity.

There was an investigation and both Felix and Dimitri were sent away, officially in disgrace; Felix would subsequently marry the Czar's niece, father a child by her, write a book explaining his version of his part in the killing, and live to be eighty. Dimitri went to America, married but never discussed the assassination; he would die of consumption when he was fifty. While Russian aristocrats and the bourgeoisie drank toasts to the executioners of the Evil One, Alexandra was convinced she had lost a guide sent by God but much worse than that: she believed that her son had been robbed of his only possible saviour. The mystic alone had seemed able to control the haemophilia of Alexei, to cause the bleeding to slow and stop, to calm the boy, to bring peace to mother and son. Now that saviour was slain by her enemies so for her, living saint had transformed into holy martyr.

A frantic Alexandra searched for spiritual links with the dead; Rasputin believed in an afterlife and, if he could help the boy in his own lifetime, he could surely help in the afterlife. She turned the full force of her furious dementia directly on Nicholas, and he buckled before the storm.

Visitors, including diplomats, who managed to get to see him found a man in a state of mental and physical collapse. He knew Russia was on the brink of catastrophe and he was certain he could do nothing to prevent it. So he did what his lady told him to do. He communicated little and seldom to anyone, even to his mother. Ministers resigned or were ejected, only to be replaced by others who stayed for no longer. The man who had been Rasputin's patron and favourite, Alexander Protopopov, remained as Minister of the Interior. The Empress believed he brought stability.

Nicholas's exhaustion was obvious and infectious. Dagmar began to believe that Rasputin had bequeathed Alexandra hypnotic powers that she used to guide her husband towards disaster. The situation demanded further desperate remedies and a plan was devised. As soon as the Czar returned to the front, Dagmar and her allies would go to Petrograd, have Alexandra's puppets arrested and send the Empress into soft exile in the Crimea. A sane and moderate government would reform moderately and all would be well. Russia needed it and the people would applaud.

Calmer voices prevailed: this was treason. If they were discovered, the ringleaders would have to be interrogated and hanged, which would destroy the very system, bringing down the dynasty that it was designed to preserve. The plan was abandoned. Dagmar would stay in Kiev. She must be seen to be above Machiavellian intrigue. But that did not stop her discussing with co-conspirators the removal of her son from the throne so that a regency could hold it for Alexei. Alexandra's mental state was far too precarious and her power over Nicholas too strong for her to remain. She needed to enter a convent or... thoughts of the icy River Neva could not have been far from anyone's mind.

Early in March there was a brief ray of light. Nicholas announced that he would purge his Ministries. Corruption and incompetence would be removed, probity and proven ability would be the sole selection criteria. Dagmar was among those who breathed easier; the firebrands would not be able to arouse revolution in a country that was at last manifestly well run.

The Czar was summoned to meet behind closed doors with the Empress. After several hours he emerged, pale but composed, to announce that no purge was intended. His mother and many others asked God to do something, for God alone could save Russia. Dagmar told Nikolai to threaten to shoot himself – "He might listen to you," she sobbed.

"It is a card I can play only once," he replied, "and I already have. She knows that if I say it, I am prepared to do it. Next time she will make him make me shoot myself, so no good will come of it." Through all their planning and conspiring, even through their prayers, a shadow moved. Try to define it and it dissolved, turn away and it was back, just on the edge of vision but never clearly seen. This spectre was the unacceptable conviction that, whatever they did now, it was all too late. They were advocates in a nightmare court of justice, still bickering over semantics when sentence of death had already been passed.

To add to the disturbance across the vastness of Russia, the peasants knew that one of their own, a holy man, had had the temerity to walk among the aristocracy and they had cut him down for it. Those effete young aristocrats had poisoned him, shot him, stabbed him, cut off his genitals and drowned his dying body in the freezing river, they said. Anger burns slow in a peasant people, but it burns hot.

Chapter 22

Winter took the land and Petrograd froze with deep, deep cold that split living trees and killed the careless as they slept. Railways froze and groaning ice burst engine boilers. Supplies of fuel and food ceased. Factories locked out their employees; horses' heads drooped in their stables for want of sustenance. Birds died where they roosted. Out on the flatlands, only trees and the tall, dead stems of last summer's purple foxgloves pierced the frozen seas of white. Rabbits do not know that digitalis in the foxglove plant grips the heart muscles, but they know not to eat it. They gnawed bark and chewed stale rabbit droppings but their flesh wasted until their skins hung on them like borrowed coats. Then those that still could, limped across the ice towards the foxglove stems.

The city's streets were silent except when rumour prompted frantic mobs, rushing to join queues for scanty, outrageously priced goods. Soon came the crimes of desperation: bakeries broken into and looted, food stores stripped and God help anyone who stood in the way. And, as always, the settling of old scores.

The ice melted and marauding mobs took to the dripping streets.

Disillusion and fury put demonstrators onto the streets by the hundred thousand. They demanded an end to the war, an end to Protopopov, an end to sheer abject misery and desolation. Russians believed they had taken all the suffering that God could ask them to take. Even Cossacks lost the will to break up the demonstrations. The military commander warned that demonstrators would not be tolerated by armed troops but he was ignored. Sectors of the police remained determined though; by night they arrested known troublemakers; by day they devoted time to recreational interrogation.

As more and more deserting soldiers joined the dissidents, gunfire rattled through the streets. Rival groups skirmished, then ran off leaving the dying to kick on the blood spattered cobbles. The Czar, 1,000 kilometres away and unable to believe this was the beginning of the end, refused changes and ordered the streets to be cleared. In the volleys of rifle fire on Znamenskaya Square and down Nevski Prospekt, Russians died amongst crawling wounded. Blood ran in the gutters of the most sophisticated thoroughfare in Russia. Nicholas heard the cries for justice and effective government, and exercised his judgement again: he sent more troops.

The difference between many soldiers garrisoned in the city and the demonstrators was no more than a uniform. Theirs was a common background, a common desperation, a common hunger. They merged and became one. Even as the reinforcements came closer, soldiers were joining the demonstrations and firing on police. Others, ordered to fire on the angry mobs, shot their officers, then clubbed the dying men with their rifle butts. Their awe of authority gone, people chased and caught policemen and suspected informers. Writhing victims were thrown onto fires, beaten to death, hauled into the air with cord biting into their throats.

Mobs coalesced and became a revolutionary army. A ragtag, motley, unstructured army certainly, but with purpose. It developed objectives and it implemented them too: the Law Courts, that bastion of privilege, became a blazing pyre for official records; prison gates were flung open; the files of the secret police were ransacked. And the Fortress of Peter and Paul fell.

Twelve years had passed since the horrors of 1905 and, though his enemies had learnt their lesson, Nicholas had learnt nothing. Revolutionaries with no illusions put the Duma to the test. It failed and Alexandra's puppet Protopopoff ran for cover. All the Ministers who could be found were arrested. Dagmar, starved of news in Kiev, could not understand what paroxysms were shaking Petrograd, why the government was so ineffectual. She blamed her daughter-in-law, who was in the Alexander Palace with her children. The whole catastrophe was the fault of Alexandra's intransigent stupidity and yearning to hold power while Nicholas was out of the way. "She must be mad," she said, and was closer to the truth than she knew.

A window shattered somewhere along a corridor and Alexandra let slip a tiny scream. She bit her knuckle; the children must not hear her terror. She listened in flickering lamplight to the crackle of gunfire far away, then abruptly so close she shuddered. Outside the Palace a thin line of sentries faced outwards. There was no talking, no meeting of eyes; they were still loyal, for the moment. Groups of dark, shrouded figures in the distant darkness beyond the shrubs seemed to grow as time passed, but came no closer. The number of servants dwindled as those who could, slipped away. There was nobody in the kitchen when she went in search of a hot drink; taps were difficult to turn and gave no water. Eggs in a bowl, precious eggs, had broken open as they froze. There was no comfort; her husband was God alone knew where. And her children were ill.

She loved them all, of course she did, but she had a duty to Russia and it was her son Alexei, poor fragile Alexei, who trod the path of destiny. Marie had a heavy cold but had escaped the virulent measles that had struck the others. All had fever but Olga seemed to be developing heart palpitations, Tatiana's ears were oozing puss and Alexei, poor Alexei's temperature was 103 degrees and rising. Alexandra desperately suppressed her panic. Had not Nicholas promised he would return next day? Nicholas would never fail them.

The Czar's train was indeed heading towards her. It stopped briefly to take on water and it was then that a galloping messenger brought news of the collapse of the Duma. The messenger had heard too of rebellious squads lying in ambush ahead. Nicholas stared into the darkness ahead, then he yelled for full steam back to the headquarters of the Northern Army. There he would have protection and accurate information.

His reinforcements had reached Petrograd, he was

told, but did no more than desert and swell the ranks of the malcontents. The Russian fleet was aflame with revolution. The fire of rebellion was bursting out across Russia like sparks in the wet ashes after a forest fire but here, the great conflagration was still to come. To a man already far beyond his wildest nightmares, this was devastating. He had agreed to replace the Duma with a ministry the people could respect, but by now, nobody was listening. He had his opportunity twelve years before and he had failed to keep faith then. The police hunt-and-kill squads would not be given a second chance.

Grey skinned and with sunken cheeks, he sat in the plush luxury of his train. His own glorious destiny was at an end. Had he ever been an Olympian? No, he had done no more than delude himself. He had been born a placid man to live a placid life. The worst he could reasonably be expected to endure was the shrill hysteria of Alexandra and the imperious commands of his mother. Instead there had been repeated bloody insurrection across this immense land, forcing him to take firm remedial action, he told himself. That action had failed – perhaps through his being too benign – and now he was being blamed, forced to declare war on his own people while fighting against alien nations. There was no way out, and yet… He could walk away.

His officers nodded sagely. Concessions would be of no use now; abdication was the only solution. A regency so that Alexei could, all in good time perhaps? There was a silence. "It's not him, sir, nor you. But a regency won't do."

Nicholas glared at the general who spoke and blind

obstinacy took him once more. He would abdicate in favour of Alexei, and Grand Duke Mikhail Alexandrovitch would serve as Regent until the boy achieved maturity. By God, he was still Czar and he had decided.

The Czar's doctor spoke quietly. Alexei was not strong. He had an incurable illness. It was at its most dangerous when he was unsettled. Being ruler was unsettling. Dr Fedoroff looked steadily at the exhausted man. "Would you condemn him to suffer as you suffer now?"

The document they put together said that the final crisis was near in a titanic battle to resist enslavement of the fatherland. Popular disturbances were undermining the fatherland's ability to withstand its cruel enemy. To enable Russia to concentrate all its energies on defeating Germany, Nicholas renounced the throne and relinquished supreme power. Foreseeing exile, it said he did not wish to be separated from his son so he passed the succession to his brother Mikhail. It instructed Mikhail to bind himself with an oath to work with elected representatives of the people. Nicholas signed it and slept better than he had for weeks.

The day came when Nicholas was due to arrive in Petrograd and there was no news of him. Alexandra, with no knowledge of the abdication, had opposed those advisers who believed the family would be safer elsewhere but now she told her immediate attendants to quickly and quietly pack essentials for the family to be ready to leave. Railway travel was far too dangerous but a closed carriage on the open road? It might be done.

At the thought of the shadowed road, the sudden challenge and the cocking of rifles, her taut calm deserted her. To see her children shot and bayoneted...

Her heart, prone to palpitations, fluttered dangerously. Knowing she must rally the courage of those who remained loyal, she took the little hand of Marie in her own gloved, shaking hand and walked the line of defenders, speaking such encouragement as she thought they would like to hear. Her voice was sharp with tension, and her stilted words punctuated by the child's incessant coughing. The men avoided looking into her eyes. As soon as she returned to her rooms she fell gasping on a lilac couch in a room where the all-pervading mauve could no longer console her. She had done all she could.

The lights went out. The table lamps, the picture lights, all died at once. Alexandra reached towards where she knew the bell was but paused. She rose from the sofa and, by the flickering light of the fire, went to the window.

The Catherine Park was in darkness, lit only by the gleam of snow and faintly silver lakes. But her eyes were growing accustomed to the dark and she knew, knew without really seeing them, that there were more of them now. Out beyond the Chinese village, around the palace hothouses, hunched figures were massing and waiting.

She had heard the trains, panting full-laden, and the long hiss as each halted for the men to jump out at Czarskoe Selo station and stamp their way through the town. She had heard the marching of other feet; a long march from Petrograd – sixteen miles, so

Benkendorff had said earlier, when she had summoned him. Count Paul Benckendorff was the sixty-four year old Court Grand Marshal. He and his lady knew that their own future was precarious but they believed their lives had been lived, they knew nothing but their duty, so they stayed with Alexandra and did their duty.

"Where did these ruffians learn to march?"

Benkendorff had gazed steadily at her. "We trained them, ma'am. These are the soldiers the Emperor sent to break up the Petrograd mob."

"So we are rescued, Benkendorff? Nicholas' soldiers will send these animals packing?"

"No ma'am, they will not. They have changed their allegiance. They are part of the mob now."

Alexandra staggered slightly. "Then they must be shot. Tell the army to shoot the mutineers."

"They are the army, ma'am."

"The troops are loyal, Benkendorff. There are three battalions behind the palace. They have artillery guns primed and ready. Russian soldiers know their duty…"

The old man kept his face down; he did not want her to see his eyes. "These are loyal for now, ma'am. Others have shot their officers and joined the rebels. Not all the army is ours."

Alexandra had felt it rising, boiling and irresistible. She tried, God knows she tried, never to let it show outside her marriage but now her fury broke. "For now, Benkendorff? For now? Is the future Czar of all the Russias to have his throat slit by soldiers in his father's uniform? In the name of God, what are you doing about it?"

He did not move. "All that can be done is being done, ma'am. We are sparing no effort in preserving the family's safety. If any harm were to befall the Czarevitch, I should already be answering for it to my maker." He turned and walked out. Without being dismissed, he had simply left the room. Alexandra stood speechless. Were there no standards left anywhere in the Alexander Palace?

But that was nearly an hour ago, and now the lights had gone out. A soft knock at the door and it was Benkendorff again, a servant behind him with a lit candle in each hand. "They have cut off the electric power, ma'am."

She kept her grip this time. "Then reconnect it, Benkendorff."

"It cannot be done, ma'am. The palace power station has been damaged. There is no power to connect to."

"Then connect to the town power supply. In the name of all that is holy, do I have to think of everything?"

"The Pevcheskaya tower supplies the town but it has no connection here since the Emperor built the palace station. We are without electricity until that is repaired, ma'am."

He looked at her and from some extraordinary corner of her memory she recalled that day, twenty-odd years ago, when he asked: "Is it prudent to suggest that the palaces are too grand to share electricity with the people?"

Nicholas had looked at him in astonishment. "Of course the palaces are too grand for that, Benkendorff. What are you thinking of? In any case, we need plenty of electricity and if the town supply fails, we should be in the dark along with them, shouldn't we?"

And so the Gothic-style building had risen, well clear of the town's nine-year-old tower, where steam pumps provided both electricity and water for Czarskoe Selo. Inside Danini's new building the most advanced engineering generated electricity for the palaces and, for security, the barracks of the guard. Until tonight, when the boilers had been smashed.

"Telephone someone, Benkendorff."

"The telephone lines have been cut, ma'am. And the water has been turned off. I suggest you rest, ma'am, and we shall see what can be done in the morning."

"Rest," she shrieked. "How can you talk of rest? How do you know these curs will let us live until morning? Is there no-one I can trust?"

He gazed at her without expression. "I shall send you a warm drink, ma'am, and pray that you find rest tonight."

"A warm drink? And how will you heat it? With a bonfire in the kitchen, Benkendorff?"

"If necessary, ma'am. Whatever is necessary. Goodnight ma'am."

She stood and tried to still her shaking. The children were safe enough. They were ill, poor creatures, but they were safe on the upper floor.

Nicholas should be here instead of wasting his talents out there on that shambling war. He had officers in plenty for that. God knows they swaggered through the Parade Rooms well enough, posed on the Grand Staircase well enough, guzzled everything they could eat and drink well enough. Could they not be trusted to order their men to shoot the enemies of the Czar? Evidently not.

There was little enough light from the candles but she knew every inch of this room. It was hers, the nest of her family – the Lilac Room. She had been twenty-two when she chose the lilac silk to line the walls and employed Roman Meltzer to design the room. Since then she had overwhelmed it with paintings, nick-nacks, family photographs, ikons, even one with a tiny chime on it, that Rasputin had promised would ring if she were in great danger – the ever more claustrophobic clutter that made her feel secure. Perhaps it had been fashionable then. Certainly it was in the same spirit of the rooms of England's Queen Victoria, the grandmother who had so profoundly influenced her childhood. Now of course, times had changed. Court ladies mocked the cosiness. Nicholas's mother was disdainful. Well, Nicholas's mother was always disdainful. "That woman of yours will bring down the Romanovs, with her hysteria and her delusions," she had told Nicholas. Perhaps she was right at that. Perhaps this was the end.

Alexandra walked up and down, picking up a photograph here, moving an objet d'art there, achieving nothing except constant movement. Her arm brushed an ikon and it fell. A crystal chime rang clear in the surrounding silence and Alexandra became instantly still; her friend was warning her – the hour was at hand and she was alone, but for his spirit. She went, almost without recognising it, out through the curtained doorway into the ink-dark Pallisander room, round familiar furniture, through into another pool of darkness she knew to be the galleried Art Nouveau magnificence of the Maple Room, and out onto her balcony. She did not feel the cold as she gazed into the darkness, trying to see the men who wanted to close in and destroy them. She heard a muttered expletive below her and looked down. "Begging your pardon, ma'am, but you shouldn't be out here, ma'am," said the sentry, his rifle held in both hands. "One of them could take a pot shot any time, ma'am. You're safer inside."

"Will you save me, sergeant?"

"If you go inside, ma'am, I'll do my best." And he saluted.

"Thank you sergeant," she said, and retraced her steps.

She heard two shots not far off and somewhere on the Grand Façade a window shattered. She was astonished to find herself thinking she must remember to have the children avoid the Garden Terrace until all the broken glass had been collected. She wondered if the girls would ever again chase one another around the Garden Terrace. Not if but when, she said aloud.

"My God," she said. "The children. The children will be terrified." She swiftly made her way through to her bathroom and climbed the steep wooden staircase to the children's rooms. Her nimbleness would have astonished those who tended her. Alexei and the girls were all asleep. There was not one of them fit and well but they slept and she was glad. She wondered what awaited them now.

Next day the numbers of malcontents surrounding the palace had increased and the next they were beyond counting. How did they feed and cleanse themselves for God's sake? They were worse than animals. Marie had collapsed with pneumonia while Tatiana and Anastasia both had ear abscesses that might ruin their hearing. Alexandra's only two comforts were the children's doctor and her cigarettes.

Chapter 23

It was Benkendorff who brought the leaflet. Alexandra Feodorovna was an empress no more, for her husband was no longer Czar. He had abdicated. She shrieked. Had all their suffering been for nothing, signed away like a gambler's promissory note on a soldiers' train?

In Kiev, court officers bickered over who would tell Dagmar that her son had stepped down from the throne to which his forebears had devoted their luxurious lives. Eventually her son-in-law, Xenia's husband Sandro, blurted out the news. Devastated and appalled, she lost her iron restraint and moaned, hitting the air with her little fists. Then she sat silent until great sobs burst out of her shaking body.

Meanwhile, having been warned he would be Regent, Nicholas's brother Mikhail attended a meeting of Ministers in Petrograd, only to be told that he had been misinformed: he was to become Czar in his own right. Far away from his lady, Nicholas had listened to the doctor and abdicated for both himself and his son. Neither Dagmar nor Alexandra yet knew that Alexei was no longer a child of destiny; he was now merely a very sick child who would wonder for the rest of what could be only a short life, what it might have been like to have been Czar.

Mikhail had endured grave unkindness from his brother but he knew that this time Nicholas had run out of options. When war had broken out, Dagmar told Nicholas that she had sent for Mikhail to return. Alexandra railed at Nicholas, her narrow views on propriety and autocracy both serving to condemn. But with the Horsemen of the Apocalypse rampant across Europe, Alexandra's bigotry could not take priority and this was a time for solidarity. Reconciled to his mother and the rest of the family, Mikhail had distinguished himself as a military man. He was the only person on Earth, other than Alexei and himself, that Nicholas could consider ruling Russia. He was the obvious choice for monarchists once Nicholas had abdicated, but Mikhail was not fool enough to accept unsecured control. He was reluctant but, if he could be guaranteed stability, he would accept this onerous burden. He demanded assurances that he would sit on a safe throne. Eventually he issued a statement saying that, without an invitation by a properly elected assembly, he would not accept the throne. There was no such invitation. Abruptly the dynasty that had ruled the largest nation on Earth for three centuries was consigned to history.

Some say Mikhail was the last Czar because Nicholas named him, but the Czars were the autocratic rulers of Russia. Mikhail never ruled; he declined to drink from the poisoned chalice. In the desperate months ahead he would try to escape Russia before the Bolsheviks closed all exits but, mistaken for a corrupt government official, he would be arrested and then recognised. In a few months' time he would stand, his hands bound behind him, with gentle rain dripping from birch leaves onto the freshly dug earth. He would feel the muzzle placed behind his ear, and nothing more.

America declared war on Germany. The muscle of the US seemed to ensure that ultimately, if the allies held on through the mud, the cold and the slaughter, Germany would lose. For the House of Romanov, the good news had come too late.

For the moment, nobody understood what was happening. The Duma, dissolved by the Czar that no longer was, reassembled to try to assert some control. In the chaos, there was nobody to point out that this was an illegal assembly. Dagmar's consciousness was filled by the knowledge that Nicholas had abdicated. It took a little time for her to dredge up the reserves of her strength. With full honours and a straight back, she was driven to Kiev railway station that evening to arrive at noon next day in Moghilev. As she stepped down from the train she saw Nicholas her son, hunched in his greatcoat, like a wraith in the swirling snow. Once they had embraced she was embedded in furs beside him and they sped away towards his quarters. Only as he spoke to her did she understand the magnitude of the catastrophe. She already knew her son had lost his Imperial crown but now she was told all: her grandson had been robbed of his extraordinary inheritance, while her other son had declined it. The drained shell of a man beside her had been the last Czar.

Everything she had lived for during half a century dissolved as though it had been nothing. Her strength left her and she broke down. Nicholas became calm, a man who found humiliation easier to tolerate than responsibility. He smoked continually and summoned the bravado to criticise his brother for cowardice in declining to shoulder the burden he had himself failed to carry. Lunch at the house was defiantly lavish but subdued and later, when mother and son returned to her train for a simple dinner, they broke down and wept in each other's arms.

During the next couple of days Dagmar came under pressure to encourage Nicholas to go abroad immediately. She recoiled from the suggestion – surely it was not all over? These were desperate times but the institutions built up over 300 years – it could not be over. Gradually she became aware that perhaps his voluntary and immediate exile would be for the best. Nicholas would always represent a threat to any aspiring group. He was the ikon that had been pulled down; there would be an urge to destroy that ikon and so ensure there was no going back. It would take longer for anger to be turned upon his family. Now was the time for him to go and if sanity returned, when sanity returned, Nicholas could answer the call of a grateful nation.

Nicholas lost his composure at the suggestion. "Do you think I lack the instincts of a gentleman?" he blustered. If he were to leave Russia they would leave as a family, he insisted, with him leading and his Empress on his arm. He was determined. Neither of them knew that this was the point at which the destruction of Nicholas, his lady, and their children became inevitable unless England offered them sanctuary, but there were those around them who guessed it. From now on the fuse was burning.

His mother looked at him and recognised that this was not a decision but another abdication. He needed to be with Alexandra; from now on their decisions would be taken only by that hysterical woman. Nicholas had needed to be Tsar to be anything at all, and now he was not even that. But he was her son and she loved him. "Give the military command back to Nikolai," she said. "He will know what to do."

Even Dagmar failed to perceive the shadows that closed about them. Advised by the head of the British Military Mission that he had begun a process to allow Nicholas to sail for England, she said that the war with Germany was unsettling and really she would prefer the family to live in her native Denmark. Nicholas rejected all offers of help to leave Russia and obtained permission to go, under escort, to Czarskoe Selo. As his train pulled away, his eyes were fixed on his mother, standing on the platform, and she gazed back, wet faced but with those large eyes clear and direct.

She waited the rest of her life, vainly believing that one day they would meet again.

Dagmar, having left an imperial escort of honour in Kiev when she went to meet Nicholas, returned there to find everything changed. No guard of honour, no imperial standard, no insignia. Soldiers lounged at the Maryinsky Palace, contemptuous as the Dowager Empress passed. With every fresh humiliation, she became more furious; once in private she exploded. She had seen the Czar carried away, a prisoner... Alexandra had brought this on them... that hysterical imbecile had destroyed the dynasty... everything the Czar had represented for 100,000 days... she had robbed her husband and his son of their rightful destiny... forgiveness? Never, never. She could never be forgiven.

Outside, days passed and the public celebrations gave way to danger. Freed prisoners avenged themselves on informers, the police, anyone connected to the judiciary. The hue and cry became common on the streets as vengeful mobs caught up with suspected oppressors. Some leaders were political but many were criminals, now freed to resume their predations, with little fear of reprisals. Overnight, walls were scarred by condemnations of the Romanovs, demands for vengeance. Dagmar tried unsuccessfully to contact her son by telegraph and messenger; even the dentist, who usually passed among them without difficulty, was not allowed to go to Czarskoe Selo.

In mid-March the former Czar and Czaritsa, accused of German sympathies, were arrested; the Danish Government moved swiftly to claim assurance that Dagmar was safe from arrest, although there could be little value in any such assurance. Her friends told her she should sink into comfortable obscurity in the Crimea but Dagmar herself remained outwardly unmoved. There was nobody now to pass on the fragments of information that fitted together to reveal trends, nobody to tell her that military morale was crumbling, that the planned offensive, scheduled for May, was becoming increasingly unlikely as around one million men a month deserted, nobody to say that the infrastructure that supported the military was no longer ramshackle – it was in ruins. She remained certain that deep down the spiritual link between the people and the Romanovs would reassert itself – until she returned from one of her routine visits to comfort the sick and injured in hospital. She had been publicly rebuffed, abused and sneered at; now she understood. The people had turned against those who loved them most; they no longer looked to the Czar as an ikon of Russia. It was all over, time to move away.

In April family members were ordered out of Kiev. Radicals in Petrograd wanted them arrested but that would have been divisive and embarrassing. The Romanovs were not alone in finding it hard to recognise that Russia was no longer controlled by them, nor ever would be again. Many would have taken up the struggle on their behalf but simultaneously strategists of all colours considered assassination.

One politician whose removal Alexandra had demanded was Alexander Kerensky. A lawyer and a radical journalist, he had been arrested, exiled, and allowed to return to Petrograd, where he defended political prisoners. He had called for the removal of the Czar, so Alexandra told Nicholas that, by legal or any other process, he must disappear from the scene. Nicholas spoke with the Okhrana but Kerensky was too high profile; it was not possible. When Nicholas abdicated, Prince George Lvov formed a Provisional Government, recruiting the man the Okhrana called 'Speedy' Kerensky as Minister of Justice. Within a couple of months the able, shifty-looking son of a schoolmaster was Minister of War. He knew that only a resounding feat of arms could establish that this faltering administration was the reliable government the people so desperately needed, so he made plans.

He wanted General Alexei Brusiloff to assemble seasoned and determined troops to launch a sudden and decisive blow against Austro-Hungarian forces.

Support troops would flood in behind them to confirm the victory.

The attack was planned to come in June and, when it did, it would succeed but, as ever, Germany would move faster than Russia. German machine gunners would reap the shock force before Russian reinforcements could be brought up. Then increasing numbers of Russian soldiers would remember other things that they would rather be doing than losing a war – like shooting landowners, burning their houses and seizing their land. Kerensky, who had toured the Eastern Front, appealing directly to massed troops for the good of Russia, said wearily: "If we were to shoot all the deserters we would kill more Russians than Germany has done."

But that defeat, the straw that would break the back of Russian resolve and force Lvov out in favour of Kerensky, was still in the unthinkable future. Spring had not yet come to the wet streets of Kiev. The city council was concerned that the Dowager Empress could be a focus of unrest there; even worse, they might be accused by revolutionary hardliners of being too gentle with her. They told her she was no longer welcome in the city. Members of the family contacted Kerensky: the Romanovs wanted no trouble, they wished to bring grief upon nobody. Could they slip away quietly, perhaps to the Crimea, perhaps to Denmark? Not to Denmark? Very well then. The Petrograd madness had infected Kiev but it would surely not reach the Crimea; there they would find peace to heal and re-evaluate.

Dagmar demanded to go to Petrograd – she wanted to be beside Nicholas. It was a last defiant cry;

not even she believed anyone was listening. In fact several agents were paying close attention. The Petrograd soviet had issued instruction that all members of the Romanov family, or agents thereof, should be located, apprehended, and interrogated as enemies of the people; Petrograd would have welcomed them, in its way. But someone else was also taking note: Kerensky's astute eye had missed nothing and he wanted Russia's allies to continue to have some confidence in the troubled Empire. Kerensky's people contacted Dagmar's son-in-law Sandro – Grand Duke Alexander, saying that safe passage could be arranged to his estate in the Crimea. Sandro was wary, unwilling to be drawn into the twilight world of clandestine meetings and negotiation, but his son-in-law, Prince Felix Youssoupov, relished the prospect.

One night a vigilant observer might have noticed a few groups of people heading briskly towards a railway siding on the outskirts of Kiev. A train waited there; no heraldic eagles, no crown insignia, no plush. But it was a train, coaled, with armed guards and ready to depart. Dagmar, in a closed carriage, was in dark clothes, a hat and a veil; her two-man Cossack bodyguard were in plain clothes, their uniforms sent on ahead. A nurse, still in uniform, arrived; it was Dagmar's daughter Olga.

Dagmar had resisted advice from Xenia's husband Sandro, who was convinced that they could exist in comfortable obscurity on the Black Sea. For her, happy memories of family life there were blighted by recollections of Sasha's last days and having to invite Alexandra to become a part of the Imperial family.

Not until her granddaughter Irina had said: "I want to go to Ai Todor. Uncle Nicki and his family are certain to want to get out of Petrograd and they're certain to go to Livadia," did the dowager agree.

Making suitable arrangements aboard the train had been impossible. Water had to be rationed, food was scarce, and there was very little privacy. Luggage had been brought in covered wagons, bundled in, taking up valuable space. Only the bayonets of their guards deterred mobs at every halt, all desperate to escape from intolerable conditions. Lying on a couch behind drawn blinds, Dagmar could not keep out the cries of fear, anger, and desperation from those who saw this train as their single hope for survival.

For day after uncomfortable day they trundled across the unending landscape. Finally they reached Sebastopol and were bundled quickly into cars to drive to Sandro's estate, a dozen miles from Yalta. And there Dagmar found peace to heal from the outrages she felt so deeply. Spring in the flower-strewn Crimea, respect from loyal troops, a little comfort.

Chapter 24

It was easy in the soft Crimea to believe that these were difficult times that would one day give way to calm, that they would all once again drive up the Nevski Prospekt past the bear on a cow statue, attend balls and dinner parties, go to the ballet and the opera, and indulge in the tittle-tattle of Court. There would be military tattoos and manoeuvres, and gallant uniforms and feast days and Fabergé eggs and visits to Windsor and Hvidore. Everyone conspired to try to convince Dagmar that it would be so.

Ai Todor, where she lived, was the estate of Xenia and Sandro, a couple of hundred acres by the sea where terraced vineyards and parkland surrounded a cluster of buildings. The main house was a small but pretty place with balconies where the dowager could sit and enjoy fine views between the narrow poplar trees. She had last been there when Sasha had been dying.

Others of the refugees – they preferred to regard themselves as temporary exiles – went to family-owned estates nearby at Djulber and Tchair. There were severe shortages, especially of money and acceptable food. The arrangement Nicholas had made to control his mother's spending had foundered: Prince Shervadshidze, still dutifully forwarding her receipts to the Court Ministry, was told by Minister Feodor Golovin to stop – they would not be paid.

Prince Felix Youssoupoff had married Irina, the eldest of Xenia and Sandro's children, three years before he was involved in killing Rasputin. A rich and adventurous transvestite, Felix had managed to convince Irina's parents that he was no longer actively gay, and then he even convinced Dagmar. Grand Duke Dimitri was unconvinced but that may have been because he continued to have a vigorous physical affair with the fine-featured Felix. At Ai Todor people either knew or guessed but there was nothing to be gained by exposure; in any case, Felix had been prepared to take the blame for murder, and he had arranged the train.

Now he and Irina went even further for the family. They travelled to Petrograd in an attempt to see Kerensky, and to refresh the memory of Feodor Golovin.

Kerensky finally agreed to grant them a meeting but Felix believed his lady could achieve more on her own, so Irina took a carriage to the Winter Palace. All was changed yet nothing new as she was led into the study where Nicholas had sat, and his father and his father before him. Kerensky rose quietly from behind the desk and invited her to be seated. What could he do for her? Irina was beautiful but uncomplicated. She simply explained that her grandmother had not been implicated in political matters. She had simply been a good wife, mother, and pillar of the society into which she had married. She was unhappy in the Crimea, living in penury under difficult circumstances that could be alleviated if Kerensky chose; he had the authority. "We should be grateful to you, and so would the people of Denmark. And perhaps many of the people of Russia."

Kerensky stared at his fingernails. "Do you really understand what the word penury means?"

Irina blushed. In a country where penury was the main cause of death, even during war, she had used too strong a word. Candour was the only remaining option. "She has led a privileged life. What she is enduring now is penury for her. Certainly, she is slowly dying from malnutrition."

Kerensky looked up. "So are most of the people in Russia," he said. "Slow starvation is endemic amongst people who have not enjoyed a privileged life. It has claimed the lives of many generations and it always will. Let me reflect for a moment."

Kerensky could charm, he could sway a mob, he could convince lesser men, but he was not good looking and he knew it; he felt insecure in the presence of beauty. His brother said: "He's the hardest bastard in the movement until he looks a woman in the eye. He can face down a hostile army and never turn a hair but put him face to face with some quality rumpo, his brain gets an erection and he's knackered."

Kerensky stood up. "I shall do what I can. Ask Citizen Shervadshidze to contact Minister Golovin."

"Thank you. I could ask no more," she said, and left.

Felix dined with Golovin, talked of old times, asked after his daughter Maria, mentioned the problem of the former Dowager Empress's finances.

He said in passing that Irina was meeting Kerensky. Golovin also recalled the past, said Maria had grown out of her youthful lack of judgement, and remarked that he was sure the problem of Dagmar's finances would be resolved. The name of Rasputin was never mentioned; it did not need to be.

Dagmar's problems eased. Her family could not afford to retain many servants but they arranged for her to keep a small household of her own. There were the two Cossacks who had come in the train. They ate and drank substantial quantities without contributing anything of value, but they would have died to protect Dagmar and she would recall that Nicholas used to say: "You can always rely on the Cossacks." He was never specific about what they could be relied upon to do, but the remark had raised a laugh at a dinner party once, so he used to repeat it from time to time. Dagmar remembered it and so the bodyguards stayed to give her peace of mind. There were also a couple of lady companions, a secretary, three maids, and two menservants. And the now invaluable Prince Shervadshidze.

Chapter 25

Under benign house arrest in the Alexander Palace, Nicholas and his family lived well enough, although they believed they were deprived and oppressed. They had most of the comforts and attendants they needed but deeply resented restrictions on their movements and the frequent insolence of their guards. Above all, what they really detested was the loss of authority. The children learned rapidly. Everyday phrases like "Fetch that", "I need this", "Go there", "Come here," swiftly disappeared. Even their personal servants and attendants encountered increasing courtesy from the family because guards, never far away, parodied any imperious demands they made. To the guards, who had never seen the cosseted luxury of Imperial life, the citizens Romanov still led a life of extraordinary privilege. They had no knowledge of courtly manners; when Alexandra glowered over Nicholas's shoulder while he jutted his jaw and blustered at their commander over some trivial remark or incident, they were genuinely as bewildered as the Imperial couple.

Nicholas bore his feelings of humiliation with some dignity for the children's sake but Alexandra found it very close to intolerable. Nicholas had been appointed by God to rule the greatest Empire on

Earth. When he had proved to be weak, God had sent her to enforce his will. Now these jumped-up, vulgar thugs told them when they might exercise and when they might not, whom they might see and if they might go out. It was beyond bearing, she hissed at Nicholas one night.

"There are people who are determined to put things right," he told her. "For their sakes and for the children we must suffer in silence."

"What people?"

"I cannot discuss it here; anyway, I don't know much but information has been got to me. There are people who will restore us to our proper position. They just need time."

"Are they from the Okhrana?"

Nicholas turned to look at her. "Good God no," he said. "The Okhrana is more likely to assassinate us than support our restoration, Alex. We have no friends there now – or none that dares admit it."

"But they used to serve you so faithfully, Nicki. What has happened to them?"

"When I was leader of the pack the Okhrana trotted at my heels and tore the throats from my enemies. Now I am no longer leader and my throat is as much in danger as anyone else's. Perhaps more so."

Alexandra put her hand to her own throat. "Are they so degenerate?"

There was no reply so after a few moments she spoke again. "Today Alexei asked if when you were Czar you had people assassinated. I said of course you didn't; what had given him such a preposterous idea? He said one of the guards had told him that, unless they were well-known, people who displeased me and our friend or you, disappeared and were never seen again."

Nicholas lay back, gazing into space.

"Did you hear me Nicki?"

"Yes, I hear you. May God forgive me. Everything I have done, I did for Russia."

"Well, now you are doing nothing and your friends are doing nothing and these ruffians are filling our children's minds with travesties of the truth. At the very least, make them let us go to Livadia. Then tell your precious friends that if they are coming, they need to come soon."

"I love Livadia but I do not think I shall see it again."

"Don't be absurd, Nicki. You know how lovely it will be now, in August. These ghastly people with their mad anarchic ideas have no control there. We can live there in peace until your friends sort things out properly. For God's sake use your authority and tell them we must go to Livadia!"

"You must not raise your voice Alex, or all will be lost. Just be patient. All will be well."

To Nicholas and Alexandra, the white Renaissance-style mansion they had built looking out over the Black Sea near Yalta had been a sanctuary from the rigours of Imperial life. Now the whole family yearned for the gentle climate, the beautiful scenery and the charm of their own palace, far away from Petrograd and the turmoil. The old wooden building in the Tartar style, where Alexander III had died, remained but another, where Nicholas had contracted typhoid, had been torn down to make way for something more becoming. This was their very own property; Alexandra had lavished huge sums of money on it, had summoned experts in architecture, interior design, and landscaping, while Nicholas had consulted authorities on plumbing, electricity, and the best facilities for watersports, tennis, and horse riding. Here they had always been free of responsibility, living life to the full, indulging every whim. In this soft environment Alexandra forgot that she needed a wheelchair, Nicholas lurked in the gardens with a huge butterfly net, the girls wound flowers into one another's hair, and Alexei could be a boy. Here at least they would be able to live as they had before. "Papa says we're leaving," Alexandra told the children. "I can't be certain so I won't say where we're going but it might not be a million miles from Yalta."

They would never see Livadia again.

Alexandra was aware that Nicholas had received Alexander Kerensky for a meeting the previous week but she had hidden herself away – she hated and feared the ferret-faced man whom in their days of power she had demanded should disappear. Her husband had not dared to explain to her the gravity of what his visitor had told him.

Kerensky lived close to reality, he knew that Russia was heavily pregnant with revolution and that birth was imminent. He perceived that his Provisional Government could be swept aside and then – just as the French revolution had – the newborn monster would feed on blood. "We must get you all as far away as possible from Petrograd. That is where the storm will rage; your being near would enrage the firebrands. Then God knows what they would do."

"I was hoping to go to Livadia," said Nicholas.

"It would be ill-advised to press the point. To be candid, I would see that as you taking refuge in luxury and privilege and so would many other people. Livadia is not for you. In any case, I have put it at the disposal of Breshkovskaia."

Nicholas blurted: "How dare you! Livadia is my personal property. My father died there and I have developed it at my own expense. And to put that criminal into MY home…" He stopped as he recognised how obviously unacceptable his argument must be to Kerensky. Breshkovskaia was a landowner's daughter who had devoted herself to freedom and justice for ordinary people on her family's lands and wherever she could have influence. She had earned both long imprisonment and legendary status for people like Kerensky. They called her the Mother of the Revolution.

A thought struck Nicholas. "Where are you living, Kerensky?"

"In the Winter Palace, why?"

"Just curious. In the Imperial suite?"

"I don't know," said Kerensky, "I expect it is. It's very ornate. More to the point, you should not concern yourself with trifles.

"As a matter of policy, I wish you no personal

harm, so I would counsel you to be compliant and hope for the best. Forget about Livadia and be thankful you are moving now. If you do not move, I doubt if I can save you. Do not tell the guards; this move is between ourselves. If they know in advance they may try to prevent it. Good may yet come for you."

"It is hard to believe you are on our side, Kerensky."

"Russia is in very great danger and your survival is worth more to Russia than your execution. For the moment, the people of Russia have more to fear from the family Romanov as martyrs than from the family Romanov as exiles. So, for the moment, we are on the same side. But I am not on your side, Citizen Romanov. I never have been and I never shall be.

"Now, Petrograd has hotheads – it is a place of great danger for you and your family. In November there will be elections, then the constituent assembly will have real authority. We shall at last be able to release you to go into exile wherever you wish; I want the world to see Russia behaving in a mature and civilised way towards its former head of state and his family, whatever was done in their name. It is my duty to Russia to ensure you are all in a place of safety until we can make proper provision for you."

Nicholas smiled wryly and said with gentle sarcasm: "Thank you Kerensky. I'm relieved to know that your concern is not personal."

Kerensky looked straight into his eyes. "In March I abolished the death penalty. It was not personal but I had a personal interest because, when you sought my execution, that felt very personal."

Nicholas flushed and glanced away. "One is sometimes prompted to do things that are unworthy when one's duty is to try to achieve the best one can for Russia."

Kerensky rose and turned towards the door.

"Indeed one is, and you did," he said. "I too am prompted but I take no notice. And I very much hope that my best is better than yours.

"There is one thing more, something you might consider to be personal. You have a rough road ahead of you, you and your family. You have always been attended by obsequious servants but there will be fewer now. You will be guarded by rough soldiers. Some of them will be deeply resentful of your past position. One of their favourite ways of exerting control is by physical assault, most particularly, by rape. They understand the humiliation involved and they enjoy it.

"Your family's situation, with the former Empress and your daughters, will be extremely dangerous. Even your son is at risk. I have formulated mandatory penalties for anyone who even tries to physically interfere with any of you, and have given those penalties such prominence and publicity that I believe, if your women behave with discretion, they should be safe."

"Thank you Kerensky. That is good of you."

"No it is not. To have done less would have been disgraceful. It is the least I can do, and it is all I can do. The means I used to add emphasis to the message will be effective, even if not attractive. I have put it about that your son's illness is the result of a virulent and contagious strain of congenital syphilis that you all carry. You have neither cause nor need to thank me."

Nicholas sat, astonished, appalled and speechless. Here was something he could never dare tell Alexandra.

Throughout their journeyings, the Romanovs were to complain of sexual innuendo, lack of privacy, and sentries at lavatory doors. Kerensky would be forced out of authority and into exile, but his defence held good to the end. The Romanovs were safe from violation, other than slaughter.

Chapter 26

Maids and footmen surreptitiously washed, ironed, folded and packed, stowing bed linen and tableware, clothing and footwear, ornaments, trivia, family mementos and ornaments in trunks and boxes. Their own modest belongings they put into holdalls they could keep close to them. By mid-August, the Romanovs, thirty attendants – servants, doctors, a tutor, and even court officials – and a small mountain of crates and chests were ready. Kerensky sent the order: a small armada of cars would collect them from the Alexander Palace at one o'clock in the morning.

It was inevitable that the preparations would be noticed. The garrison officers had been waiting, and this order was what they had been expecting: they blocked release of the cars. Kerensky had no choice: flushed with vodka, these soldiers were perfectly capable of going to the palace and bayoneting the family, bringing international disgrace on the Provisional Government. Also, Kerensky could not allow troops to flout his authority. With only his driver as bodyguard, he went to the barracks. All through the night he discussed the situation with them. They demanded action but he kept the discussion going; whatever they insisted upon, he discussed. Kerensky was known: he had been a socialist when declaring socialism invited persecution; he had defended radicals, knowing that doing so would bring the Okhrana to his door. Uneducated soldiers were no match for a man of his intelligence, commitment, and reputation. Gradually the anger faded, the men tired, their resolve faltered.

The dawn light of August 14, 1917 glinted on the cars as they drove, nose to tail, to the palace. The family held back; they would be the last to leave. Servants scurried out and in, struggling and sweating to load cases and trunks into and onto the vehicles. Eventually the luggage was organised and in broad daylight the family, accompanied by three dogs, said farewell to old Count Benckendorff, then descended the steps and boarded the limousines to the station.

For four days Alexandra lay exhausted as their train chugged eastward, across farm and woodland, into the foothills of the Ural Mountains. At Tiumen she had to be carried onto the steamer that would take them upriver to Tobolsk, although she felt sufficiently well to stand praying at the rail as the boat passed Rasputin's home village. She held an ikon he had given her and said she could pick out his roof.

At Tobolsk station the servants had to unload the boat and, for the fourth time, load the family's luggage, onto cars this time. Their destination was the governor's former residence but soldiers had been bivouacked there for months; it was filthy, dilapidated and, Alexandra stated forthrightly, utterly disgusting and unacceptable. She turned imperiously from the mansion on Freedom Street and returned to the steamer. The cabins were inadequate and the lavatories were a disgrace but they would have to do until some kind of order was restored to the house.

The situation had never arisen before: they were under detention but they were giving orders. There was no precedent, and anarchy had not yet reached this remote backwater. Until a new hierarchy was established, everyone was still uncertain so, when someone spoke with evident authority, everyone still did as they were told. The house was repaired and redecorated; what fabrics and furnishings they had brought were used, more were taken from the boat and requisitioned from other houses. Within a week Alexandra deigned to bring Alexei, now in great pain from internal bleeding, to their new home. The family settled in and Alexei's condition improved.

Inspectors, sent by Kerensky to ensure that conditions were appropriate, reported that all was well except that the plumbing gave trouble. Sewage disposal was by septic pits, which had been neglected. Once the pits were emptied the drainage system began to work again.

Dagmar heard that Nicholas and his family had been moved to Tobolsk. This was deeply disappointing – Livadia would have been accessible to her. But she knew a cleric, Archpriest Hermogene, who had two attractions for her: he was an open-minded innocent and he was in Tobolsk. Years before he had examined a young man known as Rasputin, whose family home was in the Tobolsk region. Hermogene declared that Rasputin's commitment to piety was beyond reproach. Later, along with others, he distanced himself from the troublesome starets. He had even asked an audience of Alexandra and begged her to have nothing further to do with the man. That was enough for Alexandra to instruct Nicholas to deprive him of the see of Saratov, which he held at the time, and that in turn was enough for him to be subsequently appointed by the Provisional Government to control the churches in Tobolsk.

Characteristically, Hermogene had forgiven Nicholas for their differences in the Rasputin affair and, when the Imperial family was no longer permitted to leave the house in Tobolsk to go to church, he regularly sent them a priest for private worship.

Letters passed between Dagmar, Archpriest Hermogene, and Nicholas – through the hands of Alexandra's trusted courier, Boris Solovief, the husband of Rasputin's daughter. Hermogene was even in touch with a Petrograd banker who would help finance an escape and knew people who could organise it. He wrote to the banker enclosing jewellery Solovief had brought from Alexandra. Handing the package to Solovief, he took the man's arm. "This will do a great good but, if it fell into the wrong hands, it could do immense harm," he said.

"I know, Father. Trust me. I will do what is right."

The archpriest was arrested, allegedly for organising a series of religious services throughout Tobolsk, when the actions of the Provisional Government were, by implication, criticised. He was not seen in Tobolsk for several weeks; when he returned he was somehow different. He said there was nothing wrong but he stayed indoors, neglected his duties, attended no services or meetings. The day after he heard that a banker had been found beaten to death in an alley in Petrograd, the priest went out and did not return. His body was found floating in a flooded quarry. Dagmar was deeply depressed when all correspondence from Tobolsk ceased but nobody could tell her what had brought it to an end.

Summer gave way to a wet fall. No news had come through since Solovief suddenly stopped visiting but anyway, all news now was depressing. The war was a ghastly massacre in squalid conditions. At home, the Provisional Government struggled for power with Bolsheviks in Petrograd, industry was grinding to a halt, marauding gangs roamed the streets, fighting with vigilante groups, and there was a continuing danger that Germany would drive through and capture the city. A triumphant Germany, Alexandra reflected, might restore the Czar to his throne. There were many possibilities and some of them were promising, but Russia was bleeding and in great pain. Well, it was Russia's own fault, she told herself. The people had turned on their masters and now they were paying the price. She lay in a darkened room or played the piano; their time would come again.

Chapter 27

Others had been more active. Innumerable cells of revolution had been maturing in the dark throughout Europe and across Russia. Like so many pupae, they were ready to emerge: they needed one charismatic thinker to give them focus. German agents approached Lenin.

Lenin was thirty years older than the twentieth century so he was into middle age when his moment came. He had spent years in exile, lecturing, debating over beer in Paris's Avenue d'Orleans, reconciling his wife Nadya with his mistress Inessa Armand. Both women were devoted to revolution and to Lenin; Nadya believed in the cause but Inessa lived for the cause and would, if the need arose, die for it. The great man moved about, avoiding police, evading secret police, establishing contacts and encouraging recruits. He sent Inessa to Petrograd to organise his network and there she was caught, having to jump bail to escape her fifth jail sentence. She ran his dangerous errands until 1916, when he wrote to her in Paris, telling her she was not pulling her weight. The message arrived as she desperately dodged through cellars and back streets to escape the closing nets of both Russian agents and the French police; she never again quite gave Lenin her unquestioning obedience.

She lost her illusions and became the one person on Earth who deliberately set out to tease Lenin, but their intellects were still in love, their emotions screamed in unison for cataclysmic change, they shared their purpose, their vision of destiny.

Lenin sat, sipping tea in the disgusting apartment in Zurich, where the weeping windows failed to keep out the smell of rendering pig fat. There was a knock at the door; he motioned Nadya to take away the tea things, himself moving quietly back behind the nondescript window drapes.

She opened the door a little. "If you want Vladimir Ulyanov, he is not here," she said.

"Yes he is," said the foremost of the three men, "and he will be glad to hear what we tell him."

They came in, and sat down without removing their hats. "Come out Vladimir Ulyanov," said the man. "You are in no danger from us. We are here on behalf of the Foreign Ministry of the German Reich." Lenin walked quietly to a chair and sat down. He said nothing.

"They have started without you in Petrograd. You Bolsheviks must move swiftly if you are to have a part in this play. You had best pack a bag, you and your friends are going on a journey."

Wind hurled hail like grit at the figures trudging in small groups towards the Swiss railway station. There were scores of them now, huddled waiting beside the train. Three cars drew up, more figures hurried to the group, then there were subdued orders. Nearly 200 people climbed into the compartments but at one carriage they found the doors already locked. From a wagon shed came a party of around thirty people, mostly men. Guards unlocked the doors of the empty carriage and they climbed in. "There is food and water, Ulyanov," said the man who had spoken at the flat. "The train will not stop for any reason in Switzerland, nor will it in Germany. If it did stop you would all be in the greatest danger. If anyone leaves the train, they will be shot. You will not be released until the train arrives. Nobody must try to open any door or window; that would be very dangerous for you all."

Lenin looked long at him then turned and climbed into the wagon. "What we do, we do for Russia," he said. The great wooden doors slid to, the iron handle was thrown over and double padlocked. "What a stroke of luck if it's good for Germany too," said the leader as he walked away with his comrades; their laughter was lost as the pistons came to life. Lenin and his cohorts, sealed in like a plague virus, were being injected into the very heart of post-Czarist Russia. Late on an April night, in the deep shadows and harsh lights of Petrograd's Finland Station, scores of dishevelled figures climbed awkwardly down from a newly arrived train that stank of human confinement. One man remained framed in a doorway, holding onto a handle and leaning out above the others. His jutting, bearded jaw and gleaming scalp made him instantly recognisable. "Comrades," he roared, punching the air, "now it begins!"

All that revolution needed was opportunity, and opportunity had come after a disastrous spate of emergencies that would have destroyed a lesser man than Kerensky. After the Eastern Front offensive failed, Kerensky had replaced Brusiloff with a national hero from the German war, General Lavr Korniloff, as supreme army commander.

Korniloff was a highly trained soldier and experienced intelligence officer who had served in India, Manchuria, and China before commanding a division, being captured by the Austrians and escaping. Small and wiry, with the eyes and cheekbones of a Tartar, he had a substantial moustache and a dandy's beard. He claimed to be non-political, seeking a military solution to rectify a situation of chaos. In truth, Korniloff was a close friend of Nikolai Nicholaevitch, sharing his faith in Imperial autocracy.

As supreme commander, Korniloff promptly demanded the right to execute mutineers and deserters. He said truthfully that the Russian army in the West had become a thieving terrorist rabble that would respond only to iron discipline. Kerensky refused so the commander resolved to take military control of Russia until peace could be restored. He sent General Krymoff to seize control of Petrograd. Kerensky had no choice but to ask the Bolsheviks, who could call up increasing numbers of people, mostly railway workers and defecting soldiers, to defend the capital. They, as determined as Kerensky that Petrograd would not come under the control of the military, raised a force of more than 20,000 to fortify and defend the city. The advancing soldiers refused to fight the defenders, just as the defenders refused to return the weapons they had been lent.

Krymoff shot himself, Korniloff was captured and imprisoned, and the danger was averted. Inevitably, soldiers who had previously served under him now conspired and helped Korniloff escape. He would die from a sniper's bullet outside Ekaterinberg, fighting with the White Russians to restore Empire and Emperor. That fighting was still going on when Nicholas arrived at the Ipatiev house there two weeks later, a few miles from where Korniloff had fallen.

The loss of such officers opened the way for extraordinary promotions in the White Army. One of the most extreme candidates was Baron von Ungern-Sternberg. He was the son of a German baron who had prospered in the Baltic marine trade until he was deported to Siberia for murdering one of his own sea captains, who had been cheating him.

The son adopted the title when his father died. Convinced that he carried the spirit of Genghis Khan within him, this lunatic went into battle on horseback in front of infantry, relished hand-to-hand combat, and administered corporal and capital punishments in person. When he felt playful, he had prisoners trussed before he debated with them whether they would prefer to be pushed head first or feet first into the firebox of a locomotive. The last words his screaming victims heard as they succumbed to furnace heat would be the Mad Baron yelling: "But it's what you asked for!"

The tide of war went against him and he retreated east to establish the beginnings of an independent empire in Mongolia but he persecuted his own followers, so eventually their loyalty faded. Mongolian communists would defeat, and capture him and then they would reveal to Ungern-Sternberg that they too could inflict protracted terminal agony.

Chapter 28

Kerensky knew he had sown the dragon's teeth. For all his socialist commitment, he was regarded by Lenin as inconsequential, wanting a better world for everyone but without upheaval. Within a month he heard that the Bolsheviks were taking control of essential units in Petrograd. Lenin had begun publicly criticising men like Kerensky for preserving the Provisional Government, while a leading Bolshevik journalist, Joseph Stalin, who had supported the Provisional Government, was now rumoured to be preparing a ferocious denunciation of 'counter-revolutionary forces'. Recognising that the hard-liners had the men, the means and the money, he left town. But, for all his massive depressions and morphine addiction, Kerensky was no ordinary politician. He wasn't finished yet.

The revolutionaries found themselves in a vacuum. They expected opposition when they entered the debating chamber of the Duma but everyone had fled. They sat down to discuss what they should do next and to their astonishment, they found that they were the government. People came and asked them what to do; when they suggested something, those people went away and did it. The head of an administration can be cut off but the limbs continue to move.

The new order took over the prisons, revolutionaries releasing many of their own people, imprisoned by the Provisional Government. They took over the Winter Palace, headquarters of the Provisional Government, and arrested Ministers. Lenin dropped his scarred suitcase in the Imperial quarters and glanced through the clothing Kerensky had left behind. There were splendid uniforms too, that Kerensky would never have worn. "Burn everything except any documents," he said. They took over railway stations, preventing the Provisional Government summoning troops to repel them. Their action was unhesitatingly brutal whenever necessary but almost bloodless and totally successful.

The revolution that had begun in Petrograd reached the Romanovs at the villas of Ai Todor, Djulber and Tchair in the Crimea a few weeks later. Parties of sailors arrived before dawn, a search warrant was produced at each house and the search began. When Dagmar at Ai Todor refused to leave her bed in the presence of a sentry, a woman came to keep watch. Dagmar endured in silence as long as she could but when she saw an officer collecting her private documents, the seventy-year-old former Empress harangued him like a fishwife. They yelled at each other over whether the peasant who had stood watch was a woman or a lady. They argued about the documentary status of an inscribed bible. Eventually the exasperated officer arrested Dagmar. Her family calmed her and persuaded the officer that she would be more trouble under arrest than with them.

Descent from inherited autocracy is hard for

autocrats to comprehend so the family submitted a formal complaint; a commission came to interview them. All the Romanovs were questioned but they felt they were being treated more as defendants than witnesses. Dagmar tried to retain dignity by making a statement but she was still questioned. When told to sign as the former Empress Maria she took the pen and signed as widow of the late Emperor.

Standards declined. Slovenly hostility greeted the aristocrats at every turn. They had to ask permission to go out, agree a time when they would return. Increasingly these requests were refused: they had become prisoners.

As the weeks passed, both food and fuel stocks declined, and so did the temperature. Dagmar caught influenza and came close to pneumonia, but she was recovering when the family's dentist – formerly the imperial dentist – paid her a visit. He had been at Tobolsk, he said, extricating from among his tools letters from Nicholas and small gifts the children had made for her. The old lady rallied marvellously. More letters were brought by a girl who ran immense risks. More for the challenge than for the few kopeks she was given, the girl travelled repeatedly back and forth, by cart, on foot, by fourth-class train, letters stowed where only the most intrepid might find them.

Across the country, rival groups, all claiming official status, stole, confiscated, and marauded. Russia was in the grip of famine; the Crimean Romanovs suffered, as did Nicholas's family, even though Tobolsk did rather better than most areas. Both parties had already pared the numbers of their servants to below what they regarded as subsistence;

now there remained only those who were indispensable. Even most of these were finally let go. If they had, in the days when they were paid, put aside some money, they might somehow find their ways to families or friends. If they had not…

Kerensky, with his vision of a liberated and just Russia, had one last roll of the dice. He had gone to the Northern Front and there his rhetoric and his reputation gathered a body of soldiers. They were never going to defeat the Bolsheviks but they tried. At Pulkova the force came under fire and disintegrated. Many across Russia despaired when they heard; amongst them were Nicholas and Alexandra. They had thought Kerensky extreme but in the new climate, he looked moderate.

Kerensky had done everything he could; he escaped to Finland and then to London. He would live in exile in the United States, warning the world of the dangers of both soviet communism and German fascism. Having repeatedly survived Stalin's assassin squads, he would die in 1970 aged eighty-nine. Korniloff had sneered: "What kind of man is it who fights a war in which millions kill and are killed, and yet refuses to use the firing squad to make men obey his orders?" There are worse epitaphs.

As soon as Lenin held the reins, he declared that there was no longer any private property. Everything belonged to the state and anyone who opposed the state was its enemy. Death to enemies of the state. Judicial killing was back, but without the judiciary.

In both the Crimea and Tobolsk, the news was received with resignation. There was only one prospect worse than Kerensky, and this was it.

Lenin had accepted that the Romanov succession might need to be severed but he insisted on exceptions. The former Czar and his line would probably need to be eliminated; senior Romanovs either taken into captivity or under surveillance in Russia were also on a provisional list to be liquidated along with all the other aristocratic riff-raff, but the Old Czar's widow and all those with her must be regarded as inviolable. "She is our passport to international respect," he told Sverdlov. "The group in the Crimea needs to be protected and released into exile as soon as we can manage it. Better if they slipped away – we don't want to provoke our own soviets."

"The local soviets won't tolerate it," said Sverdlov. "They want a chance to clean out the stable, to show their commitments like the chance we're giving the Special Purposes squad in the Urals. They are determined to draw a line so that the Whites can never recreate the autocracy."

Lenin ran his hand impatiently over his shining scalp. "I share their determination but we must wait, even in the case of Special Purposes; we must prevent any of the soviets doing anything hasty. They can probably have all the rest but Britain and Denmark regard Maria Feodorovna as sacrosanct. If we kill her, she will become an ikon in America too. They are all degenerate societies, they cannot last – we know that. But for a while we shall need to co-exist with them. We are weakened by this Czarist war with Germany, and the war with the Whites, and with dissent. We must have peace with Germany, we must defeat the Whites. We must grow strong again before we make more enemies."

"What about the dissent? Counter revolutionaries will gather around the Crimea Romanovs. Already they are calling the old woman a living ikon."

"Dead ikons are more dangerous than living ikons. Their Jesus was no threat until he had been crucified. We have not come this far to give our enemies a martyr to fight for."

"She is not alone. There is the nucleus of a dynasty there."

"They're just a smattering of daughters and sons-in-law, mostly degenerate. They have nothing to do with the succession. Without the Imperial authority they will just wither."

"Nicholas Nicholaevitch is there. There were those who wanted to make him military dictator."

"That means nothing; he refused it. Anyway, it would hardly be our brightest move to string up the most popular soldier in Russia. When we are strong, we shall do whatever is required. Until then, we must show restraint."

Sverdlov shook his untidy head. "What about Sergei's widow Elizabeth? If anyone deserves to be saved, it's her. She's popular – she has devoted herself to the poor, given all her property away…"

Lenin's expression reminded Sverdlov that there were no friends in a revolution, only people who were useful to each other, and only for a time. Lenin said: "I'm not talking about saving people. I am serving the interests of the revolution. What we do with Russians is nobody's business but our own; if we liquidate a doddering old Dane that might be one liquidation too many.

"Sergei's woman is a German, so she doesn't have much support, she has devoted herself to superstition, while the property she gave away belonged to the people anyway. If you are killing rats, comrade, you don't have time to pick out the ones that don't have fleas. The facts are that the Romanovs we need to eliminate are dead or in our hands. The Romanovs in the Crimea can do us far more harm dead than alive. They are desperate to get out of the country and will stay out, so let's keep them alive, then leave the door ajar for them to slip out as soon as is expedient."

"So what do you want me to do? Go to the Crimea and tell the soviets there what they can and can't do?"

"That's not necessary," said Lenin. "We can use ordinary channels to exert pressure. And I shall send a guard to protect them from the soviets; I know a man who could lead them. He solemnly told me that the Imperial House of Romanov was a domestic liability when alive but would be an overseas liability dead. And he's right."

"Zadorojny? He's not happy about the Special Purposes project."

"And he has a point; we shall pay a heavy price for that, but I'm coming round to the view that it must be done. I think Zadorojny will agree to go to the Crimea, if only to make sure that Maria Feodorovna lives long enough to die in Denmark. What do they call her there, anyway?"

"Kesjerinde Dagmar. It's after some legendary queen who was so virtuous that her God allowed her to return from the dead."

Lenin laughed. "There is no God, Comrade, so we shall have to hope Zadorojny can handle it."

Chapter 29

In December new guards moved in. On the first day they brought the entire group together. Dagmar, small, frail, and past her three score years and ten, stood at the head of the staircase, looking down at them. The guards' leader, Zadorojny, walked to the foot of the stairs. He was a very large man, tall and broad shouldered.

"I'd like you to come down and join the others," he said conversationally. "We intend to conduct a roll call."

"You must do as you choose but I shall not come down, nor shall I participate."

There was silence.

Almost casually, Zadorojny drew his revolver and, his arm straight and unwavering, aimed it up at her. "Is that your final word?" The silence was palpable.

"It is."

Nikolai glared at the big man but did not move.

Everybody heard Zadorojny cock his revolver. "What name shall we put on the papers?"

Her chin came up. "I am Maria Feodorovna, widow of the late Emperor."

Zadorojny lowered his gun. "Thank you Comrade Feodorovna. I hope everyone else will give their names as clearly." He walked out as one of his grinning men started checking names from a list. Dagmar stormed away with as much dignity as she could muster.

Afterwards Nikolai stood at a window, gazing out onto the moonlit landscape. He glanced round as he heard a step and was surprised to see Zadorojny. He moved quietly for a big man. "You could have got yourself shot in there, comrade," said Zadorojny.

"If I had intervened? Yes, but I decided you wouldn't fire. Also, shooting upwards accurately is more difficult than many may think; everyone would have turned at the shot and I could have reached you before the second. Anyway, it would have been ill-considered and I don't think that is how you do things."

"I want to talk to you about that."

"About what?"

"About you having the sense to work things out."

"How do you know?"

Zadorojny grinned. "I served under you."

"So have most of the scum who want to cut our throats."

"I know. You won't remember me but I was an officer and, I like to think, a pragmatic patriot. That's why I'm here. In Sebastopol, they think they might want to cut your throats. In Yalta they know they want to and they'd like to do it now. In the Soviet Offices we have agreed that your throats are worth more to Russia uncut."

Nikolai pondered. "The Soviet Offices. Would those be the Imperial apartments at the Winter Palace?"

"Used to be. Yes, I remember it well, as I'm sure you do. That's probably where your lot planned the wars that beggared Russia and killed all those millions of people. Not now though. They're the Soviet Offices, where we plan how to save lives. Yours, and that obstreperous old woman's, just for a start."

Nikolai smiled. "Don't call her that. You have already deeply offended her. If you call her an obstreperous old woman, she will get herself killed just to thwart your plans."

"Plans? I don't have any plans. I'm sailing on a torn sail and a broken oar."

"I thought you were going to say that," said Nikolai, feeling more cheerful than he had for months. "Perceive, evaluate, and respond. It's how I handle unexpected contingencies too."

"I know that," said Zadorojny. "I've been there when you've done it and I've got shrapnel in my arse to prove it."

The Danish Government tried to negotiate Dagmar's release to go to her homeland. They had no desire to anger a powerful neighbour and trod with great care but they pointed out in March, once the Bolsheviks had seized all her property, she was of no further value to them and, should she come to grief, she could cause Russia immense embarrassment.

Danish newspapers stated she was being moved as

preparation for return to Denmark, but they were wrong. The Ai Todor party was told to pack for departure. "We are being taken to Petrograd," declared Dagmar. "There we shall either be restored or murdered. The world has gone mad."

Zadorojny held a meeting with Nikolai, Peter, and Sandro. Through moderates at Sebastopol, he knew that the Yalta soviet was planning to exterminate the Romanovs. "Surely they can't just come and shoot us," said Sandro.

"They are the law," said Zadorojny. "If they decide that you are criminals to be executed, they can write their own piece of paper."

Nikolai asked: "So where do you stand while they are executing sentence of death upon us?"

"If we try to protect condemned criminals from the rule of law then we are accomplices and they will be justified in exterminating us too. We intend to stay alive and we want to keep you alive too."

"Well," said Nikolai, "you have perceived and evaluated. How do you plan to respond?"

"Do you have any suggestions?"

"Yes, as a matter of fact I do," said Nikolai. "Djulber, my brother's house, may be absurd with its Arabian pretensions and minarets and all that, but it is fortifiable. A company of men would have a much better chance of defending it than they would here."

The big man smiled. "You're absolutely right. Djulber is a damn silly house but we are going there because we can defend it if necessary. I have fifty-seven men, armed with rifles and machine guns. I also have one or two procedural aces up my capacious sleeve. I think we can give Yalta a run for their money."

Nikolai and his lady Anastasia went on ahead to help Grand Duke Peter and Militza prepare for the invasion. Dagmar, still convinced that the jocular Zadorojny was leading them to their deaths, followed with Xenia and Sandro. On arrival, Dagmar looked round without enthusiasm. She loved her daughters, was fond of Nikolai, tolerated Sandro, and preferred to have very little to do with the Montegegrin sisters. "Please go to no trouble on my account," she said. "I have virtually nothing with me; the most modest room will be more than adequate." She was shown to the master suite, which she accepted without hesitation. As her ladies fussed about there, she heard noises immediately outside so she went out onto the balcony. Against the view of foothills rising to dramatic mountains, a machine gun swung on ropes. Men shouted above and, turning gently, it was hoisted upwards out of sight.

Two days later trucks arrived, decanting a couple of dozen assorted Bolsheviks from Yalta outside the gate. Two guards went to them, asked them to wait and invited three to come forward to talk.

"We have come for the Romanovs," said their leader. "We have a warrant for their arrest for crimes against Russia."

"A warrant in whose name?" asked Zadorojny.

"It is signed by the leader of the Yalta soviet and by his deputy," said the visitor, pulling a document from inside his coat.

"I too have a warrant," said Zadorojny. "It instructs me to keep these prisoners safe until the authorities in Petrograd require me to turn them over to the national government. To them, not to you." He too pulled a document from inside his coat.

They exchanged papers but, while the visitor opened Zadorojny's, the big guard simply waited. The man scanned the document closely, then handed it to his companions. Heads close together they examined it. Their leader faced up to Zadorojny. "We could destroy this document, say we have never seen it," he said.

"What good would that do you? You have read that I must send a report each week to Petrograd. If there is no report, Comrade Vladimir Ulyanov will require to know why not. He will want to know what has become of us and of this document that bears his signature.

"Comrade Ulyanov values loyalty and obedience to Russia above all else. I and my men are loyal and obedient to him and to Russia. Are you?"

In the silence that followed there was a sound from the staircase, a rattle, exactly like someone feeding an ammunition belt into a machine gun.

Nikolai watched discreetly from the back of a balcony as the three men rejoined their companions and drove away. Descending the staircase he found Zadorojny gazing through the cracks in a board-covered window. "How did you do that?"

"I told them I had a warrant to protect you, signed by Valdimir Ulyanov in Petrograd," he replied, gently waving his document.

"I didn't know that. May I see the warrant?"

"No."

"Why not?"

There was a pause before Zadorojny replied. "Because you can read."

That night Peter unlocked his cellar door. He personally selected wine, wine for the Dowager, wine for the entire Romanov party, wine for the guards. Plenty of good wine for the guards.

Chapter 30

In Tobolsk through the long winter there had been many rumours of escape plans, each of them embraced by Alexandra until it crumbled. Britain's King George was alleged to be behind a plan to take the family out by boat but nothing ever came of it, perhaps because George V really wanted nothing whatever to do with the embarrassing Romanovs. Beyond all else, he feared an eruption of Bolshevik anger in London.

Before dawn one frosty morning, carts drew up outside the Tobolsk house. Commissar Yakovleff had been ordered to take the former Czar for a meeting in the Bolshevik's capital of Moscow. It was, he said, all a matter of regularising his situation as a former head of state. Alexandra decided to go with him, taking Marie. The other girls would stay to look after Alexei, who was haemorrhaging again; Yakovleff had promised that they would follow in a couple of weeks if the boy was well enough. Dr Botkin insisted that straw was found to make the carts more comfortable and they set off.

The roads were pitted and rutted, so the carts needed frequent repair. Rain and thawing ice made the journey worse and they spent the first night on the floor of a derelict house. From before dawn until well into the evening the carts lumbered on until, near Tiumen, a cavalry escort met them and took them to the train station. They were too exhausted to undress but, pulling off their outer clothes, fell on the bunks and slept. They did not know that Soviets in both towns of Omsk and Ekaterinberg wanted the honour of hanging the former Czar; Yakovleff did know and he was nervous.

They were waiting, grim-faced and implacable, as the train pulled to a hissing halt in Omsk. The Omsk soviet believed Yakovleff was a traitor of the revolution – he was taking the former Czar to the East so he could escape through Vladivostok, they said. "They are mad," cried Alexandra. "Do they suppose I would leave my little ones and flee the country without them? Let me speak to them."

Yakovleff raised his hand. "My men and my authority from Moscow are all that stand between you and those men, who want the honour of killing you both," he said. "They would shoot you on sight, so stay in this compartment with the door closed. Do not touch the blinds.

"I shall telegraph Moscow and seek further instructions." Moscow told him to turn back to Ekaterinberg, so the train took on fuel and water while the weary travellers prepared for another day in transit. At last the pistons slowed at Ekaterinberg but there, the scene was even more terrifying.

Unshaven men of the regional soviet were waiting but this time there was no discussion. Two manned machine guns were trained on the train doors. Soldiers stood in spaced ranks down both sides of the train, each with his rifle cocked and ready. "Hand over the prisoners or we open fire." It was as simple as that.

Yakovleff demanded an assurance that the prisoners were in no immediate danger and they were shepherded into a car. Escorted by a truck full of armed soldiers, the former Czar and his party arrived by car at the Ipatiev house in Ekaterinberg.

Nicholas Ipatiev had done well for himself. He had developed systems and techniques that improved safety underground. The mines were profitable, producing iron, asbestos, manganese, platinum, and above all, gold, so the hazards had been neglected. Too often the groan and crash of shifting rock, the dust and the invisible gas brought death to toiling miners. But the hazards had done more than crush, entomb, suffocate, and poison: they had reduced productivity and closed valuable veins and seams. Ipatiev could not interest the mine owners in compassion but profitability was a horse of a different colour. They listened, they paid, and they sent their engineers and overseers to learn from Ipatiev.

Ipatiev was a man of good family, of influence in the town so, when at the beginning of the century, he built himself a family mansion – it was a grand one. The Ipatiev house stood on a hill, on the corner of Voznesensky Prospekt. Ornate and impressive, it reflected the status of a man of standing.

Sokolov had been shown into the study and Ipatiev came to meet his old friend, the magistrate. Their friendship was not intense but mutual dependency over the years had created an intimacy that would pass in a poor light: they were useful to each other.

"Tea?"

"No thanks. It's bad news, Nicholas."

"I had not supposed it would be anything else. What is it?"

"We're going to requisition this house."

Ipatiev span round. "Are you mad? This is my family home, my livelihood – I teach here. My reputation stands or falls by this house…"

"I know, I know. It was going to be either your house or my house, so I withdrew from the discussion. They said yours was larger, grander. We need a big house for what they have in mind."

"I won't permit it. Do you have any idea how long it took to build – and what it cost?"

"I'm afraid you will either permit it with a signature or you will go to prison while they forge your signature. There can be no question. They're determined and short of time."

"It's not them, it's you, you sanctimonious swine! You come here threatening me. How dare you…"

Sokolov watched Ipatiev, whose voice trailed off. "I have got you the best deal you could have under the circumstances. I don't want you to be grateful but it will keep you and your family alive, at least for a while." They stared at each other.

Ipatiev sat down and slumped. "What is it you have in mind for the house?"

"You wouldn't want to know."

"I do want to know. If we are to be made homeless, I insist on knowing."

"Very well, Nicholas. We believe that important prisoners, enemies of the people, will be coming here. There will be forces who wish to lynch them; there will be forces who wish to release them. Either way, we shall be held accountable for their security. This house has been named a building for special purposes."

"Put them in the prison for God's sake!"

"You are missing the point, Nicholas. These have been very important people. They may be very important people again. We cannot put them into prison cells. Their friends would be displeased. We cannot release them because certain other people would be infuriated. We need to make a fine house secure and then put them in it until we know what is to become of them."

"And then what?"

"Then you will get your house back, with compensation for the inconvenience and any damage or deterioration that may have occurred."

"Why should it have been damaged?"

The man shrugged. "These are troubled times, Nicholas. Furniture might get damaged, decorations…"

"Are you mad? I'm not going to leave my house furnished, least of all when it's going to be used as a prison."

"Yes you are, Nicholas. You and your family are going to take your personal effects and the piece of paper I am about to give you, and you are going to go away. The house will remain, complete with fixtures, fittings, and furniture. Ready for the prisoners and their guards to take up occupation. You can clear out your mining equipment – in fact you had better do that. Send it over to my place if you can't find anywhere else; the guards will need some of the basement rooms to be empty and available, I expect.

"We are doing you a favour. I believe the soviets are going to become more powerful and more extreme. I have read their propaganda; people like us with fine homes are likely to be named as enemies of the people. They say all property is theft. People with property are being named already as thieves. I am going to have to stay and take my chances, Nicholas, but you are being invited to go to safety for the duration. Bring this document back when the wave has passed on, and all should be well." He held out two sheets of paper.

"How much compensation?"

"Be fair but not greedy. You should be all right."

"Will you be here to honour this paper?"

"God knows. It is signed by bigger fish than me. You need to sign both copies, then I'll take one back. It should be good but anyway, it's all you are going to get. Be glad of it and go."

"When?"

"You must be gone by tomorrow night."

Again Ipatiev was astonished and appalled. "Two days? Why two days?"

"The timber is arriving this morning to build a barricade around the house to make it secure. You need to leave tomorrow night at the latest. It will be a bad place to be, believe me. The labourers have already started whitewashing the windows." His patience snapped and he stepped close. "Get out for God's sake, you fool. It's my guess this house will become an abattoir before long but whatever happens it won't be a place where I'd want anyone of mine to be."

Ipatiev stared. Then he said: "Who are these people that are so important?"

"They are on their way to Ekaterinberg now. Try to imagine the most important people who are imprisoned at the moment but don't tell me who you are thinking of."

"They're going to be murdered here, aren't they? You are going to wipe out the Czar and his family, here in my house."

Sokolov stood silent for some moments. "Not if I can help it," he said, "but I take my life in my hands in saying it."

He passed the two sheets to Ipatiev, who scanned his face before looking at the papers, then slowly signed them both and handed them back.

One he folded carefully, slipping it into an inside pocket of his jacket. The other he handed back and then moved towards the door. Turning, he said: "This is not as I would wish it but like everyone else, we must make the best of it. Your wisest course is to go quietly and make as little noise as possible. If I were you I would go to England or Denmark. When it's over, we shall meet again." He held out his hand. "I wish you and yours happier times." Their hands clasped and their eyes met.

Within six months Sokolov stared unfocused as a

uniformed Bolshevik behind him put a revolver to his head. Ipatiev had taken his advice, and lived. It was into his vacated house that the Romanovs came and they stayed for two months. Initially the party was allocated three rooms: a bedroom, where Alexandra, Nicholas, and their daughter Marie slept, a sitting room where the doctor and menservants had their blankets, and a smaller room where the maid erected her camp bed. A couple of weeks later they were given more space after the other girls arrived with Alexei, who was feeling better despite the rigours of the journey. Almost immediately he fell climbing out of bed and was again in dreadful pain. He shared the corner room with his parents, while the girls slept together in an adjoining bedroom, so none of them slept much while he cried in the night. Now they had five rooms. Immediately below the girls' bedroom was an empty room with striped walls.

Ekaterinberg, like the rest of Russia, was in turmoil. Opposition to the Bolsheviks was developing into civil war. Bands of deserters were claiming authority, liberating other people's goods and property for their own use, and loyalists were plotting to liberate and restore the Emperor. Ekaterinberg became isolated, with white Russians holding all lines of communication.

Chapter 31

Lenin needed peace to concentrate on civil dissent, but Ludendorff had made no secret that the German High Command's intended to subjugate substantial regions of Eastern Europe. Kaiser William had been revealed, by the war he did so much to create, as the vain, inadequate, contorted character he was. He dispensed bluster, bombast, and medals but even the trenches shown behind him in publicity photographs were phony; he never went near the realities of war.

The High Command now controlled the German war machine and it demanded territorial gains. Lenin and his fellow revolutionaries detested the Western allies; they would much have preferred to have been on the side of Germany and would, in the post war years, encourage German aggression towards those adversaries. But they had not sought revolution so that they could give territory to Germany. When they began negotiations to extricate Russia from a war bequeathed them by a now defunct administration, they found Germany intransigent: they would be required to pay an immense tribute before they would be allowed to escape.

Lenin withdrew from negotiations with Germany, saying that, once they realised that Russia was breaking off hostilities, the rest of the allies would be out of the war within weeks. It was the signal for a million German soldiers on the Eastern Front to prepare to invade. The prospect of another phase of total war, with still more massive loss and humiliation, was too much for Lenin. Within a fortnight Russia had come back, hastily negotiated and agreed peace. On the third day of the third month of the fifth year of Russia's war, that war was over. As Dagmar perceived, the war had been fought over territory, millions had died and multitudes suffered, and at the end, territory was sacrificed. Bolshevik Russia had committed the very treason that Alexandra was alleged to have been planning.

Almost overnight the Brest-Litovsk Treaty robbed Russia of Finland, Estonia, Latvia, Lithuania, Poland, and a wedge of Romania. With them went three out of every ten subjects of the Empire plus most of its coal reserves and nearly half its industrial capacity. But equally abruptly, it stopped bleeding to death. This starved, ruined, crippled giant still lived and breathed. Hope bloomed in the spring sunshine.

Petrograd was awash with alcohol, pillaged from merchants and palace wine cellars. Crime, drunkenness, looting, murder, and rape ran riot. Troops, ordered to destroy stocks of alcohol, fell drunk and insensible among the rioters.

The revolutionaries had a greater bogeyman in their nightmares than Germany; it was their own shadow. A man who throws out his lady to marry his mistress has created a vacancy and, what is worse, established that he is capable of an act that he might repeat. Russia had collectively done away with the Czar and the Duma; the country had espoused the revolutionaries that had courted it for so long. If it grew tired of Bolsheviks, who might it flirt with and then substitute for them?

The Okhrana was gone, fading into the shadows, but now a new monster emerged, seeking out corruption. The Cheka began small and puritanical but rapidly grew fat on the fruits of power. The death penalty was restored. Across Russia thousands were recruited to the Cheka, trained in its ways, given rights to arrest and detain, educated in interrogation, and then given the power to hold summary trials and to summarily execute sentence.

Purge upon purge would be used to eradicate threats, whether it was real or imagined; red terror would be followed by black horror and still the slaughter would go on, for decade after decade. But before it could sterilise society, the Bolsheviks had to give Russia the peace it craved at any price. Then they would be able to check the cellars for people who had exactly the same motives as their own. Nobody fears sedition more than those whose sedition has put them in charge – the handgun to the head had come of age.

Lenin moved his capital to Moscow but he still had as many problems. The war was over for Russia but there was still the possibility of the Czar being liberated and restored as monarch in Siberia. There were few true revolutionaries but his strength lay in the multitude of spear carriers, people who obeyed because they believed the revolution would bring better days. They would be disillusioned sooner or later and Lenin recognised that a soldier who turns his coat once might have little compunction in turning it twice.

Troops were moved into Ekaterinberg to withstand a possible assault by monarchist white Russian soldiers. The security of the Romanov party was important; options were discussed and plans prepared to take them to Moscow. Then the plans were abandoned – safer to stay put.

Alexandra received secret messages of hope from prospective rescuers; prepare a sketch of the rooms with windows, said one, and she did. Put in details of obstructions, like large pieces of furniture. She smuggled it out by a nominated visitor whom the guards seemed to trust. The whole party made ready for a hasty departure, even the servants lying fully clothed all night, waiting for a whistled signal, then gunfire, and rescue. The whistle never came.

Avdieff, the guard commander, took Nicholas aside next day. "There's something you should see," he said, and handed over Alexandra's sketch. Nicholas stammered that perhaps his lady had not realised the sensitivity of such a drawing. Avdieff laughed. "Do not disillusion her, comrade," he said. "It keeps her out of trouble; she enjoys writing to me and I enjoy writing to her."

Avdieff took his file to the head of the Bolshevik secret police in Ekaterinberg, Jacob Yurovsky. "They are planning to escape," he said. "I wrote these letters and that woman replied, but what other letters do they receive? We have a machine gun on the roof, men both inside and outside all day and all night but how can we be sure?" Scrawny little Yurovsky had a reputation: he did not allow mistakes to occur. He telegraphed Jacob Sverdlov, who even in his twenties was already a veteran of revolution. He had been repeatedly imprisoned and interrogated before the revolution. Now he was a leading member of the Central Committee. People said, "Lenin thinks, Sverdlov achieves." On this occasion Sverdlov was decisive but suspended sentence.

"Take control yourself at the Ipatiev house," he told Yurovsky. "If you even suspect that there is a risk of their escape, wipe out the entire nest. Leave nothing for the whites to venerate."

Chapter 32

The ending of Russia's war with Germany meant extreme change in the Crimea. The advance guard of the invading Germans could arrive almost any day. Bolsheviks panicked and at Ai Todor Zadorojny predicted they would come to burn out the nest before the conquerors arrived. "They're terrified the Krauts will put a Tsar back on the throne and then they will be compared with the Ekaterinberg soviet and blamed," he told Nikolai, Peter, and Sandro. "They don't want that. We can't defend this place against large numbers of armed troops."

"What do you suggest?"

"I know of a wine cellar. It's large and obscure. It's some way from here. We can transport your people there, lock you in and, when Yalta demands to know where you are, we shrug. The Krauts will be better for you and they will be here very soon."

Nikolai grinned. "You don't like Germans much do you?"

"I don't like Royalty much but I'm doing my best to help. My men would give the pay they haven't received to be locked into a wine cellar and you, you're hesitating. Will you go?"

Sandro shook his head. "She'll never go

underground to hide from that rabble."

"Oh for God's sake," said Zadorojny, and there was sudden silence. Then they all laughed. "If he existed, anyway," he said. "She's one old woman and you lot are staking everything on whether she's prepared to do the sensible thing. Isn't one of you prepared to pick her up and carry her into the cellar?"

"Certainly not," said Peter. "Are you mad?"

Nikolai grinned. "It's not her way and it's not our way. It may be absurd and it could get us all killed but we won't, and that is all there is to it. Give us what arms you can and leave us to it."

"You're all bloody crazy," said Zadorojny.

Nikolai laughed and said, "You're absolutely right, not that it matters."

More news came from Yalta: they were planning to attack in force. "I'm sorry," the big guard commander told Nikolai. "I'm going to have to go and get reinforcements from Sebastopol."

"Will you be in time?"

"I don't know but I'll do everything I can. While I'm gone my men will defend you if that is necessary."

Night was closing in when he left. As dawn gilded the hills next day a German column arrived. This was on a different scale from anything the guards could oppose. Trucks rolled up by the dozen, stopped in lines, hundreds of uniformed men formed up as though they were on a parade ground. A pre-war Benz drove to the gate of the big house and out stepped Field Marshal Hermann von Eichhorn. A veteran field commander who had faced Russia's invasion of Prussia, Eichhorn was a Prussian military stereotype: fat, bald, arrogant, brutal, and bemedalled.

Dagmar said he was not to be admitted to the house but Peter overruled her. Eichhorn and his three aides waited in the salon. Nikolai declined to meet them: "I'd have to shake hands with him you see, and I'm damned if I'll shake the hand of that bastard."

Peter said: "I'll talk to him but he is a field marshal and they say he's to be military governor of the Ukraine. Sandro, I'd appreciate it if…"

"We need to talk to him," said Sandro. "I'll come."

"He was only made up to field marshal last winter," muttered Nikolai.

Eichhorn was at his most conciliatory. He had been instructed personally by the Kaiser, in a telegraphed message, to come straight to the Villa Djulber and make sure that the Kaiser's much-loved relatives were safe and well. He was delighted to see that the two grand dukes were in good health. The Dowager Empress and the Grand Duke Nicholas Nicholaevitch, they too were well? "The Kaiser is delighted they are no longer on a different side and wants them to come to Potsdam," he said. "It is for me to have you escorted to safety in Potsdam."

"Thank you," said Peter stiffly. "They are indisposed at the moment but they are generally as well as can be expected. I shall tell them of Willie's invitation and we shall respond as soon as we can."

"The Kaiser will be relieved they are unharmed. So much has happened since he last saw them. So very much."

Afterwards Sandro told Nikolai: "And then he smirked. I could have hit him, and by God I would have enjoyed it."

But Eichhorn wanted no confrontation with the Romanovs. Russian soldiers and guards were an entirely different matter.

"My men are securing the area," he said. "They have disarmed the men who were holding you prisoner. They have also captured their leader, who was returning with a rabble from Sebastopol. He is being interrogated and then we shall hang him. We shall hang all the ringleaders, and then the rest. The ranks don't riot if they think they will escape death."

"Unless of course, you wish to dispose of them yourselves." He smiled as though he were inviting the two Russians to come on a picnic. "I expect you have some unpleasant experiences to requite."

Sandro spoke quietly but forcefully: "Zadorojny and his men have defended us with their lives. They have done everything possible to protect us from Bolshevik elements, and that rabble to whom you allude was coming to reinforce them in case we were attacked. If any harm is done to any of them, the Dowager Empress will protest to your Kaiser in the very strongest terms."

Eichhorn stared back, amazed. Then he beckoned one of his aides. "Go and stop the interrogation," he muttered, leaning close to the officer. "Don't let them damage any more of the prisoners. Get a doctor to repair any that need it." The man hurried out.

"I don't understand," said the field marshal. "These men are loyal to the Tsar?"

"Not exactly," said Sandro. "But there are different factions amongst the Russian people. All I need to say is that these men have treated us well and deserve to be treated well in their turn. Zadorojny is our friend and ally. We need to talk to him and then his men will be no trouble to you. The Dowager Empress will want them rewarded. She will also wish them to remain as our guards and protectors for as long as she feels it is necessary."

"It was nice to see von Eichhorn nonplussed," said Sandro later. "He stared out the window, shaking his head and murmuring: 'Fantastiche. Fantastiche.'"

Nikolai chuckled. "Rewarded was a nice touch. A very nice touch. That gives von Eichhorn a challenge."

A few days later Nikolai stood outside the house, smoking a cigar. It was good to smell the machinery of war again. He heard the big man coming towards him but he did not turn.

"It is not over. Here in Russia, it is not over," said Zadorojny. "The changing will continue and from the blood and the chaos, Russians will make a new Russia. Perhaps it will be better, perhaps not. But it will never be the same again."

Nikolai stared into the distance, the mountain against the stars. "Will you be a part of it, that new Russia?"

Zadorojny shrugged. "I don't know. Perhaps I will make it, perhaps not. I was close to being hanged a couple of days ago but the people I have been trying to rescue, rescued me. Thank you for that. I will try. I will go to Moscow. That's where action begins now.

And you?"

"I shall stay close to the Empress… to the old lady until I can be sure she's safe. Then, my lady wants to go to Nice. That's where old Russians go. It's a good life there. You could do worse…"

"Me in Nice? It seems no more likely than you in Lenin's Moscow."

"No, I suppose not. You know, I wish I had recognised your qualities; you should have been on my staff in the old days. You're too good for the god-forsaken land that Russia will become."

Zadorojny frowned. "Now you're talking merit and meritocracy. That was heresy with your lot and now it's treason with mine. Truth is, I have my rank."

Nikolai nodded. "One of these days somebody is going to hang you for telling the truth, Zadorojny."

"That is my inevitable destiny. Still, there are worse ways to go, and worse reasons than destiny."

"Destiny," said Nikolai thoughtfully, "is not all it's cracked up to be."

There was a long silence and then, without a word, Grand Duke and jailor turned and embraced each other.

Spring came, and Easter. They celebrated and went to live in homes they or close relatives owned in the area. There were no Fabergé eggs but surely sanity was returning to Russia. German control had brought calm to their area and now the war with Germany was over, everything would settle down. Soon they would travel to Czarsko Selo for the summer. They would be reunited with Nicholas and the children, and

Alexandra of course. Nicholas would be Czar again. Plenty of time then for Fabergé eggs.

Dagmar lived in Harax, a villa belonging to Grand Duke George Michaelovitch. The main house would have looked more appropriate in Scotland than on the Black Sea at Alupka. "We want to live in a place in the English manner," George had said proudly. He was unaware of the difference when Architect Kraznoff responded by building him a mansion in the Scottish bourgeois mock-baronial style. When Dagmar moved into the house she did not know where George was, certainly not that he lived in very Russian surroundings: the SS Peter and Paul fortress in Petrograd; there he would be shot in 1919.

It was at Harax that the Yalta Bolsheviks, having suffered the humiliation of being repelled by Zadorojny three miles away at Ai Todor, had beaten the resident steward so severely that he died.

The house was large and luxuriously appointed but it was not built on the scale of Russian palaces: Dagmar was comfortable, a guest in the master suite, able to walk straight out onto a canopied balcony where she could sit and read in the honey-scented air. But she would not have called her quarters grand.

Irina suggested to her that it was absurd for a uniformed Cossack to play nightly bodyguard in a corridor designed for the tartan dressing gowns of Lowland pretenders. Dagmar reacted robustly: she always had a Cossack sleep outside her door and she always would. The bodyguards would under no circumstances be relieved of their nocturnal duties.

George's lady had found it convenient to quarter

all servants in a lesser building built nearby for the purpose. During the day, servants and attendants assiduously attended to aristocratic needs but when Dagmar retired, so did they, all except the bodyguard. "She's no trouble at night," said one of her ladies in waiting, in that way people have when they believe that the weight of years is so great a burden that it has become a disability.

Their courier, the plain peasant girl, had last brought letters from Tobolsk in March, when the family was unhappy but reasonably well. The girl had set out again for Tobolsk with replies but somewhere on the journey someone, for purposes of his own, investigated, and discovered the letters. Since then they had heard nothing.

Chapter 33

The family in Ekaterinberg had noticed the difference immediately their guards were changed, as though a door had been left open in midwinter. Avdieff's men had been untutored amateurs; they had sneered, criticised, stole. They knew the rules and the penalties and they stayed clear, just.

Now Yurovsky and his men controlled them. There was no humour now, not even the customary sniggering; pilfering not only ceased but jewellery was collected, listed, sealed in a box, and returned to the family "to retain for more appropriate times". Cleaners were brought in to scrub the filthy floors. Another machine gun was hauled onto the roof. The household became austere but well ordered, efficient.

Food was still coarse, but it came regularly at noon. Brought in from a nearby canteen, it was given to them to serve themselves; the maid reheated the remains in the evening. They found it almost inedible – Alexandra was now desperately thin – but the stability cheered them all; they appreciated order. Through all the changes, Kerensky's gift had endured. Nicholas remembered with gratitude the man whom Alexandra had wanted to disappear. No guard ever laid hand on a Romanov woman. Not while they lived.

Outside the house, disorder ruled. White Russians, led by Czech divisions, had virtually encircled Ekaterinberg. There was little doubt they would lay siege and would almost certainly be victorious. On 5 July workmen were brought in to install iron bars outside the windows of rooms occupied by the Romanov party. Nine days later one of the last messengers to make the hazardous journey arrived in town; he was the regional war commissar, with a message from Moscow, a message too important for the wires, to deliver only to Yurovsky.

The story is well known. Twelve men were briefed on what they were to do – two of them recoiled and had to be replaced. Twelve revolvers were cleaned, oiled, and loaded. Yurovsky saying: "If you're not man enough to do the job you can't be trusted to clean the weapons. You can put buckets of water out on the terrace, and you'll help clean up afterwards. There will be plenty for you to do." Yurovsky showing astonishing compassion in sending the kitchen boy Leoniv Sedneff away to visit his uncle. Yurovsky had a fourteen-year-old brother and for a moment he weakened; it was the only occasion. Alexei was a boy too, but that was not relevant.

Soon after one o'clock the next morning, Yurovsky wakened Dr Botkin in the Ipatiev dining room where he laid his mattress each night. There was fighting in the streets. Everyone needed to gather in a safe room downstairs until the violence eased. It was for their own security. Botkin retrieved his false teeth from a glass, pulled on his clothes and wakened the family. They dressed, the girls lacing themselves into stiff corsets. Nicholas carried Alexei, both of them dressed in soldier shirts and caps. The boy, long-legged in his father's arms, looked for his spaniel, calling out: "Has someone got Joy? He must be saved too."

"Don't worry," said his father. "Marie is bringing Joy."

"She always does," called Alexandra, as she limped along behind, holding the handrail. They laughed.

"What about me?" asked Anastasia.

"You always bring joy too, Stasia," said her mother. "You all do."

The girls followed, one carrying a Pekinese dog and another pulling a black, brown, and white spaniel by the collar; the third of their dogs had disappeared at Tobolsk at the same time that Alexei's attendant Nagorny had gone missing. The guards said the sailor had left, taking the dog with him; the children believed Nagorny had been shot and the dog had died trying to defend him. Dr Botkin, balding and attentive, shepherded Alexei Trupp the valet, Anna Demidoff the maid, and the cook, Ivan Kharitonoff down the stairs. Out onto the court under a starless sky, then through a door into the lower room.

Nicholas sat Alexei on one chair and put another beside it for Alexandra. He placed a third and sat down at the boy's shoulder. Yurovsky said that a publicity photograph was needed, to establish that the family members were alive, well, and in Bolshevik protective custody. Please gather in a line behind the chairs. Men filed into the room, Yurovsky announced the group had been sentenced for crimes against the people and sentence would be executed immediately. As Nicholas stuttered incredulously the squad opened fire.

Yurovsky had instructed that head and heart shots would minimise blood spillage. He and his deputy fired straight into the foreheads of Nicholas and Alexandra but as the parents' bodies dropped they felled children, making further killing shots difficult. The room became a bloody massacre, with screams, arterial blood spurting, and dogs yelping in terror. Yurovsky swore, pulling a sword bayonet from his belt. The maid stepped forward, seeming to try to embrace him as blood poured down her bosom. He brought the heavy blade down across her skull and as she sank down he jerked it free to strike again and again. Most of his men were standing appalled. Only two were dispatching the wounded. One sank his bayonet repeatedly into Anastasia as she lay propped against the wall. Yurovsky kicked out as he saw Alexei raise himself on his elbows. He put two shots into the boy's head, then fired again to silence the whining dog that scrabbled at a closed door.

As abruptly as it began, it was over. There was silence. Blood ran thick on the floor. Swirls of gunsmoke merged into a haze. Here and there a limb twitched, a muscle relaxed.

They stepped back, opened a door, went out onto the terrace. Yurovsky admitted to himself that he needed a drink. In the darkness there was the sound of vomiting from one of the men. Suddenly a spaniel hurtled out, dodged amongst their legs and disappeared into the night. There had been two dogs; he had shot one. Well, a dog could do nothing.

Yurovsky went to the buckets of water, washed the blood from his boots and hands, then turned.

"Wash well. Don't forget this blood is diseased. Now we have done half the job. When we have had a drink, we finish it. There will not even be relics for the Whites to worship."

Meanwhile, the world went on as though nothing had happened. In the Crimea, Dagmar sipped tea, trying to suppress a feeling that something dreadful had occurred. On the Marne, exhausted Germans prepared to retreat from land that had cost the violent deaths of millions. Citizens of New York were celebrating the subway opening on Lexington Avenue. Behind a barn in the Ural foothills a bedraggled spaniel called Joy cowered in the dark, too traumatised to whimper. Dawn stained the Eastern sky.

Chapter 34

Seventeen of the fifty-three Romanovs in Russia that year died violently. Four Grand Dukes – three of Nicholas's cousins and an uncle – were brought dishevelled to the rim of a mass grave in the SS Peter and Paul Fortress and shot, tumbling down like unstrung marionettes. Another Grand Duke accompanied Ella, another nun and several princes when they were driven to an obscure site in Alapayevsk. There the guards clubbed them with their rifle butts, then hurled them alive down a mineshaft. The guards waited, listening. When they heard cries and screams of pain, they tossed a couple of hand grenades into the darkness.

Mikhail's body had slid into the woodland grave near Perm, five days before the massacre at Ekaterinberg. Johnson, his secretary, just had time to marvel that even the Bolsheviks gave precedence to the Grand Duke, before the same muzzle touched his head too.

"They are expendable, so let there be no mawkish sentimentality," said Lenin. In August he had time to reflect on mortality after crashing to the ground himself, shot by a rival socialist. A couple of years later he too knew the agony of inconsolable loss.

Inessa had been beside him, body and soul, through so much. Now she was in a group foraging for food to supply a troop train. She had not eaten for two days. It was only water, water in a deserted house – people usually fled at sight of marauding troops, if they had the strength. She drank it and thought no more, until a few hours later when the stomach cramps began. He wasn't even a real doctor, the medic who came to look at her, but he recognised the irresistible diarrhoea, the grains in it like rice, the twitching muscles and the waxy skin. "Drink plenty of water," he said, backing away. "Stay away from her. It's cholera." For the Grand Dukes' unwrapped remains there were ignominious unmarked graves; for this extraordinary woman, illegitimate daughter of a French opera singer, a state funeral in Moscow's Red Square. Privilege is like the cash that the Romanovs scorned to handle. It only seems to disappear; in reality it simply changes hands.

The Central Committee inherited a land impoverished and disheartened by external and internal warfare. Now the German war was ended it could still make of Russia a controlled empire, a power base from which to bring the world into a brave new era. Once the stench of war was gone on the wind, the secret police could sniff the air for revolutionaries and monarchists, knock doors at midnight, interrogate, reinterrogate, and then... it could be an ice pick, poison, a knife in the eye. But a bullet behind the ear remained favourite. You could rely on a bullet behind the ear.

Between 1918 and 1921, more than one million people would flee from Russia; there is no record of how many died violently because they could not escape. Some were lucky; Lenin the thinker dealt comparatively gently with other philosophers. They had to go – Russian philosophy was too integrated with Russian theology for them to remain – but even the iron man could not bring himself to have those refined brains blown out. Leading intellectuals were gathered in Petrograd, put aboard an outbound ship, together with wives and children, and told not to come back. Most of them gravitated to Paris and, being wise, they never returned. Years later Joseph Stalin, who then controlled the Soviet Union, would offer Russian émigrés in France safe passage back to their homeland. Some took him at his word and went. The Cheka liquidated them.

Field Marshal von Eichhorn made sure the Romanovs were safe but that benign attitude did not extend to the native people; his brutality earned him der Militärverdienstkreuz – a military cross – in June and an assassin's bullet at the end of July. Two days later telegrams arrived announcing that this had been a fateful month in Ekaterinberg too. Nicholas was dead.

Dagmar seemed to have been destroyed by the news. She locked herself away and forbad anyone to mention even the possibility that her son had been killed. Photographs were framed and hung around her rooms. She went into denial because that was the only way she could survive. He was not dead, Nicholas was not dead, he could not be dead. It was a litany that had flooded through her consciousness nearly fifty years before. "Saint Nicholas, worker of miracles, I begged you then for a miracle but you gave me nothing. I have built you a cathedral. What more must I do? Would you fail me again?"

She had shrunk at Ai Todor, where food was rough and sparse. At Djulber, the food had been no better but she had taken a little wine. Now she ate virtually nothing and withered. The kitchens were instructed to prepare nourishing broths to restore her but the dishes returned untouched.

Information arrived in fragments. The White Army had captured Ekaterinberg but found Ipatiev's house empty. The bodies of Ella and the others at Alapayevsk were found; they had been injured but it seemed most of them had starved to death. The children and their mother were believed to have died with Nicholas. Civil strife was tearing Russia apart; peace with Germany had cost an immense price in territory and now Russians were at war with Russians.

Germany was still pushing hard on the Western Front but there was desperation in the air now – it was all or nothing. The German troops that had menaced Russia could not go to the West – they had to stay where they were to consolidate their Eastern conquests. The Kaiser's forces gathered all the strength they could to dishearten the rest of the alliance, attacking the British in the muddy bloodbath of Flanders, occupying Helsinki, advancing on Amiens, attacking at Noyon and on the Aisne; finally, in July, Ludendorff began another offensive near Reims. That ancient city again trembled to the thunder of artillery batteries in the region while deep underground, in vast caverns carved by slaves of Rome, an immense army of champagne bottles lay rank and file, slumbering in the dark, entombed behind false walls indistinguishable from the surrounding limestone. The French, like the Russians, had learnt how to survive invasion.

The German war machine was spent. Old men and boys glared defiantly over the sandbags towards Europeans who were reinforced from across the Atlantic and from the British Empire. Germans learnt how Russians had felt, facing better troops, better trained and better armed. Loss after loss eroded the German High Command's confidence. Ludendorff, having paid too high a price for expansion to the East while failing in his Western offensive, departed ignominiously in October. On 9 November Kaiser William was forced to abdicate; two days later a general armistice was signed. Germany's war with her other adversaries was finally over.

From the eleventh hour of the eleventh day of the eleventh year of the century, the Allies grimly rejoiced in victory, but they celebrated without Russia. Having soaked up the agony and horror of war through four blood soaked summers and bitter winters, for the sake of 253 more days Russia had traded victory for defeat.

It was the end for the German Kaiser. William had servants pack the uniforms and medals he valued so highly and he fled from his unforgiving country. The man who modelled himself upon Napoleon went into ironic exile; he would strut no more through the imperial pastiche of Potsdam. One day he would watch from sanctuary in the Netherlands as another man, with an even more ludicrous moustache, led his beloved Germany to destruction or to glory. The man the defiant remnants of Scotland's Highland Regiments had called the cocky wee Kaiser died in

1941, too soon to know that Adolf Hitler was also to taste the bitter ashes of failure. Russians would then retrieve the territory they now regarded as stolen by the Boche, and exact bloody vengeance.

And the people? The people would suffer. They always do.

Armistice meant the German troops would have to evacuate the Crimea. Surrender had been followed by the collapse of Germany's ruling dynasties so Potsdam was no longer an option for the refugee aristocrats. The Germans began to withdraw, leaving White Russians controlling the area, Tartars protecting the Romanovs.

Revolutionary fervour had become a sea of fire sweeping across the steppes and out into the extremities of the land. Aristocrats, landowners, employers – skorum eaters – were smelled out and slaughtered. The Russian faith in heritage ran deep, so families died with those who were condemned: scotch the snake and burn out the nest.

The Russian faith in Mother Church also ran deep, but Mother Church preached ethics, compassion and – worst of all – the Tsar. Lenin had claimed all church property for the state. Now the Church had no authority, no property. Drunken mobs caught priests and made them run the gauntlet, goaded between two rows of vengeful men with farm implements, to reach a grave. Pyres burned and the stench of charred flesh hung heavy.

But chaos was coalescing: in increasing areas, a sort of administration was administering. White Russian armies fought and advanced, but they were doomed by numbers, condemned by declining morale. Lenin had been right: without a Tsar, their cause declined. There was a system developing across Russia. It was clumsy, cruel, and often ineffective, but it developed. The Reds would master the land, indiscriminate slaughter would be replaced by methodical liquidation. Autocratic control would again become complete, but not under the little father of all the Russias. The eclipse of the Romanov sun would leave Russia in a deadly gloom for generations.

"You have come to tell me it is time," said Dagmar.

Nikolai looked at her puckered face; it had to be said. "It is past time. All arrangements are made."

"You could leave me here."

"No, Maria. We could all stay here except you, and it would make no difference. You must go. You are the last Olympian. You are the Empress. For Russians who love the Romanovs, Russians who love the Church, Russians who hate what is happening: you are our only ikon. And the other nations, they are clamouring for you to leave. The diplomats are…"

She had tilted back her head, lids heavy over the dark eyes. "Having denied sanctuary, they want to salve their consciences? Now there is nothing to save, they want to play saviours? Is it only a game, Nikolai? Is that what it was all the time?"

He waited. "For Russians, Maria, you must go. If it is a game, the queen must make her move. Step out upon the square. We pawns are nothing without your leadership."

She stood up. "If you say we must go, Grand

Duke, then we must go.

"Let everything be done as the organisers want it done but I shall go alone to church before I leave. You and you alone will escort me there, and then escort me to whatever they have planned for me."

Nikolai shook his head. "British battleships are stood off Yalta to take us off, Maria. There may be German deserters in the area, there are certainly Reds closing in, and Whites can't be trusted. There is no time to go to church. The British will not wait."

She gazed at him steadily. "Tell them," she said, "that they can go without me or they can go with me when I come to them from church. The choice is theirs."

Chapter 35

She knelt in the chapel beside the sea. In her gloved hand lay an egg, a little jewelled egg, the last of the many Fabergé masterpieces she had been given by her two Czars. It was decorated with the Order of Saint George.

Saint George, guardian saint of Moscow and of Georgia. Saint George, the soldier saint, who held on when his own nation turned upon him, who took the pain and the humiliation and kept the faith. Who faced the headsman's sword and did not flinch. She held it tight, the little egg. *It is over now and they are dead. Nicholas and Alexander, Nicki and George and Mikhail, all are gone. My Czars and all my little ones. He bled, he must have bled, the little one, and how he must have hurt. Yet while I breathe I shall not say it's so. Long live the Czar; give thanks to good Saint George.*

I must not weaken; I am the last Olympian left alive. George, guardian of Moscow and of England, be with me now.

As she stepped outside she saw the silhouette of Nikolai against the early morning sky. He was her sole companion in what had become an alien land, and she felt completely safe. "You still look like a Czar," she said.

He lit her cigarette. "And you still look like an

Empress, comrade," he said softly.

She laughed. "Was it a worthy aspiration after all, serving the Czar?"

"It was not an aspiration, it was my destiny. I have fulfilled mine, just as Nicholas and Mikhail and Alexei have fulfilled theirs."

"Don't," she said. "Don't say they are dead. I know all that I know, but don't say that they are dead. These are words that should not be spoken."

"Very well. I shall not say that they are dead, Maria. We need to go – HMS *Marlborough* awaits and Commander Toby Pridham will be anxious."

Still she stood, knowing her feet rested on Russian soil.

"Where will you go," she asked, "to England?"

"No. I still have some resentment over the armaments we waited for but which never came. And I should not wish to show respect where our Imperial family was denied sanctuary. No doubt His Majesty and the British Government had their reasons but I should not again feel able to accept the word of an Englishman."

"Perfidious Albion," said Dagmar smiling. "So how will you serve the Czar now that there is no Czar?"

"It's a difficult habit to break, Maria. The Czar served the people so I shall serve the Czar by serving the people," said Nikolai simply. "I shall go to Nice and do all I can for Russian émigrés, until we can return."

"You find you can accept the word of the French then?"

"I never trusted the people who trusted Napoleon," said the soldier, grinning, "so I have nothing to lose on the Riviera. Anyway, we outnumber them there and that is where I can do most good. You will go to Denmark?"

"I shall go to England and my sister, although I may not stay – perhaps I shall live in Hvidore."

Like Dagmar, Alexandra had changed beyond recognition since those innocent days in Copenhagen. They had recaptured their youth each year when they spent time together, especially in the estate they had bought together at Hvidore, in Denmark, but they were growing old now, and things could never be the same. Alexandra was becoming increasingly deaf and was usually a little confused. She had not fully recovered from the death eight years before of her domineering husband King Edward, nor had she established a satisfactory role for herself in the new King's Court. King George's Queen Mary had been deeply offended when Dagmar had pressed her sister to emulate the Dowager Empress and demand precedence at the funeral. Mary had given way at the time but made it plain she would not welcome any further interference. In England, Dagmar could not expect to be much more than a personal guest of her sister, and then only for a limited time.

The people of Denmark regarded Dagmar as a heroine but even this was an obstacle. Her nephew King Christian X balanced both monarchic survival and his finances with infinite care; any diffusion to the spotlight of popular loyalty could cause him problems and he had no contingency budget for Olympian guests. He had made clear that he was not in a financial position to help maintain his aunt's luxurious household: he would of course provide what humble hospitality he could but Dagmar must remember her childhood – this Court was not opulent, as others she had experienced might have been. He said he had heard that Romanovs never asked the price of anything. "Here we must count the cost of everything, and confine our expenditure to essentials." It sounded to Dagmar as though a red carpet of welcome would be regarded as an unwarranted extravagance. Well, perhaps she could learn to count the cost of things, though it hardly seemed likely. Poor artistic Prince Shervadshidze had fallen ill and quickly died only a few months ago; Nicholas had made an excellent choice there, but now she was without the man she had called her abacus.

She roused herself from her thoughts and spoke as they walked. "Is that HMS *Marlborough* out there? Why have they got so many lights on? Do they want everyone to know they are there? They don't seem to realise that Russia is at war with Russia."

"They are a proud people, the British, and the allies have beaten Germany. Excuse them a little arrogant stupidity."

"In this light she looks little larger than the Imperial yacht."

"It is deceptive at this distance," said Nikolai. "She is a battleship with more than a thousand men aboard. I expect the British will be able to accommodate you all in respectable discomfort, just as they did, those of us who attended their King's funeral. What a farce that was, with Kaiser Bill prancing about, trying his Prussian best to upstage everyone and humble George, King of England, trying not to be noticed. They brought credit on neither autocracy nor pseudo-democracy. And that wedding of the Kaiser's daughter, just before…"

"Stop trying to divert me with Montenegrin tittle-tattle. Wherever I go, things will be very different for me," she said. "I suspect autocracy will be a difficult habit to break, Nikolai. I shall have to begin to try to care whether the Toby Pridhams of this world are anxious."

Nikolai chuckled. "I imagine it would take more than a few minutes' delay to bring your liaison officer out in a lather. He was involved in destroying the German cruiser *Konigsberg* in East Africa during the war."

"Was he indeed? Then he is taking some risk coming here to be my ADC – the Germans wouldn't take kindly to the gallant Lieutenant, whatever may have been agreed. I shall have to consider endowing him with an honour… the Order of Saint Stanislas, I think."

"Are you sure that a Stanislas is entirely appropriate?"

"What may or may not be appropriate is not the major consideration, my dear Nikolai. What really matters is which insignia I happen to have to hand, and I know I have a spare Stanislas lying around somewhere. Let me take your arm. We are leaving the largest Empire in the world, where I was Empress. I should like to depart as I arrived, on the arm of a dear friend who understands my heart."

They went unchallenged between the armed

Marines deployed defensively on the beach around a hastily built wooden jetty. As they walked down the shaky structure, Pridham, in immaculate whites, stepped forward and saluted. "The others are all aboard, Empress," he said. He noticed that she was wet-cheeked as he helped her into the pinnace, but she smiled and thanked him. Perhaps she wasn't such a harsh old autocrat after all.

Nikolai saw her safely aboard HMS *Marlborough*, but he was to leave on HMS *Nelson*; the British, with precise administrative care, had allocated HMS *Marlborough* to the close relatives of Alexander II, and HMS *Nelson* to those of his brother Nicholas. As she saw him standing in the tender, hand raised in farewell, she seemed to hear a voice say: "This is Nicholas's cousin my dear. Your Nicholas is Nicholas Alexandrovitch; this young man is Nicholas Nicholaevitch, son of my brother. We call him Nikolai and he has a role to play in Russia's destiny."

At the last she stood alone, small and fragile, large eyes watching her empire disappear below the horizon, in the light of another day.

Chapter 36

The last Olympian arrived in Portsmouth one bright May afternoon. There were no bands, no celebration. The Queen Mother Alexandra explained to her on the way to Victoria Station that the British Government wanted good relations with the Russian government so Dagmar's 'visit' was 'delicate'; it could be only a family affair. Other passengers had been cleared from the platforms to enable the King to informally greet his aunt. As swiftly as was decent, the party was whisked away to royal residences. Dagmar spent most of her time with her sister at Sandringham but the glory days were gone.

Alexandra was deaf, vague, and forgetful. Her sight was failing and with it, her temper. Dagmar was lame with lumbago, shackled by having neither money nor understanding of economy. She had difficulty concealing her contempt for a royal family that betrayed the name of its bloodline because it was expedient. At dinner one evening she raised a soupspoon to her mouth and asked: "What is this?"

"Windsor soup, ma'am."

"Windsor soup? Food for cowards," she said. Time to go.

There was a band in Copenhagen in August when

Dagmar quit England to live in Denmark but again, no sense of occasion. Dagmar wept as she realised that, even here, she was an anachronism. For a time she lived in Christian IX's palace but he grew increasingly annoyed by her profligacy and envious that the press thought her the best part of Royalty. Influential friends tried to help her financially but she was unskilled in money matters. Dagmar returned occasionally to England but found little comfort there.

One in three of the fifty-three Romanovs living in Russia at the beginning of 1918 died violent deaths there during the following months. More than one young woman subsequently claimed to be Nicholas's daughter Anastasia. A publicity campaign made saints of the Imperial family, even campaigning to change the Western spelling of Czar to the more respectable Tsar. Bickering between family factions over who could now call himself Emperor – Little Father of none of the Russias – roused the old lady's contempt, as it disgusted Nikolai, living in Nice. He regularly attended services at the cathedral there, gazing at the Divine Face of Our Lord Jesus Christ and remembering a young man who died when he was himself only a boy.

Once when Dagmar visited, they paused by the gatepost engraved with the legend 'Remember 1865'. Leaning on Nikolai's arm, she said: "The émigrés in America call me the Old Ikon, you know. I don't care for that at all."

Nikolai laughed. "Here they call you Our Lady of Tears."

"What stuff and nonsense," she said. "What tears I have shed have been more from frustration than grief.

Weeping is not for me – I am an Olympian, the last one. None of these squabbling Romanovs is capable of being an Olympian."

"Not one," he replied. "But then what do I know? I was never an Olympian either."

"You were invited to be one. You had the qualities but you wouldn't climb Olympus."

Nikolai gazed up at the golden Imperial eagles and the cupolas, confident against the brilliant sky. "Perhaps... if I had been able to see the future, Empress, I might have denied what I regarded as my destiny. If I was wrong, I apologise."

They walked on. "I forgive you," she said. "I am content with the past, as I remember it. Now I have walked enough." Nikolai raised a hand, the open Bentley that had been following rolled forward and they stepped in behind the driver. Down the Avenue Nicholas II and smoothly into the Boulevard du Tzarewitch.

Nikolai glanced at his watch. "Shall we take coffee Maria?"

She sniffed. "You have been here too long, Nikolai. I shall take tea."

Chapter 37

She was tired, so very tired as she knelt with bowed head. Then she slowly raised her eyes to the flat stone monolith. The smell of the pines was a comfort as she read: "DIGTEREN HANS CHRISTIAN ANDERSEN." He would have enjoyed the smell of the pines.

She was still for so long that the two waiting women looked at one another, moved as if to approach, then stopped.

She thought deeply before she whispered. "It IS like a biscuit. Being a princess is like a biscuit. It is sweet, even delicious. But it breaks in pieces and is soon gone."

Then suddenly, her face came alive and those large eyes were dancing, as they had when she was a girl. "No. It's not at all like a biscuit. Being a princess is the most marvellous experience in the whole world, you scale Olympus to be a god amongst gods and to live as only gods can live…"

She breathed deeply, her eyes fixed on another world. Then she said softly, "And being a princess shatters your heart. But there is no path back down from Olympus. There is only a precipice.

"You asked me to tell you and I have. Now we

both know so you can rest, Storyteller, and so can I."

The old lady raised a gloved hand, perhaps in farewell, and her attendants came to her, lifting and supporting her as, slowly, so slowly, she moved away.

POSTSCRIPT

Dagmar was living at Hvidore in 1925 when Alexandra died of a heart attack at Sandringham. The two sisters owned the Danish estate jointly but even King George felt uncomfortable about being seen to make Dagmar homeless by selling the half he and his sisters inherited. Three years later, aged eighty-one, she slipped into a coma from which she did not awake.

Although the remains of some slaughtered members of the Romanov family, including Alexei and Mikhail, still lie somewhere in the endless Russian landscapes, others have been recovered and reinterred in the vaults of Petrograd, or Saint Petersburg, as Russians are now told to call it. That is where Dagmar wanted her bones laid too but until the end of the twentieth century, Russian bureaucracy, Danish politics, and rivalries amongst residual Romanovs prevented her repeating the journey she made in 1866.

Now at last she lies with the others.

Printed in Great Britain
by Amazon